Somewhere out there, more soldiers were bearing down on them. As the gunshots got louder, Delta looked up from her position behind a palm tree and saw they were from Megan's rifle; she was racing toward the clearing.

"Megan!" Delta yelled over the roar of the chopper and the rifle blasts. "Over here!"

For endless moments, Delta waited until she heard the heavy footsteps of someone plunging through the jungle. Sweat dripped down her chest, wetting the center of her bra; she wished she still had her shirt on. Lifting her rifle, she took aim. Through the cross hairs, she saw Megan's sweaty, bloody face. "Over here!" Delta yelled, keeping her rifle poised and ready.

As Megan stumbled forward, out of the jungle, Delta shot two soldiers in hot pursuit. Both men's backs blew out as two well-aimed bullets tore their bodies apart. Moments later, Delta helped Megan up and checked her rifle's ammunition.

When she finished examining the AR-18, Delta looked at Megan's bloody face. "You're bleeding. You okay?"

Megan nodded. "A bullet grazed my cheek. Think I was unconscious for a moment, but I'm back. Nothing to worry about, love."

Delta nodded. "Get to the chopper." Delta scanned the edge of the jungle, waiting for more soldiers to appear.

"What about you?"

"Right behind you, love." Quickly kissing Megan on the lips, Delta gave her a shove toward the chopper.

"Delta?"

"Yeah?"

"Don't leave me."

Delta grinned. "Never. Now move it!"

❧ ❧ ❧

# TROPICAL STORM

## LINDA KAY SILVA

RISING
TIDE
PRESS

Rising Tide Press
5 Kivy Street
Huntington Station, NY 11746
(516) 427-1289

Printed in the United States on acid-free paper.

Publisher's note:
All characters, places and situations in this book are fictitious and any
resemblance to persons (living or dead) is purely coincidental.

Publisher's Acknowledgments:
The publisher is grateful for all the support and expertise offered by the
members of its editorial board: Beth Heyn, Hat Edwards, Pat G. and
Candy T. Special thanks to Edna G. for believing in us, and to the
feminist and gay bookstores for being there.

First printing July, 1997
10 9 8 7 6 5 4 3 2 1

Edited by Lee Boojamra and Alice Frier
Book cover art: Peggy Mocine

Silva, Linda Kay 1960-
        Tropical Storm /Linda Kay Silva
                p.cm
ISBN 1-883061-14-8
Library of Congress Catalog Card Number 96-69424

# DEDICATION

This one, like my heart, is for Connie.

Never could a writer be so fortunate as to be loved by another writer. Our love of words, our pursuit of knowledge, and our endless streams of conversation breathe fresh life into both my creative spirit and my eccentric life.

You are the beginning and the end, and everything in between, and I am blessed to have your light in my life. Thank you, Sweetheart, for everything you do, for everything you think, and for all that you are. I love you.

A most special thanks for Kathleen—my guru, my mentor, my friend. Delta may come and go, but you and I have forged a forever friendship. Thanks for your love and guidance.

Heather—always there, always supportive. You are my definition of a true friend. You are most wonderful.

My mom and dad— who keep helping me make my dreams come true.

My non— Alzheimer's may have taken your mind, but I will always hold a part of your heart. Thanks non, for showing me how to be.

Katherine V. — For your quiet wisdom and path-forging ways.

For my sisters: Sherry, Sloan, Bonnie, Kin Kin and Sally— You make work fun, laughter easy, and bitching an art. I love you guys.

# 1——

"**What** do you mean, 'Megan is missing'?" Delta quickly changed the phone from her right ear to her left as her feet hit the floor. Missing? *How in the hell could Megan be missing?*

Turning on every light as she made her way to the kitchen, Delta grabbed a pen and pulled a memo pad across the counter. "Define *missing*."

The voice on the other line sounded curiously detached, and Delta heard an intake of breath. "Megan went out on one of her excursions three days ago and ne—"

"Three days? Megan's been gone for three days, and you're only calling me now? What's the matter with you, Liz?"

"I'm sorry, Delta, but it isn't what you think."

"What I'm thinking is, why in the hell did it take you so long to call?"

"Megan and Augustine left three days ago for La Amistad Park after receiving a hot tip about some poachers. I'm sorry, but I..."

"What kind of hot tip?" Delta switched channels on the portable phone to reduce static.

"I don't know. Megan didn't share much about her poaching activities with us, Delta. She'd just whisk in here for a change of clothes and then be off again. She's spent more time chasing poachers than working on her internship."

Delta's mind was already ticking off a list of things she'd need to do. They would need binoculars, sturdy backpacks, maybe a first-aid kit. "So, she and Augustine went off to some park after poachers, and no one has seen them since?" Grabbing a pencil off the calendar, Delta scribbled notes in the margin. It was March 10th, and Megan was due home in less than two weeks. March 22nd was the only date highlighted in yellows and oranges.

"Right. Megan changed her clothes, talking excitedly about the trip, and barely mentioned that she probably wouldn't be home that night."

Cradling the phone between her shoulder and chin, Delta pulled on a pair of jeans before grabbing her favorite high tops—the ones she bought after the fire had melted hers down like a plastic plate. "When she didn't return the next day, what happened?"

"We just figured she stayed an extra night. You should see her down here, Delta. Megan has really changed. She's totally into this macaw preservation thing. It wouldn't have surprised us if she would have stayed an extra week."

"But?"

"But she would have called if she were going to stay longer. It's not like her to just up and go and not tell us where she is or how long she's staying. She's been very considerate that way."

"Are there very many phones in Costa Rica?"

The line was silent, and Delta realized the absurdity of the question.

"There are plenty of phones here, Delta. Terry and I have called everyone we've met here, and no one has seen them since they set out for Chirripo."

Lacing up her high tops, Delta looked at her ankle holster and wondered if she would be able to go armed. "Chirripo? Is that the name of the rain forest?"

"Yes. It's the name of a smaller park bordering La Amistad."

"What about this Augustine fellow? Any word on him?"

"We don't know much about him. I'm telling you, Megan has been pretty secretive since hooking up with this guy."

Delta went back into the bedroom and flung open her closet door so she could retrieve an empty duffel bag. Then she opened her drawers and grabbed various pieces of clothing. From the top of the closet, she tossed in her binoculars, a rain poncho, a compass, and her favorite hiking pants. "Any family? Last name? Anything?"

"We spoke with his mother. She lives in Rivas. Doesn't speak any English, though."

"How did you locate his mother?"

"Terry went through Megan's desk and found the name of a small village. We had a friend check it out for us."

"And?"

"And the family is not real worried yet. The mother doesn't think Megan is with him. You know...these people are Catholic, and..."

"I get the point." Grabbing her duffel bag, Delta brought it with her back to the kitchen. "Have you notified the authorities?"

"I just got off the phone with the American Embassy."

Delta looked around and plucked the SOX baseball cap Sal had given her off the floor. Then she grabbed the toiletry bag and tossed it into the duffel bag before cinching it closed. "And what did they say?"

"She's one of a dozen or so people reported missing in the last couple of months."

Delta paused for a moment before straightening up. "A dozen or so? Don't they find that a bit strange?"

"This is Latin America, Delta. People come down here to disappear on a regular basis. The Costa Rican government doesn't get overly excited about it unless it's someone important."

"Megan *is* someone important." Adrenaline kicked into Delta's system like gasoline in an engine.

"I know that, but Central America has excellent hiding places. You can really get lost down here, so a missing person *isn't* high priority."

"I see." Delta's blood suddenly ran cold.

"Delta, I'm scared. Terry and I don't know if we should stay, come home, go looking for her, or what."

"For now, I need you to stay there."

"We've heard horrible stories about these dangerous poachers. We shouldn't have let Me—"

"Liz, Megan does whatever Megan wants, or needs, to do." Delta paused as she stared at the wallet-sized photo of Megan underneath a refrigerator magnet. Pulling it out from under the magnet, Delta put the photo in her chest pocket. "It's one of the reasons we love her so much." Delta walked into the living room and looked around for other items she might need.

"Delta, I'm really sorry."

"Don't be." Tossing the duffel bag on the couch, Delta opened up a hollowed-out edition of Winnie-the-Pooh and removed a wad of emergency cash. "Okay, Liz, here's what we're gonna do..."

# 2——

**When** Delta swung her front door open, less than two hours had elapsed since she'd hung up the phone with Liz. Her lover was missing, and there was only one other person she knew who could help get her back.

"Ready?" A short Latina woman with long black hair and serious, fierce coffee-brown eyes entered briskly, carting a blue duffel bag similar to Delta's over her shoulder. Barely legible on her bag was "River Valley Police Academy" in worn white letters.

"I have a million vacation days, and Gina sends me with her prayers. You have me as long as you need," Connie said, quickly brushing passed Delta. She was a good seven inches shorter than Delta's five-nine height, but her intensity more than made up for her lack of height.

Closing the door behind her, Delta nodded. "Thanks. Get the tickets?"

"Went one better," she answered, picking up a half-filled cup of lukewarm coffee and taking a sip. It didn't matter how old or how cold, Consuela Rivera loved coffee. "The next flight for San Jose doesn't leave until tomorrow, so I made a few calls and arranged for us to hitch a ride on a military transport."

Delta waited for Connie to finish the cup of coffee before continuing. She'd known Connie forever, and knew it was useless trying to get information from her until she was damn good and ready to give it. "I didn't know you had any military connections."

"I don't. Sal and Josh do. They made all the calls. Even offered to come. I told them I'd call if we needed them. No use bringing everybody down there until we know what's what."

"They're good people."

"Yes, they are." Connie walked into the kitchen and opened the pantry door. After quickly surveying the contents, she withdrew a box of granola bars, a package of raisins, and a half-eaten fruit roll-up.

When it came to good people, Consuela Dolores Maria Rivera was at the top of that list. For seven years, she had been Delta's best friend, partner in crime, and mentor. She was the yin to Delta's yang, and there wasn't anything they wouldn't do for each other. Connie and Delta, Delta and Connie; the two were as inseparable as butter and toast, and when it came to solving hard-to-crack crimes, they had no equal.

Tossing the box of granola bars to Delta, Connie continued rummaging through the pantry. "Damn, Del, don't you ever eat at home? Mother Hubbard's cupboard looks stocked compared to yours." Reaching for a bag of dried apricots, Connie tossed those to Delta as well.

"Costa Rica has stores, you know."

Connie pulled her head our of the pantry and glared hard at Delta. "Right. Your lover is missing in the jungle and you want me to believe you'll stop to go grocery shopping? Tell me another tale, my friend."

Delta bowed her head, trying to hide her grin. No one knew Delta better than Connie, and not just because Connie was a genius. Connie and Delta were soul mates who had managed to find each other early in life. They fed off each other in a relationship which could only be called symbiotic, both ebbing and flowing when needed. They complemented each other's strengths and weaknesses, possessing a nearly psychic bond between them that even their lovers did not understand.

Closing the pantry door, Connie opened her duffel bag and made room by jamming some of the other items down. Then, she opened an overstuffed kitchen drawer and started pawing through it.

"Is there a flashlight in this mess?"

Delta walked over and instantly plucked one out.

Connie snatched it from her and turned it on and off.

"Anything else?" Delta asked.

"Still have that Swiss Army knife?"

Delta opened the junk drawer and pushed through the jumble before finding the knife. She continued rummaging through the drawer looking for its black leather holder. Connie walked over to the roll-top desk and sat down. She jotted some numbers down on a notepad. As she set her pen down, she noticed a lavender envelope with unfamiliar handwriting neatly stretched across it. Connie opened the envelope and found a card with a black-and-white picture of Emma Peale, from the 1960s show *The Avengers,* on the front. Inside, the card read:

To My Favorite Cop.

If you're ever in Rio, look me up—

You're the best! In crime and passion—

T.

Shaking her head, Connie put the card back in the envelope and slipped it into the interior pocket of her jacket.

"Found it!" Delta announced, proudly displaying the oft-used first-aid kit.

Connie looked at the kit and sighed. "Geez, how often have you used this thing?"

Delta looked at it and grinned. "I've been stabbed, shot at, and nearly burnt to death. How often do you suppose?"

Connie's smile mirrored Delta's. "Let's hope we don't have to use it this time out."

Taking one last look around her house, Delta quickly jotted a note to Megan and taped it to the refrigerator. "What about our firearms?"

Connie shook her head. "Not unless you want to spend a week in their jail trying to explain why we're carrying them. This is a country without an army, Del. They pretty much frown on civilians packing."

"But we're not civilians," Delta replied.

"Down there we are. Besides, we probably won't need them, and it's not worth the risk of being deported before we even get started. Trust me on this one, Del. Latin American countries frown on foreigners toting guns around, especially Americans."

Delta frowned as she reached for her Swiss Army knife. "How about this?"

Connie nodded as she yanked her bag closed. "Never leave home without it."

As the two women reached for their duffel bags, Connie lightly touched Delta's shoulder. "You scare me when you're this calm. You okay?"

Delta's green eyes slowly filled with tears. "I've been on autopilot ever since she left. Just working and trying not to get myself killed until she comes home and tells me she wants to be with me. I've been marking off the days on my calendar each night in anticipation of her coming home. I wasn't...I'm not ready for this, Con."

Connie hugged Delta. "Ready for what? A trip to a foreign country? Come on, Storm, you're ready for anything."

Delta pulled away and gazed into Connie's coffee-brown eyes. "I'm not ready to be without her."

"For all we know, she could be having the time of her life. You can't start thinking like that or you won't be any good to us."

Delta opened the door and stepped out, wiping her eyes with the back of her hand. "You should see my other thoughts. I keep pushing away the idea that she's all alone and afraid."

Connie squeezed Delta's shoulder. "Alone, maybe. Afraid? Not Megan."

Delta nodded unconvincingly as they stepped out on the porch. *She may not be afraid, but I sure as hell am.*

3——

"I'm scared," a small, red-haired woman whispered, folding her hands around her body to still the shivers.

Megan put her arm around the woman and pulled her closer. At nearly six feet, Megan had a hard time getting comfortable in the small tent they'd been assigned upon arrival.

"So am I, Siobhan, but if you just keep doing what they tell you to do, you'll be fine." Megan reached behind her and tightened the ponytail of her long blonde hair. Her hair, like the rest of her, was covered with a thin layer of dust after working all day, its usual luster dulled by the dirt and grime she'd been exposed to for the past several days.

"But they shot that one poor man, and he didn't even..."

Megan placed her fingers over Siobhan's mouth to quiet her. "Shh. They're coming for us. When they get here, don't panic, and don't act scared. These bastards really get off on a woman's fear, so be strong. Look brave, and you'll be fine. Stare them straight in the eyes." Megan let go of Siobhan and peered out of the tent through one of the metal eyelets. All around the camp, guards dressed in green army fatigues carried rifles over their shoulders. Some chatted in Spanish while others looked out into the bleak darkness of the surrounding rain forest. It was nearly dusk and the guards would soon retrieve the women, once more, to provide the nightly *entertainment.*

The thought of what these men wanted disgusted her. Megan had spent the better part of her life providing the form of sexual entertainment these men took for free. A wry smile flickered across her face at the irony of her situation: Three years ago, after meeting Delta, she'd left prostitution behind to start a new life; now she'd have to rely on that very past to save it. What a bitter taste that left in her mouth. How could she have come so far, only to wind up at the beginning?

When she'd left the streets and a life spent on her back, Megan Osbourne had discovered an entirely different world, one which she wholeheartedly embraced. She loved being up in the mornings, drinking coffee with Delta, watching as the dawn turned into day. The sunshine, the warmth, the way it seemed to make people happy were things that escaped her during the years she'd prostituted. Like a vampire cleansed of the curse, Megan rejoined the land of the living and discovered that being awake in the day was so much better than the life she'd been living at night. Once she'd had a taste of Delta's world, she knew there was no better place to be. Megan enrolled in the university to sample more of it, and became hooked; hooked on Delta, hooked on knowledge, and hooked on living a real life. But it wasn't enough. She wanted more, so when her paralegal professor offered up a number of Latin American internships, Megan's hand was the first to shoot up. Costa Rica sounded like a wonderful place, and Professor Juan Carlos' background in environmental law was just the ticket she needed. She had always wanted to travel, to see things she'd only read about in magazines. She wanted to taste a culture very different from her own. What Megan wanted most now was to live.

"Megan, I...I don't think...I can do it," Siobhan said, starting to cry. "I can't just...just lie there while these...oh, God, they'll kill me."

Megan stroked Siobhan's back. Poor young woman. Siobhan had never been out of Ireland, and now, she was afraid she'd never get back. Megan herself had had similar thoughts the day she was captured after wandering too far from camp.

Her mistake had probably cost Augustine his life, but Megan could not dwell on that. Since she was snatched from the stream, Megan made a commitment to herself to do whatever she needed to do to stay alive. She would eat dirt if that's what it took, but she had made her mind up that she would do anything they asked of her, as long as it meant she would see Delta again.

Delta. How long had it been since she'd gazed into those intense emerald eyes? It felt like an eternity. Three months ago, Megan had needed to find herself, to see the world and her place in it. She needed to completely let go of the girl prostitute and embrace Megan Osbourne, the woman. And here, in Costa Rica, it was as if she had risen from the dead, and found a nearly insatiable thirst for life.

At first, Delta had balked at the idea of her three-month excursion, but in the end, she'd understood why Megan needed to go. This wasn't about their relationship—it was about Megan's relationship with herself. What Delta didn't know—couldn't know—was that in the rain forest, Megan had discovered that she wasn't as far away from herself as she'd thought. She realized that she simply needed to find that one thing that would motivate her every morning. She had to find the spark and ignite it within herself. And in a few short weeks, she had done just that.

When Professor Juan Carlos first introduced her to his nephew, Augustine, Megan thought he was just a *Tico*, or native Costa Rican, with nothing better to do than visit with his uncle's foreign interns. She couldn't have been more wrong.

The moment Augustine introduced Megan to all of the incredible sights and sounds of the rain forest, she fell in love with it. Every morning, amazing sounds filled the fresh air, and the beauty tickled and teased her senses. It was the most tranquil place she had ever been; the perfect place for finding who she was. She discovered not only peace and serenity in nature, but also a passion she never knew existed. In a matter of days, she learned that Augustine wasn't a bored young man visiting his uncle; he was a bounty hunter tracking down poachers who illegally entered the rain forest to remove various exotic, and often endangered, species for profit. Lots of profit.

On their first trek out, Augustine showed her the scarlet macaws. Megan was captivated by their long, red tail feathers waving in the wind, by their magnificence. Augustine went on to tell her of the horrible way the birds were captured, and Megan knew then and there that she had found the direction lacking in her life. On that day, Megan discovered a purpose greater than herself, and it was the first time in her life she felt like she was finally traveling on the right path.

For the first part of her stay, she and Augustine spent hours observing the splendor of the rambunctious parrots— how they chatted to each other as they flew, how they lovingly preened each other, and took turns feeding and caring for their young. The idea that someone was forcibly removing them from their beautiful habitat made her sick. When she saw their brutal entrapment at the hands of the poachers, she could no longer just watch. She had to stop them. That commitment had brought her here.

And where, exactly, was here? Megan had no idea. She knew they were somewhere deep in the rain forests of La Amistad Park in the Talamanca mountains, but precisely where was anybody's guess. As the largest international park, it took up ten percent of Costa Rica's land. It would take a very determined individual to rescue them. That individual was Delta Stevens.

Poor Delta, Megan thought. She'd be so worried. No doubt, she was either on her way to or already in Costa Rica. That was the kind of woman Delta was. She would tear this tiny country apart to find Megan. No proverbial stone would go unturned—on that, Megan would bet her life. The problem would be staying alive long enough for Delta to find her.

"They're coming," Siobhan whispered, pulling away in fear. Megan, yanked from her thoughts, listened intently. Yes, she could hear the crunching of their military boots as they made their way along the narrow trail.

"Please, Megan, I could not live with myself if they defile me. I...I am to be married back home, and he..."

Megan's heart dropped at the sight of this cowering woman. Siobhan was probably right about not surviving the ordeal of repeated rapes and nightly sodomies. Not many women could. Even if Siobhan were able to survive the physical abuse, her spirit would be crushed.

Megan quickly learned to recognize who the "used" women were when they returned to the mines following their personal nights of terror: their hollow, empty eyes and shrinking posture betrayed spirits that had been broken. The nightly ritual of *entertaining* their captors was eating away at their will to live, for, like prostitutes, they were beaten and humiliated by their captors. Now, fear filled their eyes as night fell...as they waited to see who would be the next victim. So far, Megan figured, nine of the fourteen women she worked the sluice with had been put into service. It was only a matter of time before the men's sexual perversions ruined the other five.

Being chosen or not wasn't as much a concern to Megan as escape was. Each night, she timed every move the guards made; she noted patterns, observed routines, did all the things she'd spent the last two years watching Delta and Connie do. Already, she knew what time the men were relieved of their watch posts. Approximately ten minutes after that, they would come to the tents to exact their disturbed notion of pleasure from their captives, which, if Megan had counted correctly, numbered nearly two dozen women, possibly more.

Four men had been brought in the day after Megan arrived at the makeshift camp, but an unsuccessful escape attempt cut short two of their lives. She hadn't seen the other two men in a couple of days and assumed they, too, were dead. Megan knew why the two men got caught. First, they left in the morning, giving the soldiers daylight by which to begin the hunt. That was their greatest error. Second, they went back the way they came, instead of risking unknown territory. Megan would not make those same mistakes when it was her time to leave.

She also knew, by the foulness of their breath, that these men drank heavily every night. This was good. If she could escape sometime between them passing out and dawn, she could get a good five-, maybe six-hour head start. And she would not attempt to go back to Rivas, but would head south toward the Panamanian border. A part of her believed they might not even bother to come after her. What chances did a lone woman have in the heart of the rain forest at night? But the way Megan looked at it, even a slim chance was better than being raped night after night by a gang of foul-smelling cutthroats who would kill them once they had everything they came for.

"Megan?"

Looking up from her thoughts, Megan sighed. "What?"

"What should I do?"

Megan studied Siobhan's soft face and forced a grin. Fingering the bone necklace around her neck, Megan released it and stroked Siobhan's back. At twenty-one years of age, Siobhan McKinnon had convinced her parents to let her take the holiday of her dreams. One day, while her traveling companion recovered from a stomach virus, Siobhan decided to explore the rain forest on her own. She had been hiking for less than an hour when she found herself being dragged into a waiting car, to eventually end up here. Alone and frightened, she was grateful Megan had taken her under her wing. Only now, the guards wanted one or both of them, and Megan wasn't sure how protective her wing would be. "I know you're scared, Siobhan. Just remember, there are people back home worth living for."

Suddenly, the flap door to their tent was unzipped and whipped open to reveal a man wearing green army fatigues and black combat boots, with a silver cross lying against his bare chest. Bending over so he could step into the tent, he glanced at Megan before squatting on his haunches in front of the opening. Grinning, he displayed teeth stained brown from too much tobacco.

"General Zahn wants two of you, especially you," he said, his alcohol breath fouling the air in the tent as he pointed a dirty finger at Megan. She still hadn't figured out if these men were real soldiers or civilian drug runners, but she knew enough not to ask. She knew fatigues were a popular item in Central America, but their weapons smacked of the military.

Siobhan scooted closer to Megan and whimpered, but the guard grabbed a handful of her hair and yanked her head back. "Whassa matter? Scared of a leetle fun?"

Megan slowly reached over and grabbed his wrist. "Leave her alone," she snapped.

Caught off-guard, the man glared at Megan, but she did not let go of his wrist. For a moment, his eyes locked on hers, hatred and anger building up like an electrical charge.

"Who gonna make me, bitch? You?" he growled in broken English.

Megan nodded. "I'll tell the general you don't think he's man enough for two women. How well do you think that would go over?"

The soldier looked at Siobhan before slowly releasing his grip. Reaching for his knife, he pulled it from its sheath and put the tip up to Megan's face. "Maybe you should put something in that mouth to keep it shut. What do you think?"

Megan carefully pushed the knife aside and whispered, "I think you're a piece of shit." With that, Megan rammed her fist into his balls, sending him sprawling on the ground outside the tent. Dropping the knife, he doubled over, grabbing his crotch as he struggled for air. Before anyone else could move, another pair of legs appeared at the tent flap.

The second soldier picked up the knife and helped his comrade Hector to a tree stump. He spoke rapidly in Spanish, pointing to Megan and shaking his head. All Megan could make out was that the general wanted them *pronto*.

When the second soldier finished, Hector held up his hand. *"Uno momento."* Megan knew he needed to catch his breath.

A minute later, the guards escorted them to a large, portable structure resembling a mobile home. It had been camouflaged so well she hadn't noticed it before. Megan wondered how they had gotten something this big so deep into the rain forest without being spotted, but then realized that these men specialized in paying people off to get what they wanted. Payoffs were commonplace in many Latin American countries, especially where drug runners were concerned. And as far as Megan could tell, that was what these men were— drug runners who were diversifying their portfolios by stealing another country's gold; another poor country that did not know there was gold to be stolen. Megan had quickly figured out that these men, whether they were real soldiers or not, were most definitely criminals, probably working for one of the drug cartels.

Reaching for the door, Megan held it for Siobhan before closing it quickly behind them. She turned to face the interior of the room, surprised to find a well-furnished living room decorated with a variety of topographical maps she did not recognize. A love seat stood on one side of the room, with a coffee table and a hammock taking up the rest of the space. A large man whose broad shoulders were covered with gold epaulets stood with his back to them, apparently studying one of the maps. After he placed a red pin on the map, he turned to them and smiled.

"I am General Zahn," he said with a curt bow, before striding over to a desk with a computer and piles of paper. His dark features were highlighted by thick, unruly eyebrows and a mustache to match. He was impeccably dressed in a khaki general's uniform bearing several bars and assorted colorful decorations. He held himself like a man used to giving orders.

Folding her arms across her chest, Megan fought to maintain her composure as he evaluated her. God, how she hated this scrutiny. "Is this what I think it's about, General?"

The General's lip twitched beneath his mustache. "Please, call me Tito. I thought Hector had explained my wishes."

"He didn't get much of a chance, but I've dealt with men like you before. It's no secret what you want."

General Zahn stepped back and studied Megan. "Believe me..." The general looked at her for a name.

"Megan. I'm Megan, and this is Siobhan."

"Believe me, Megan, you have never met a man like me, and you haven't the first idea what a man in my position might want."

"I'll spell it out for you. R-A-P-E."

The general's face registered acknowledgment. "Ah, yes. I apologize for my men. They are not always...how should I say...genteel?"

Megan felt Siobhan move behind her. She had not uttered a sound, but Megan could sense her fear. One thing remained clear: Siobhan would not mentally or emotionally survive a rape. Just the thought was already devouring her. Like so many of the other captives, Siobhan had been a student trekking through Latin America, carrying the telltale backpack of a wanderer, of someone who would not immediately be missed. Some of the other students had been studying various flora and fauna in the jungle, so their abductions wouldn't be missed until well after Zahn had his share of *Tico* gold.

"Gen...Tito, what would I have to do to ensure that Siobhan, here, is left alone by you and your men?"

General Zahn's eyebrows raised slightly. "Do? My dear, are you suggesting that I make a deal with you?"

Heart pounding, palms sweating, Megan stepped forward. She'd seen Delta do this before: throw an opponent off-balance by doing the unexpected. Perhaps if she didn't act like a captive, he wouldn't be so quick to treat her like one. "Every man has his price, General. But I'm sure that's not news to you."

General Zahn stared at her.

"What's your price, General? What will it cost to make sure she's unharmed?"

General Zahn slowly reached out and touched Megan's hair. On her first visit to San Jose, the Costa Rican capital, Megan realized Latino men were fascinated by, and attracted to, blondes. Never in her life had she seen so many men turn their heads when she walked by. She'd grown used to the many wolf whistles and lascivious expressions yelled to her in Spanish, but she also realized that it was all bark and no bite; it was a part of the machismo culture of Latin America. They might admire a woman from afar, but they usually respected her space.

Pulling at his mustache, General Zahn smiled. "You are either very brave or very foolish."

Megan grinned. She had met dozens of men like the general when she was on the streets in River Valley. Just because he was wearing a uniform didn't change what lay beneath it.

"Fortunately for you...," the general continued, releasing Megan's hair, "I like women with courage. Who is she to you that you risk your life?"

"She's a human being, General. And I don't think she'll survive what your men have in mind. She's a good worker. It would be a shame to lose her because of your men's perverse sexual needs."

"You believe she can't handle my men? What about you?"

Megan nodded as she pulled her trump card out. "Can and have. Spare Siobhan the nightly horrors, and I will willingly do whatever *you* please."

The general stepped up to Megan. He smelled of sweat and cheap cologne. "You'll do what I wish anyway."

Megan did not move from his hot breath. "Perhaps. However, it could be so much more enjoyable for you if you were inclined to leave her alone."

An evil glimmer twinkled in his eyes as he wrapped a meaty arm around Megan's shoulders and pulled her closer to him. Now, the smell of cigar and fruit blended with his hot perspiration. "Oh, I think you will be very enjoyable. What is my prize if I do as you want?"

Megan's lips were inches away from his as she tossed her trump on the table. "You can be like your men and rape an unwilling victim—"

"Or?"

"Or you can have the most incredible sex of your life with a woman who made a very comfortable living pleasing men back home."

General Zahn was so taken aback, he dropped his arm from her shoulder. "You? A whore?"

Megan nodded. "Not just any whore. A very expensive one. So you see, General, you can fuck a limp rag doll, or you can enjoy what I guarantee will be some of the most exciting sexual experiences of your life. The choice is yours."

General Zahn looked from Megan to Siobhan and back to Megan before shaking his head. "I think too little of you...*como se dice...*"

"Underestimate?" Megan supplied for him.

"*Sí.* I underestimated you."

"Men usually do. Beauty does not mean absence of brains, General."

The general strode over to Siobhan and looked down at her, his disdain apparent. Then, without warning, he backhanded her across the face, sending her sprawling against the wall. Megan started toward Siobhan, but the general's abrupt glare at Megan told her that would not be wise. Turning back to a whimpering Siobhan, General Zahn spat, "You are a miserable dog to let this woman deal for your mercy."

Siobhan held her reddened cheek and started crying.

Throwing open the door, the general grabbed Siobhan, yelled something to Hector in Spanish, and then pushed Siobhan out the door. When he closed the door once more, he locked it behind him. Megan wondered, for a brief instant, if she hadn't overplayed her hand.

"Please," General Zahn said with a sweep of his hand. "Sit down." Like Jekyll and Hyde, he instantly turned from brutish dictator to charming paramour. The transformation made Megan aware of just how dangerous this unpredictable man was. And she had learned enough from Delta to know that unpredictable enemies were the most menacing.

Sitting on one side of the plaid love seat, she watched as he poured two glasses of brandy. Handing her one, he sat next to her on the sofa. "I may be living in the jungle, but I am no barbarian." Sipping the brandy, he rolled the snifter around in his palms. "I bring home and comfort any place I go."

"And that includes women?"

"My men sometimes lose control, Megan, but I have never taken a woman against her will. I come from a small village near Bogota, where women are held in high regard."

"So high, you kidnap us, then enslave and rape us?"

General Zahn was no longer smiling. "Take care how you speak to me. We may show regard to women where I am from, but we do not allow their disrespect."

"I apologize. It is just so difficult hearing about respect when I see the way your men treat us."

The general shrugged. "Men who are content are more alert and productive. I do not wish to stay in this jungle any longer than I must."

Megan set her snifter down and let her eyes take in the room. Near the computer sat a small fax machine and cell phone. *Must have a portable generator supplying power. If I could only get to that phone...*

Turning back to the general, Megan sighed. If she could get just one call out, she was sure Delta and Connie would find her, knew they were already looking. They had to be. As she realized there was communication equipment nearby, Megan's hopes rose. She understood from years on the street how vital hope was to everyone's survival—and she was going to survive this, no matter how many greasy, dirty men touched her body.

"How could a woman as beautiful and intelligent as you prostitute yourself?" the general asked.

Megan held his gaze. "Americans do whatever it takes to survive."

General Zahn inched closer, the leering grin now back on his face. "Like spend the night with me?"

As his face neared hers, his fierce brown eyes bored into hers. Nodding slightly, Megan stared back into his eyes.

He might touch her body, but he would never break her spirit.

Never.

# 4——

**San Jose**, Costa Rica, was much like any American city: too many cars, too much smog, and not enough trees. Still, Delta was surprised by its overall modernity. She had half-expected to land on a dirt runway somewhere outside a small village, not this hustling bustling city complete with taxis, buses and traffic lights. *Connie's right: I need to get out more.*

"Why do we call this place underdeveloped?" Delta asked Connie as they waded through customs.

Connie finished her discussion with the customs agent before answering Delta. "They *do* speak English here, Del. Keep your voice down, will you?"

Lowering her voice, Delta spat, "Then why are *you* speaking Spanish?"

Connie grabbed her bag and headed out of the customs area. "It's their native language. You stand a better chance of getting answers if your questions are in Spanish."

"Then I'm screwed."

"Why? Because the extent of your Spanish is *taco* and *burrito?*"

"Don't forget *cuarto de baño.*"

Connie shook her head. "No, *you* don't forget. The way you eat, you'll probably use that word the most."

Grinning, Delta pushed opened the glass doors and was hit by the tropical heat and humidity—she hadn't anticipated that at seven in the morning. But then, Connie had warned her. In fact, what hadn't Connie told her about this tiny country? Nine hours of Costa Rican history on the plane and Delta thought she would surely strangle Connie.

"This reminds me of Hawaii," Delta said, stepping out into the moist air.

Hawaii. She and Megan had gone to Hawaii right after Miles's killers were sentenced. It had been one of the most romantic trips Delta had ever experienced. They spent their days on the beach, shopping, reading, just enjoying each other's company. They did the glass-bottom boat ride, the windsurfing, the parasailing, and endless hours of snorkeling. Megan's lust for adventure, her desire to experience everything on the island was equal to her sexual appetite At night, they took long strolls along the beach, slowly undressing each other in the surf. It was the vacation of their lives. How long ago it seemed.

Now, Delta was afraid if she slowed down long enough to think about possibly losing Megan, she would be paralyzed with fear. She had to keep focused and remain calm. Megan needed her to think clearly and rationally.

"So...where do we start?" Delta asked.

Connie peered at her watch and stretched. "We've got reservations at the Gran Hotel. We'll make calls from there to firm up our plan. I'm still not sure I like the idea of splitting up. You don't speak a lick of Spanish—"

"But you said some *Ticos* speak English."

"Some. Not all. If you're talking about going to the town where Augustine lives, we'll be traveling through towns where it's Spanish only. Didn't you read any of those brochures I gave you on the plane?"

Delta shrugged as she watched two cabs pull away from the curb. Actually, they looked more like minivans with rusty racks on top than they did taxis.

"Del? You okay?"

Turning toward Connie, Delta shrugged again. She felt so out of place, so foreign, so...alone. They were in a country

Delta knew nothing about, looking for the most important woman in her life, and she didn't know where to begin. "It's hard, Con. To slow down and make plans when it takes everything I have not to jump in a taxi and head somewhere, anywhere." Delta looked out at the crosswalk as a family of four scooted across. "I'm afraid to think about never seeing Megan again."

Connie laid her hand on Delta's shoulder. "Then don't think about it. We'll find her, Del. We may have to tear every inch of this country apart, but we are going to find her."

Delta glanced up at the sky; it looked like it might rain. "How can you be so sure?"

Hooking her arm through Delta's, Connie led her across the street. "Because you're Delta Stevens, that's why. Come on. Let's find our hotel."

After registering at the Gran Hotel, one of the better cheap hotels in the city, Delta sat on the veranda and sipped excellent coffee, while Connie made arrangements with the car-rental agent at the front of the hotel. Setting down her third cup, Delta looked out at the bustling street from their corner table on the veranda. She pulled out the picture of Megan she'd taken off the refrigerator—it was one of Delta's favorite pictures. Megan's long blonde hair was tossed casually over one shoulder, and her opaline eyes gazed meaningfully into the camera. Megan was beautiful by anyone's standards, and her smile could melt Arctic glaciers. It was that smile and those eyes which had captured Delta's heart a few years ago, when their worlds were light years apart and heading straight for each other. Delta was a beat cop who felt prostitution was a victimless crime. Megan had been a prostitute whose best friend, Miles Brookman, was a cop, and who was brutally killed one night. Megan had helped Delta and Connie bring down the men responsible for his murder. In the ensuing weeks, Megan and Delta fell deeply in love. Since then, Megan had been helping Delta and Connie catch criminals. She never doubted the two supercops would have found their perp with or without her, but it was still fun to be a part of the process.

Some time later, when Connie's life was endangered by an old college rival, Megan had set aside her studies to help find him before he could do Connie any harm. Megan fit so easily into Delta and Connie's equation that she soon became part of their family.

It wasn't easy for many women to understand the ties that bound Delta and Connie together. Hell, Delta wasn't sure *she* understood it herself. Gina, Connie's lover, referred to the relationship as symbiotic. Symbiotic. Delta had had to look it up: *Two organisms that need each other in order to survive.* That probably was a good way to describe them.

The blare of a car horn brought Delta back to the present. She was acutely aware that Megan needed her help, and she didn't even know where to start. For a change, her gut instincts were silent. It was as if once she deboarded the plane, her intuition was left sitting on the seat. Megan had come here to find herself and now...she was literally lost. Irony cut its wicked teeth on Delta's heart, and she cursed her intuition for failing her.

As she stared at the picture, Delta wiped a stray tear meandering down her cheek. She would be no good to Megan if she let her emotions run wild. She had to remain levelheaded, and in control. She needed to think clearly and plan accordingly. Thank God Connie had come with her, or else Delta might be running through the streets shouting Megan's name.

Glancing up from the photo, Delta studied her best friend with amazement as Connie gesticulated and spoke to the man from the car-rental agency. Delta had to smile. Connie Rivera was, quite simply, the most remarkable woman Delta had ever known. Fluent in five languages, possessing a black belt in karate and two degrees from MIT, there was nothing Connie could not do. No doubt about it, Connie was the best. And it wasn't just her job as Research Specialist in the police department that Connie left behind to help Delta; she'd also left her pregnant lover, Gina, to fend for herself. Not many women would be as understanding as Gina had been in accepting the conditions of Delta and Connie's relationship. Like Megan, Gina was both understanding and accepting. Together, the four women made a nearly unbeatable team, and anyone entering any of their lives soon learned that Delta and Connie were a package deal. Like the strongest twine, Delta, Connie, Megan and Gina's lives were interwoven so completely that when one was in trouble, the others came running to help. If Gina weren't pregnant, she would be sitting across the table from Delta at this very minute.

Sighing heavily, Delta set the photo on the table. She had faced many dangers in her career as a cop for the River Valley Police Department, but none had prepared her for this. This was a different type of fear seeping into her soul, like a slow-acting poison that debilitates the victim. Right now, it took all her strength not to drown in the "what ifs." What if Megan was hurt? What if Delta couldn't find her? What if...

Watching Connie conclude her conversation with the car-rental agent, Delta picked up the photo and dropped it in her shirt pocket. When Connie sat down, she looked in her empty mug and signaled to the waitress.

"What was that all about?" Delta asked.

"At home, if you want to find out how to get some place, you ask a cab driver. Here, you ask the rental agent."

Delta shook her head. "How in the hell do you know so much?"

Connie's eyes narrowed. "I read." Waiting until the waitress poured her more coffee, Connie continued, "You okay?"

"I'm all right. Just thinking about Megan, that's all."

Connie checked her watch. "What time did you say Liz was meeting us?"

"Eight-thirty. What time does the embassy open?"

"It's probably open now. Here, things tend to open early, while it's still cool. You won't find much going on in the midafternoon, when it's very hot."

Delta started to respond, when a young blonde woman walked up to their table. "Delta?"

Delta nodded as she and Connie both rose.

"I'm Liz."

Delta reached her hand out and shook Liz's. "Hi. I'm Delta. This is Connie. Have you heard anything?" Delta asked, pulling a seat out for Liz.

Liz shook her head. "Nothing. Augustine's family is sick with worry. They say he's never stayed away this long." Liz sat down in the chair with exaggerated weariness. "They've called his father. He'll be flying home on the next plane back." Liz said something in Spanish to the waitress before returning her attention to Delta. "It took all night to get hold of Augustine's family. Some of the smaller towns here have only one phone per town."

"You're kidding."

Liz smiled. "You're in the capital now, Delta, but some areas are extremely remote. Don't let San Jose fool you. There's a wilderness to this country that's every bit as wild as Africa or the Australian outback."

"And you think Megan is in that wild?" This came from Connie, who was busy scratching notes on a small notepad.

Liz reached into her large purse and pulled out a book that Delta immediately recognized.

"Megan's journal."

Handing it to Delta, Liz nodded. "She takes one into the field with her, but uses this one at night. I thought you might find something helpful."

Delta took it from her and flipped to the last entry. In Megan's neatly scripted handwriting, it read:

> Tomorrow's the day. I have to admit I'm a little nervous, but reporting them doesn't seem to make a difference. Augustine assures me we can do this, but I'm still hesitant. We're going deeper into the jungle

after them—it should be exciting. I understand the wildlife is much different the deeper you go. The Bribri tribe is still living there, so we will have to be careful not to overstep our bounds. Well, the days are positively flying by, and soon, I'll return home to Delta—a much better woman than I've ever been. I've missed sharing my life with her, but I'm sure I can convince her to come back here with me. Once she sees it, I know she'll fall in love. Well, gotta go—

Delta handed the journal to Connie. "Was there anything else in her room that might help us?"

Shaking her head, Liz sighed. "I left everything just the way I found it. I figured you'd want to take a look for yourself."

Connie flipped to a few pages before the last entry and quickly read the short entries. "She mentions something here about climbing Chirripo. Is that a mountain?"

Liz frowned as she thought. "Climbing Chirripo? Yeah, it's one of the main mountain peaks of the Talamanca mountain range, but she never mentioned going there to me."

Connie set the journal down and studied Liz. "Something bothering you?"

Liz returned Connie's gaze with confused eyes. "La Amistad and Chirripo are huge. If she really went there, she'll be impossible to track down."

"How impossible?"

Liz looked out into the streets of San Jose and shook her head. "I don't know. I'm not as into the rain-forest thing as Meg was. Sorry."

Delta glanced at her watch. She'd had enough talk. It was time for some action. "Let's assume she and Augustine were going to La Amistad in search of poachers. Just how big is it?"

Connie quickly flipped open her guidebook and read aloud. "'La Amistad is 193,929 hectares.' Whew."

Delta shrugged. "And that translates to what?"

"Approximately 479,000 acres. Give or take," Connie calculated.

"That's wild rain-forest acres, Delta. It's not a stroll through the park, even for an experienced guide." Liz wiped the sweat beading on her upper lip.

"What can you tell us about the poachers they were after? How serious a threat are they?"

Liz's demeanor changed immediately. "Very dangerous. From what Megan has shared with us, poaching on this scale nets the poachers thousands of dollars, but the risk is huge. Get caught poaching here and you're going to spend some decent time in one of the horrendous Costa Rican jails. It's not like in the United States; these guys will shoot anyone who threatens them or gets in their way."

"Do you think Megan and Augustine posed a serious threat to them?"

Liz thought for a moment before answering. "It's possible. Meg told us that a scarlet macaw goes for anywhere between one and three grand in the States; more in the UK and Canada."

Delta nodded. She had already purchased a blue-and-gold macaw as a welcome home present for Megan. She well knew the price of one of those gorgeous birds. "And they might net how many in a week?"

Liz shrugged. "Ten, twenty, maybe more. Exotics, dead or alive, are big business in rain-forest countries, Delta. These guys play for keeps."

"Aren't they worth more alive?"

"Sure. But only one out of every seven wild birds caught makes it to the US alive, so they have to catch a lot to make money."

"This makes me sick," Connie said, shaking her head.

Liz nodded. "After they catch the birds, they tape their wings, beaks and feet with duct tape, anesthetize them with brandy or whiskey, roll them in newspapers, stuff them in shoe boxes, and then put the shoe boxes in the hub of the wheels of their cars in order to get them across the border. That doesn't include what happens to them once they're out of the country."

Delta sighed sadly. No wonder Megan had so wanted to make a difference. "Disgusting."

"Yeah, well, so are the prisons here, so you better be careful if you're going in there after her."

Delta and Connie exchanged looks. Delta knew what Connie was thinking. "Liz, I think we should take a look at Megan's room. Maybe there's something there that might give us a better idea of what we're up against."

Connie motioned to the waitress, said something to her in Spanish, and handed her a five-hundred *colones* bill. "Where does Augustine's family live again?"

"In a small town called Rivas. It's right outside La Amistad."

"Address?"

Liz grinned. "They don't use any. Just ask for Señor Augustine Riner's *finca*. The people there are very friendly. They'll point you in the right direction. Just ask."

Delta gulped down the remainder of her coffee, pushed her chair back and rose. Connie glanced up at her, apparently annoyed by this gesture. "Where do you think you're going?"

"I can't just sit here. There's work to be done."

Reaching across the table, Connie took Delta's hand. "Thrashing about will only cost us time. We need more information before we go off running into the jungle. She could be right here in San Jose for all we know. Now, sit down and have another cup of coffee so we can figure out our next move."

Slowly returning to her chair, Delta sighed and struggled to keep from crying. "Sorry." Running her hand through her short, curly hair, Delta sighed again. It had been her nature in the past to run headfirst into danger. Doing so now would only endanger Megan; and that wasn't something she was about to do.

"It's okay," Connie answered softly. "We have to be smart about this, or we could wind up chasing our tails.

We need to get as many answers as we can before charging into the jungle."

"I know," Delta replied weakly. The anxiety she had been fighting to suppress was successfully breaking through the surface of her well-constructed facade.

"Just hang in there. We'll find her." Connie turned to Liz. "Would you mind taking us back to your pension so we can have a look at Megan's room?"

Liz nodded. "Sure."

Connie looked out at the street. "What's Juan Carlos think about all of this?"

Liz shook her head. "He thinks Augustine is quite the lady's man and swept Megan off her feet."

"What?" Delta practically jumped out of her chair.

"It's just part of the Latin culture, Delta, it's nothing to—"

"I couldn't give a shit about culture, Liz! Hasn't he done anything to find her?"

"He did make some calls for us, but I'm afraid Juan Carlos won't be much help to us."

"I think he should be our first visit." Delta rose as she said this.

Liz reached out and touched Delta's hand. "He's not here."

Delta stopped and glowered down at Liz. "What do you mean he's not here?"

"He had business in Nicaragua, and won't be back until tomorrow."

"He isn't worried, then?"

Liz shrugged. "Believe me, Juan Carlos believes Megan fell under Augustine's charm and is spending some romantic time with him. That's how they think down here."

Delta slowly lowered herself back to her seat. "So, he didn't bother sending anyone after her or check to make sure this Augustine guy wasn't taking adv—"

"It's nothing like that, Delta. He's a really nice guy who's devoted to saving animals in the rain forest. Megan showed an interest and they became friends. But that's all. Megan made it clear she was not available. *Tico* men respect a woman's space, unlike some of the other Latin American men. Augustine was just a friend."

A sigh of relief escaped from Delta's lips. "And you're sure he understood Megan's boundaries?"

Connie leaned closer to Liz. "What Delta wants to know is, is there any reason why we shouldn't suspect that Augustine had abducted her?"

Liz shook her head. "I never saw him treat Megan like anything other than a friend or a student. He was always very respectful. If he had any romantic feelings for her, I wouldn't know."

Delta pushed her chair back once more and stood up. "Let's get to the *pension* and see what we can find."

Connie glanced up at Delta.

"Now, Consuela! I won't wait any longer."

Connie slowly rose, taking Megan's journal and stuffing it in her purse. "What about the embassy?"

Delta considered this a moment. "Why don't you go to the embassy, and I'll go to Megan's. We might as well cover as much ground as we can." Delta smiled to the waitress as they made their way from the veranda to the front of the Gran Hotel.

Connie gazed over at Delta. "I still don't like the idea of separating."

"It makes the most sense."

Sighing, Connie acquiesced. "All right. Meet me back here in three hours, and don't go anywhere else."

Delta nodded and said softly, "Thanks."

"No problem. You take the Jeep." Connie pointed to the red Jeep in the parking lot before turning to Liz. "You take Del back to your place. I'll get a taxi."

Delta took the keys from Connie. "Good idea. Come on, Liz." Hopping over the curb, Delta started for the Jeep.

"Storm?"

Turning just as she put the key in the door, Delta answered. "Yeah?"

"Don't go off half-cocked," Connie warned, fully aware of Delta's MO when patrolling the streets. Delta was as unconventional as they came when it came to bringing down the bad guys. "And take this." Tossing Delta a map, Connie watched as she snatched it with her free hand.

"Right."

"We're not in River Valley, Del. Remember that."

Closing her fingers around the keys, Delta unlocked the door and jumped in. They might be out of their element, but solving crimes was what they did best.

5——

**Morning** sun filtered through the large green leaves of the overhanging trees. Shafts of sunlight caressed the camp as a light breeze rustled the smaller leaves. The only sound louder than the birds and insects was the sound of tents being unzipped.

*"Buenos días!"* one of the guards announced as he folded the tent flap back. As he held his hand out to help Megan through the opening, the guard grinned at her.

"No thanks," Megan said, brushing past his outstretched hand. Shielding her eyes from the sun, she realized there was something different about this morning. "It's later than usual, isn't it?"

The guard, still grinning, nodded. "*Sí.* General Zahn want you sleep late. You good for his...*como se dice...* temperature?"

Megan looked at him. "That's temperament, Paco, and you can march right back there and tell him that I don't want any special treatment. He may get me in the evenings, but I don't want anything from him once the sun comes up."

The guard, still smiling, said in broken English, "No make him happy."

Stretching, Megan bent over and helped Siobhan from the tent. "I don't really care."

The guard looked at Megan and shook his head. "No smart, *señorita*. The general is *muy feo* when *enojado*."

"I'm sure he's ugly even when he's not mad. Go on, Pedro...take my message back to him."

The guard shrugged. "Whatever you say."

As they were led away, Megan asked Siobhan, "You okay?"

Siobhan looked up at Megan with empty eyes. "I don't know how much longer I can do this."

Megan put her arm around Siobhan's shoulders and walked close to her as they started their descent into the mouth of darkened caverns covered by overgrowth. After four days of this daily trek, they were all too familiar with the rocky path. At first, Megan figured they were being led to their deaths. And in a way, they were—they were being worked to death. Already, one woman had collapsed, and when she refused to work, they shot her in the back of the head. This seemed to motivate the others the next day.

"I know you're scared," Megan whispered to Siobhan. "But you must have courage."

"Courage? How can I? And how can you just keep going, knowing they'll probably kill us when they're through?"

Megan stopped. "Kill us? Where'd you get that idea?"

"They killed your friend, Augustine, didn't they?"

Megan blinked her eyes quickly. "That was different. Augustine knows the rain forest. He could have gotten us out of here. He was a threat. To the Colombians, we're just weak women. We're not really considered very threatening."

"Exactly. They were afraid of him. And they'll be afraid to let us go, too. They'll do the same to us when we're finished."

"Then we must not finish."

Siobhan stopped. "What?"

Gently pulling her along, Megan lowered her voice. "Tell the others to slow down just a little. We must buy ourselves some time."

"Time? Time for what?"

"Time for me to think of a way to get us out of here."

6——

**An** hour and a half after her fruitless search through Megan's possessions, Delta drove into the town of Rivas. The first thing she noticed was its size...or lack thereof—one main street...and the major mode of transportation was by foot.

So far, Liz's description of life outside the city of San Jose was right on the mark. The Pan-American highway was the only real highway in the country that didn't have yard-long potholes, sections of gravel, or one-lane bridges. Once outside the metropolitan area, the scenery was lush and green—every shade of green imaginable. Numerous small houses dotted the countryside. But they weren't houses like Delta was used to seeing at home. These almost looked like airy barns and small sheds. Few, if any, had glass in the windows, and almost every front door was wide open.

But what struck her the most were the smiles on the people's faces. Everywhere she went, people waved to her, as if she were some long-forgotten relative. They seemed so happy, so carefree. But then, Delta figured, given the beauty of their surroundings, it was no wonder. This country was a postcard. Everywhere she looked, she saw another Kodak moment. There were rolling hills, lush valleys, cliffs covered with the forest green of coffee trees. Every available field was home to at least one kind of fruit-bearing tree or shrub. In areas too steep for tree growth were dark green coffee plants flowing lazily over the cliffs and hillsides. There were small farms rolling across the expanse, some with white cows and an occasional bull. Nothing had prepared her for the raw beauty that lay before her. Suddenly she understood why Megan had fallen in love with this place.

Delta pulled up to the first building she saw, locked the Jeep, and walked across the street to a bar with a long, unrecognizable name—*Los something-or-other.* Reaching into her back pocket, Delta withdrew the pocket traveler Connie had forced on her on the plane. She looked at the front of it and grinned. *I don't even know how to use it.*

Nearing what looked like an outdoor bar, Delta watched several children running across the street, their laughter filling the tropical air.

"Hey!" Delta shouted. All five children immediately stopped. Flipping open the pocket guide, Delta knelt down in front of the gaggle of kids.

*"Hay alguien aquí que habla inglés?"* Delta asked, butchering the pronunciation.

The children shook their heads. The oldest child couldn't have been more than six or seven.

"Shit," Delta said, rising and jamming her hands on her hips. The children giggled at her. They might not know English, but they knew enough to see that she was a frustrated traveler who had just sworn. Pulling Megan's picture out, Delta showed it to them. The children all crowded around to see it and began chattering among themselves. Finally, when all the talking died down, the oldest-looking boy shook his head.

*"Gracias,"* Delta said, putting the picture back. As she started toward the bar, she turned back to the kids for one last try. "Augustine Riner?" she asked hopefully.

The group nodded in unison. *"Sí! Vive aquí!"*

Delta quickly flipped through her guidebook, looking for the word for 'where.'

Before she could find it, they all pointed down the street, while chattering again among themselves. Suddenly, Delta had a feeling that she'd landed in Munchkin Land, and that she, too, was dogless.

"Uh, *Señor Riner's casa?*" she asked, pulling out the fourth Spanish word she knew. The children stopped talking and the oldest boy took her hand and started pulling her down the street, followed by the flock of curious children. If only there were a yellow brick road...

About a hundred yards from where the Jeep was parked, they came to a little house with no glass on the windows, and the front door wide open. This was a far cry from River Valley, California, where windows and doors were often protected by bars, security gates and guarded driveways, and where people owned attack dogs for pets.

Unfamiliar with Costa Rican customs, Delta stopped at the door, even though the boy was motioning for her to enter.

"No way, kid. Where I come from, walking into someone's house uninvited is asking for a bullet between the eyes. I think I'll just wait here." Delta smiled at the children behind her and thanked them again. They seemed perplexed by her unwillingness to enter the house, and one of the smaller girls said something to the group before taking off down the street. Delta had read somewhere (or was it one of Connie's oft-told tales?) that gypsy children lured tourists into desolate areas so adult gypsies could mug them. Delta watched silently as the girl disappeared down the street. Where was she going? For the cops? For her dad? Her gut instincts kicking in, Delta surveyed her surroundings for a way out. Connie, as usual, had been right: Delta was way out of her element here, and all the street savvy she had acquired over the years was all but useless to her now.

Starting down the path, Delta decided retreat was the better part of stupidity, and would try the *Los-something* bar again. When she looked up, the little girl who had left a moment ago had returned with a teenage girl in tow.

"Great," Delta muttered. "Now, I'm a tourist attraction."

When the two girls rejoined the group, everyone started talking to the teenager at once. How anyone heard what was being said was beyond Delta. What she *did* understand was that they were all giving the new girl their version of finding this bumbling American tourist. The new girl, who was much older than the others, held her hand up and the children all stopped talking. She pointed to one older boy, who chattered away a moment, before beaming proudly that he had been the chosen one. The new girl then turned from the group, sized up Delta, and then stepped in front of her.

"I'm Bianca," she said. "What's your name?"

Bianca's crisp, clear English was sweetness to Delta, who was beginning to feel like she'd fallen into a foreign film.

"My name is Delta. You speak English?" Delta asked slowly, afraid Bianca might only know that one line.

Bianca smiled and nodded. "And quite well, too."

Another huge sigh escaped Delta's mouth. Finally, someone with whom she could communicate. Delta studied the young girl in amazement. Bianca had beautiful caramel-colored skin and a lovely face surrounded by shiny black hair down to her waist. She regarded Delta with big, intelligent brown eyes. *She could be Connie at that age,* Delta thought, for the similarities in their expressions were uncanny.

Bianca grinned as Delta squatted there. Bianca looked about 13 or 14 but Delta couldn't be sure. "Your English is very good," Delta said.

Bianca's smile grew. "I am home on holiday. I attend a private school in Canada."

Ah...illumination at last. "Oh, I see."

"I am also fluent in French, but I'm afraid there's no use for that here. Maria says she thinks you are looking for someone."

Retrieving Megan's picture once again, Delta held it out to Bianca. "A friend of mine disappeared a few days ago.

We think she was traveling with—"

"Augustine Riner."

Delta's eyes grew wide and her heart seemed to skip. "Yes!" she said eagerly.

"He is gone, also. That is why his family is not home. His brothers went looking for him on Talamanca, and his mama and sister are in San Jose." Bianca looked at the picture of Megan with intense eyes. "The boys had spoken of a beautiful woman traveling with Augustine. She is very pretty." Handing the picture back, Bianca said something to the children, who scattered like leaves in the wind.

"But you haven't seen her?"

"No. We knew Augustine was taking some woman into the forest, but that was the last anyone heard."

"How long ago was that?"

"Four days."

"How long has his family been gone?"

"They left two days ago. Augustine is very responsible and doesn't like to worry his mama. Something has happened to him, or he would have called."

"What do they think happened to him?"

Bianca looked away. "There are rumors...I don't know..."

"What?" Delta's voice was hard and sharp, as if she were speaking to an adult. Yet this precocious girl certainly spoke and acted like a grownup. "I'm sorry, I didn't mean to snap at you."

Bianca patted Delta's hand. "Costa Ricans don't gossip. It isn't right to speak lies of someone, and anything you say that is not the truth is a lie."

Delta studied her for a moment, unsure of what to say. "Then tell me as much of the truth as you know."

Bianca grinned. "You're asking me to guess."

"I'm asking for help."

Bianca's eyebrows knitted together as she thought. "Some of us believe Augustine is a tour guide, but others...well, people around town know of his hatred for…what are they called in English? Poachers?"

"He does that for a living?"

"We do lots of different things for a living here. Augustine has a special relationship with animals. He goes into the forest all the time."

Delta gazed into Bianca's face. "What do *you* think he was doing in the rain forest?"

Rubbing her chin, Bianca thought for a moment. "I'm not sure. My brother, Manny, might know. He and Augustine are good friends."

"Where's your brother now?"

Bianca glanced up at the sun and then down at the shadow of the streets. "He's usually at the bridge about now. Want me to take you there?"

Nodding, Delta looked up at the sun, and wondered if she would ever be able to tell time by the solar clock. "I'd really appreciate that."

Bianca headed for the road. "Delta, huh? Isn't that Greek?"

Delta nodded. "Yes, it is."

"Delta what?"

"Stevens. Delta Stevens."

"Well, Delta Stevens, it is awfully brave of you to come deep into a country without knowing its language or customs."

Delta followed Bianca onto the main road. "I came with a friend who is fluent in Spanish."

Bianca stopped and shook her head. "Spanish? That might work in San Jose and out here, but if you're going into the forest, it won't help you one bit. The natives here have their own language and not even *Ticos* can understand it. Sort of like your Native Americans, I would imagine."

Delta stared at her. "How old are you, anyway?"

"Me? Almost sixteen. But don't let my age fool you. There's a reason I'm in a private school so far from home."

Bianca continued walking until she took a turn down a gravel road. "We have to stop at my house first to get Kiki. My mother doesn't like me going to the bridge without Kiki, just in case something happens."

Delta smiled at Bianca and wondered, only for a split second, if the trees were going to start throwing their fruit or if a witch was going to land on top of a house and start tossing fireballs. "In case something happens? What could happen on a bridge?"

Bianca parted the low-hanging branches of a fruit tree and waited for Delta to pass before responding. "*Los cocodrilos*, is what can happen."

"Los what?"

Bianca grinned and shook her head. "Crocodiles, Delta Stevens. Big, fat, ugly crocodiles."

"Crocodiles?" Delta said, her mouth hanging open. "You're kidding, right?"

Bianca set her hands on her hips once more, a gesture Delta would come to know quite well. "What did you do? Hop on a plane without the faintest idea of where you were going?"

Delta nodded sheepishly. "Something like that."

"Then you know next to nothing about the forest or its animal life?"

Delta nodded again. "Zip." Delta waited for Bianca to respond, but the girl only shook her head. "Look, I heard my friend was missing and here I am."

The two did not talk again until they reached an even smaller dirt road outside of town.

"Is Kiki your sister?"

Bianca laughed. "I suppose you could say that." Putting her hands to her mouth, Bianca yelled, "Kiki! Kiki, come here!"

"Oh. She's your dog."

Bianca rolled her eyes at Delta before putting her fingers in her mouth and whistling sharply, a skill Delta had tried so hard to master when she was her age, but which she never quite got the hang of.

Seconds later, there came a rustling from the trees. Glancing skyward, Delta watched a black-and-white monkey leap with lightning speed and precision accuracy from tree to tree. When it reached the lowest branch, it wrapped its tail around it and slowly lowered itself to Bianca's head. Reaching with tiny, leather-like hands, the monkey released the branch and sat on Bianca's shoulders with what could only be called a grin on its face.

"This is Kiki."

With wide eyes, Delta simply stared. She had seen monkeys once when her fifth-grade class took a trip to the zoo, but she'd never been this close to one.

"You can pet her. Just hold your hand out slowly so she knows you aren't trying to grab her. Monkeys hate being grabbed.

As much as she wanted to, Delta could not move.

"Don't be scared. She only bites people who grab her or aren't nice to me. Really. Just reach your hand out."

Delta stared at the tiny face of a monkey who looked like she would laugh if she knew how. Her sparkling little eyes, smiling face, and rosy cheeks made Kiki appear to be a happy monkey. The chirping sounds coming from her as she picked through Bianca's hair were much like those of a baby.

"What's she doing?" Delta asked, watching as the monkey parted Bianca's hair with her nimble fingers.

"Grooming me. Monkeys look for lice and other bugs on each other as a form of bonding. Kiki loves to do it even though she never finds anything."

"Then why doesn't she stop?"

Bianca giggled as Kiki tickled her ear. "They don't do it for results, they do it for contact and warmth. She loves me."

Slowly, tentatively, Delta put her hand out to Kiki, who stopped her grooming long enough to look at Delta's hand. "Hi there, Kiki," Delta said in a voice she reserved for her cats. At the mention of her name, Kiki completely turned toward Delta and blinked both eyes. Her pink little face framed in white fur looked so soft and inviting. As Delta's hand neared her, Kiki reached one of her hands out and grabbed Delta's index finger. The first sensation that coursed to Delta' brain was the softness of that tiny black hand. It was the softest thing Delta had ever felt in her life. And it wasn't a paw—not really. It looked and felt too much like a hand to be called a paw.

"Hold your arm out stiff and she'll use it as a bridge to climb on your shoulders. Just don't be afraid, and don't pull away."

Delta did as she was told, and Kiki scurried onto Delta's shoulders. To maintain her balance, Kiki's tail hugged Delta around the neck. Delta was surprised at the strength of the tail, as it gripped her. It felt like the time one of her grammar school classmates brought a boa constrictor to class and Delta held it around her neck during recess.

Bianca started back down the path. "We'd better get going or we might miss some action."

"Action?" Delta said, as she caught up to Bianca. "What do you mean?"

Bianca grinned as she turned around and then started to skip away. "You'll see what I mean. Come on!"

The bridge crossed over the river's bend for fifty yards, and mixed technology and nature in bizarre fashion. What surprised Delta were all the people with picnic baskets lined up along the bridge. People had binoculars; some were kicking back in lawn chairs, while others spread out a blanket to sit on. One obvious tourist couple had a camcorder on a tripod, but even they seemed to be anxiously awaiting the arrival of something. As Delta looked at the various faces surrounding the river, she realized that, with the exception of the two tourists, the rest were all *Ticos*.

"What's going on?" Delta whispered as if they were in a theater.

Bianca shrugged. "Anything. Everything. Sometimes, but not very often, nothing." Bianca waved to a couple of people before starting over the bridge.

"You've lost me."

Bianca grabbed Delta's hand and pulled her faster. "Three times a day, the wildlife becomes active around here. Natives and knowledgeable tourists come here to just hang out and see what happens today. It's our version of TV, only way better."

Delta didn't know what to say. All about her were people with ice-chests, cracking open a Cerveza and crunching on some kind of snack. Like in the movies, just before the lights go out, people were visiting, laughing, chatting and preparing for the main event. Delta wondered what the big deal was about a couple of crocodiles. Weren't they simply giant lizards? They certainly weren't the most beautiful creatures in the world. Wasn't Marlin Perkins eaten by one?

"But what's the big deal?" Delta asked, pulling Kiki's hand from her pocket.

"The 'big deal' is that last night, at five, when the macaws start to leave the forest, en route to the cliff's shores, this one macaw came flying out before he realized that his mate wasn't with him. He did this excellent U-turn in midair, squawking the entire time, like he was really mad. When he met his mate, he got even louder, as if he was yelling at her. It was pretty funny."

Kiki wrapped her tail more tightly around Delta's neck and hung like a necklace on her chest. "Sort of like a television show, then."

Bianca nodded. "You never know what's going to happen out here from one moment to the next."

Delta looked out into the forest in the distance. "Are there a lot of macaws in there?"

"Tons."

"And your brother is supposed to be here?"

Kiki suddenly jumped from Delta to Bianca. "Manny's one of the few people in town with a job other than farming. He's a tour guide for a company in the city. It's a pretty good job, really. He works one week on and one week off, and today is his last day on."

"He brings people here?" Delta asked, looking around.

"Sometimes. He will today. This group is a bunch of environmental scientists from Germany. Or was it Sweden? Anyway, he'll be coming out of the forest any second. Then he'll go down the road and catch their bus. Oh...look over there."

Delta peered over the bridge's edge and did a double-take. What she had originally thought were logs were actually crocodiles floating lazily in the water next to the river bank. About twelve feet from the bank's edge, the river picked up speed rapidly as it raced around the bend for destinations unknown. The crocodiles seemed to defy the current and floated with just their eyes, the tips of their noses and parts of their backs protruding from the water. They were a tannish-beige color. Of the five she could spot, their length ranged from five to fifteen feet long. How animals that size could float was beyond Delta, but there they were, hanging out like there was nothing better to do.

"I feel like Jacques Cousteau," Delta whispered.

"I've traveled all over the world," Bianca whispered back, "but no place in the world compares to my home here. My teachers say everyone feels that way, but my home is different. My home is so alive, so real."

It might be real to Bianca, but to Delta, it was surreal. She had spent so much time in the city, she had stopped imagining the possibilities beyond its concrete walls.

"How long before your brother arrives?"

Bianca shrugged. "Hard to tell. I'd say within the hour. Our buses have to deal with potholes the size of tennis courts. They'll get here when they get here."

For the next half hour, Bianca pointed out scarlet macaws eating, playing and preening each other. She showed Delta smaller green parrots, two four-foot-long iguanas, a pair of howler monkeys, whose deep-throated sounds contributed to their names. She showed Delta six-inch-long grasshoppers, various waterfowl which cruised along the bank looking for food, and a variety of reptiles and amphibians out sunning themselves. It was a strange and wondrous world to Delta. And without Bianca's practiced eyes, she might not have seen any of it.

As the young girl started to point out another bird, Kiki made a very strange, high-pitched noise.

"What's that about?" Delta asked, as Bianca suddenly froze.

"Shh. Something's going to happen. Look!" Pointing in the direction in which Kiki was staring, Bianca turned Delta's attention to a fifteen-foot crocodile which had just surfaced near the bank. In a flash faster than seemed possible, the crocodile leapt from the water, grabbed a bird that had wandered too close to the edge, and returned to the depths of the river as quickly as it came.

"Holy shit! Did you see that?"

Suddenly, the water under the bridge erupted like a volcano, as a huge tan crocodile thrashed violently about as it grabbed a white heron that had strayed too close to the water's edge.

"I can't believe it," Delta uttered, shaking her head. "Unbelievable."

The crocodile, now holding the heron in its ominous jaws, shook the bird back and forth in a powerful display of viciousness, before plunging back into the water. The crowd around the bridge cheered their good fortune. They had just witnessed a sight most wildlife photographers would wait a lifetime to see.

Bianca nodded and beamed proudly. "Better than TV, huh?"

Delta nodded vigorously. "Much better. If I lived here, I'd come here every day."

"Many do."

Delta looked out over the river which flowed through the rain forest just ahead. "I imagined someplace completely different. I kept hearing words like third-world and underdeveloped."

This made Bianca laugh. "Hardly. We've let the rest of the world think that so they'll leave us alone. We're afraid Americans and Europeans will find out how lucky we are and then we're doomed. Look what happened to Hawaii."

Delta cast her gaze down at this girl-who-would-be-woman. There was so much more to her than her precocious nature. "How come you're so smart?"

Bianca shrugged. "My father is a Canadian diplomat. He sent me to the finest schools in the world."

"I thought you were Costa Rican."

"I am, silly. I live with my mother when I'm on holiday. My father comes home whenever he gets the chance. It's a good arrangement for them, because my mother enjoys her time away from him."

"Why didn't she just go to Canada with him?"

"And leave all this?"

Suddenly, a flock of screaming, squawking scarlet macaws took flight. Delta could only look up at them in wonder. With their long tails waving grandly behind them, they were fireballs against a blue, blue sky. Their powerful wings beat quickly and majestically as they sliced through the air. These incredible birds were the reason Megan was missing, and, in this instant, Delta was truly beginning to understand why. Two by two they left the rain forest, squawking back and forth in what could almost pass for laughter. Some flew higher than others, but no matter what the distance, no one could miss the bright red tails waving as they flew. They were like splashes of red paint on a blank canvas. Everything about them took Delta's breath away. "God, they're beautiful."

"Nothing like them in the world, that's for sure. Hey, here comes my brother."

Glancing at the other end of the bridge, Delta watched a young Costa Rican male pointing toward the macaws while talking. He couldn't have been more than twenty-one or twenty-two. He had short, curly black hair, a smooth caramel complexion, and piercing brown eyes, much like his sister's. Delta studied him as he helped everyone load onto the bus. He was very gentle with an elderly couple who had a hard time getting up the steps.

"What makes you think your brother knows anything about Augustine's disappearance?"

"Manny knows a lot about everything that goes on here. I think he's a spy, myself."

"Will he tell us if he knows anything?"

"*Us?* He won't tell *us* anything. He'll tell *you* whatever it is you want to know. Manny is a sucker for green-eyed women. One look at you, and he'll tell you where Amelia Earhart is."

Delta laughed. "How old did you say you were?"

Bianca picked a leaf off a tree and handed it to Kiki. "Age is just a state of mind."

Shaking her head, Delta stared down into Bianca's dark eyes. "You remind me of a woman who would have said the exact same thing."

Bianca grinned. "Smart lady."

Delta grinned back. "The smartest."

7——

"I wish the embassy could have been more help," Liz said before dropping Connie off at the Gran Hotel. After saying her good-byes, Connie grabbed Megan's journal and the note Megan had left for Liz and Terry, and ran upstairs to her room. But even before the door was fully opened, Connie knew Delta was not there. Not there, nor would she be there any time soon—she just knew it. Checking her watch, Connie shook her head. It was a little after one, and Delta was already late getting back. *Damn! Never should've left her to her own devices.* But the reality was that sometimes, stopping Delta Stevens from doing what she wanted was as impossible as stopping the rain.

Tossing her purse on the bed, Connie heaved a sigh. "I should've known."

Suddenly, there was a knock on the door. Throwing open the door, Connie half-expected to find Delta standing there.

"Pardon, *señorita*," the concierge said, bowing his head. "But your friend call. Left these note for you." Handing Connie a piece of notebook paper, he grinned and started back down the stairs.

Opening the note, Connie read:

*Nothing at Megan's. Went to Rivas. Will*
*return tonight. Don't worry.*

*Love, Storm*

"God damn you, Storm," Connie muttered, crumpling the note and missing the trash can with it. She had christened Delta *Storm* when Delta was just a rookie storming headfirst into any fracas or investigation, with little regard for rules or regulations. Even now, years later, Delta still stormed into battle before taking inventory. Connie remembered how on one occasion, when Delta thought there were children in a burning building, she'd raced in, forgetting her childhood fear of being burned alive—which was what almost happened to her. Connie could only hope Delta wasn't storming around the countryside now. "We're not in River Valley," Connie said softly, feeling the same dread she had felt the night Delta went into a warehouse after a killer and was shot.

Tossing the rest of her things in her bag, Connie hustled downstairs to the concierge, arranged for another rental car, and made the only phone call she could think of making.

"Hello?" came a small voice on the other end.

"Thank God you're home. It's Connie, and I need your help."

8———

**When** Megan reached the opening of the mine, she cast one last longing look at the bright sun. It made her realize once again how much she loved being a part of the magic of daytime living. Ever since she'd been snatched by General Zahn's men, she'd spent grueling, backbreaking hours in the cavern, panning, separating, sluicing, and chipping gold from the walls of this great underground cavern which had become their daytime prison. Day after day, she and the others worked their fingers until nearly bloody, panning in the crevices of the underground stream, or shoveling loads of silt into sluice boxes so that tiny gold flakes would not escape.

Escape.

Megan had thought of nothing else since her abduction. But even if she were to escape, where would she escape to? There was nothing but wilderness out there, and without a guide, escaping into the forest might result in an even swifter death than if she stayed with the general. But...which was worse? Dying as a free woman in the rain forest, or as a slave at the hands of a killer?

"Megan?" came Siobhan's soft voice from behind her.

"Yes?"

"I...I don't know how to thank—"

"Don't thank me, Siobhan," Megan replied, looking over at the guard who had followed them down. Yesterday, her group had toiled to separate the gold; today, they moved beyond the separation area toward the panning place. While panning, they stood in knee-high water which flowed in from an underground source. It was a back-bending, neck-straining job, and Megan was dreading every second of it. Unlike the warm Caribbean waters washing on the shore, the water entering the cavern was icy. "I only did what I thought was best," Megan added. She had to smile. How many times had she heard Delta say that very thing? How often had Delta used that phrase to justify going out on a limb? Megan's smile disappeared as quickly as it came. Where was Delta now?

"You're a good person, Megan."

This put the smile right back on Megan's face, not because it made her happy to hear, but because it was just too ironic. Before Delta Stevens jumped headfirst into her life, Megan wasn't a good person or a bad person—she was a non-person by societal standards—a prostitute who fed off the lust of men all too eager to pay a high price for her services. She'd been a person on the fringes of a system that didn't want her and didn't know what to do with her.

"I've never met a woman as strong as you, Megan," Siobhan said in a low voice as she peeked over her shoulder.

"Thanks, Siobhan...I had good teachers."

Siobhan nodded as she entered the dusty chamber first and went down to retrieve the special screening equipment lying on the bank. "I don't think I understand. Your teachers were strong women?"

Megan took her screen from Siobhan. "In a manner of speaking, yes, they are. I am fortunate enough to run with a very special group of women who have showed me the joy of living. Before them, there wasn't much joy in my life. But now...now I have a lot of living left to do, and I'll be damned if I'm going to die in this hellhole." Megan glanced up at the entrance to make sure the guard had not come down to listen.

"You're still thinking about leaving, aren't you?"

Megan nodded as she removed a small nugget from the screen.

"But two men have already been killed trying to escape, and you're just..." Siobhan lowered her voice even more, "...a woman."

"Just a woman? If I had a dollar for every stupid person who ever thought that of my Delta, I'd be a rich woman. Gender doesn't make you better, Siobhan, attitude does. Miguel and Jorge were caught because of poor planning. I'll know everything I need to before I take off."

"Then you really are going?"

Megan nodded as she pressed her finger to her lips. "You bet. And the key to what I need is somewhere in the general's trailer."

Siobhan stepped gingerly into the water. "You will come back for us?"

Placing her screen in the water and scooping up a pound or two of heavy silt from the bottom of the stream, Megan joined her. "Siobhan, you have my word. If I get free and reach help, I'll be back for you all."

Siobhan pushed the hair out of her eyes and stared up at Megan intently. "Promise?"

Megan looked down into Siobhan's pale blue eyes and nodded. If this was the weight of the world that Delta chose to carry on her shoulders, Megan was just beginning to feel its enormous weight. She was also beginning to understand why Delta could never say no.

"Yes, Siobhan, I promise."

# 9——

Delta didn't have very·much experience with men being attracted to her, but she didn't need to be hit over the head to recognize that Manny Decoubertin had fallen into her emerald eyes and couldn't get out. From the moment Bianca introduced them, Manny couldn't stop staring at Delta. Even now, as she wrapped up her story about their arrival in Costa Rica, Manny was intensely gazing into Delta's eyes.

"So, we need to know where Augustine was going in his search for poachers," Delta finished, wondering whether Manny had heard anything she'd said.

Manny stood about two and a half inches shorter than Delta, which, by Costa Rican standards, was still pretty tall. Whenever she spoke, he narrowed his already intense eyes toward her, clearly giving her one hundred percent of his attention. When she finished her entire tale, Manny asked his first question.

"And you believe your friend was with Augustine?"

Delta nodded. "Sure of it. Megan would never just traipse off without telling anyone else. That's not like her at all."

"Perhaps she and Augustine—"

Delta held her hand up to silence him. "Not a chance. She's...spoken for back home. Contrary to popular belief, not all American women are loose." Delta glanced down at Bianca, who gave her a small grin. "Besides, disappearing isn't her style. Look, I don't want to be rude, but if you can help me, great. If not, I really need to be on my way."

Manny glanced over at Bianca, who nodded to him.

"But I swore to Augustine I would not tell," Manny explained. "A man is only as good as his word."

Bianca slid her tiny hand into his and squeezed it. "He could be in trouble for all you know."

Manny shook his head. "Augustine knows the jungle better than anyone."

"Still..."

Manny returned his gaze to Delta, who nodded. "Bianca's right, Manny. Augustine could very well be in some kind of trouble."

"If he is, how could one woman help him? Augustine is a strong man, but you—"

Delta's left eyebrow rose in its characteristic question mark. "What I am, señor Decoubertin, is a cop in the United States; a highly trained professional capable of taking care of herself and those around me. You might be surprised at what this one woman can do."

Manny grinned patronizingly at her. "My sister says the same things, but we are not in the United States or Canada. If Augustine needs help, he will not need it from a woman."

Delta and Bianca exchanged a roll of the eyes. Men, it seemed, were the same simple-minded sexists with a genuine lack of understanding about the female of the species no matter what country they came from.

Releasing a frustrated sigh, Delta turned to Manny. "Listen, I don't have time to sit here and debate your macho-man views on women. If you can't or won't help me, fine, but I'm going after them with or without your help." With that, Delta turned on her heel to begin her walk back toward town.

"Now look where your *machismo* has gotten you, Manuel! Go after her. She won't last an hour in the forest by herself," Bianca said.

As Delta started across the gravel road, she felt Manny approach her from behind. She slowed intentionally, and Manny reached out to touch her shoulder. In a move so swift it would have done Connie proud, Delta grabbed his hand, stepped back into him, and yanked him over her shoulder. He landed on the ground with a thud. Planting her foot squarely on his chest, Delta regripped his hand so that she now held him in a painful thumb lock. The whole move took less than three seconds.

"*Merde!*" he cursed, grimacing under the pain from the thumb lock.

"Point number one, Mr. Manny, you weren't listening when I said 'highly trained.' Point number two, I may not last an hour alone in the rain forest, but I can kick the ass of anyone stupid enough to get in my way. And point number three, this 'woman' is going into that fucking forest one way or the other, so lead, follow, or get the hell out of my way!"

Delta glared into his face, expecting some sort of macho response. Instead, she was surprised to see him grinning up at her.

"All right, all right. I'll help you. But you must promise me one thing."

Delta did not release his thumb. "That depends."

Manny forced a grin through the pain. "Teach me how you do that."

Helping him up, Delta looked hard into his dark eyes. If he hadn't developed a crush on her before, he sure had one now. Delta knitted her eyebrows together and looked over at Bianca, who shrugged.

"You asked for that, Manny," Bianca said.

Manny brushed his butt off and nodded. "I would like to buy you a drink. Maybe we could start over."

Nodding, Delta motioned for him to show the way. "One beer. Then I have to go."

After ordering two Imperial beers and one Coke, Manny pulled a stool next to Delta's and smiled. Yep, it was a crush all right, and Delta was resigned to looking into puppy-dog eyes that gulped her in like a diver taking in air.

Removing her sunglasses, Delta began first. "Okay, Manny, you start. What do you know about Augustine's little excursions?"

Manny cast a reluctant look over at his little sister, who nodded for him to go ahead. With some trepidation, he began. "Augustine mentioned the girl to me."

Delta winced. "She's a *woman,* and I know they were going after poachers. That's no secret. Just fill in the blanks for me."

"And then what? You think maybe you can grab a machete and go looking for them?" Manny asked.

When the scruffy-looking bartender handed her an Imperial, Delta gently pushed it back to him and smiled. "Coke, *por favor.*" Even after playing softball in one-hundred-and-five-degree heat in Redding, California, Delta had never acquired a taste for beer, preferring, instead, a Diet Coke. "I'm not one of those people who sits around waiting for someone else to solve my problems, Manny."

"You'll have your share of problems if you try to do this alone."

"I'm not alone. I have a friend. And as soon as she gets here, I'm going into that jungle. So, why don't you tell me what might make this journey a little easier."

Manny studied Delta for a moment. "You believe they could be in danger?"

Delta nodded. "Don't you? We're talking poachers. Surely you know more about them than I do? Don't *you* think they're dangerous?"

"The stories...," Manny started, but something stopped him from finishing his sentence.

"Manny, like many *Ticos,* thinks the poaching stories are exaggerations." Bianca blew a stray strand of hair away from her face.

"I don't know much about poachers or preservation, or scarlet parrots, for that matter," Delta responded. "What I do know is the person who means the most to me in world is out there somewhere, and I don't have time for bullshit answers."

"If Manny won't help, I will," Bianca offered, tossing a peanut to Kiki, who had been playing under their rickety stools. "Kiki and I could be a lot of help."

Waving one hand in the air, Manny brought his beer bottle to his mouth with the other. "*Hermana*, the rain forest is no place for the inexperienced, whether they're girls or boys."

"I'm not as inexperienced as you think, Manuel. Kiki and I have been more places than you know. She's an expert, you know."

Manny looked at his little sister with a mixture of admiration and angst. "The part of the jungle we're talking about isn't a place where even Kiki would be safe."

"Then go with us," Delta stated flatly.

Manny cut a look over to Delta. "Us? You would take a child into the jungle? That shows how very little you know about the jungle."

"I am not a child, Manuel, and you know it. Besides, I'm smarter than you and would probably be just as much help." Bianca crossed her arms in defiance.

Manny shook his head. "You would give mama the shakes."

"Mama knows I am capable, Manuel. She gives me the credit I deserve."

"You aren't capable, sister, you are bored and want an adventure."

"So?"

Delta held her hands up for them to stop. "Time out. Manny's right, Bianca, it would be wrong for me to put you in danger. If Manny won't go, neither will you."

"But—" Bianca began.

"But nothing." Smiling warmly into Bianca's eyes, Delta laid her hand on Bianca's shoulder. There was so much more to this young woman than she'd imagined. And if Delta had the time, she'd find out just what lurked behind this woman-child, who, indeed, appeared every bit as bright as her older brother.

"Back home, I go up against the unknown every day of my life. I run down dark alleys after people who would love to see me dead. I've been trapped in burning buildings, not knowing whether or not I would ever get out alive. Handling the unknown is what I get paid to do. It's my job. It takes a great deal to scare me," Delta said, looking out the window and watching the children play with Kiki.

Bianca glared at Manny. "No wonder Augustine goes without you. You are a coward."

Before Manny could respond, three dirty, sweat-drenched men entered the bar. They spoke a brisk Spanish in low, husky voices—unlike the free-flowing, melodious Spanish Delta had heard since she'd arrived. This Spanish sounded somehow different. Perhaps, Delta mused, it was a regional dialect.

As the three men hoisted their legs over the barstools, Delta carefully watched Manny's outward appearance change as he, too, eyed the strange men. Something about them clearly raised Manny's hackles. Without a word, he slid off the stool, reached for Bianca's hand and slowly walked towards the door with her. Delta hopped off her stool and followed them outside.

"What was that all about?" Delta asked, putting her sunglasses back on.

Manny took Delta's arm and pulled her across the street. "Shh. They're Colombians. Drug smugglers."

Delta started to turn around, but Manny placed his arm around her shoulder and continued walking down the street.

"Are you sure?" Delta whispered. "What are they doing here? They looked like—"

"Quiet," Manny said under his breath. "They first came to town ten days ago for supplies. They speak to no one, and no one speaks to them."

"Then how do you kn—"

"We are not stupid."

Bianca shook her head. "They come to town about every three days."

"So, this is their third trip?" Delta asked, feeling a familiar tension inside her gut. "Tell me everything they've done so far."

Manny continued walking away from the bar with his arm around Delta. "They come in, sit at the bar for a few hours, drink *guaro*, and then go collect their supplies."

"Then where do they go?"

"Back to the forest. La Amistad's rain forest crosses over into Panama. We figure they have found another way to transport the drugs through Central America to Mexico."

Delta's eyes narrowed. "We?"

"My friends, of course. This is a small town. Everyone knows what everyone else is thinking. We think they've found a place to cool off while the authorities look for them. What better place than a rain forest?"

"So, these men come and go as they please?" Delta fully faced Manny. There was something else he wasn't telling her. Was this the reason he did not want to go into the rain forest? Was he afraid they might have to deal with men who probably had already killed? Or was there something else?

Manny laughed. "Being simple doesn't mean being foolish, Delta. We want no trouble with these men, so we leave them be. Don't make more of it than that."

Suddenly, a flash of energy jolted Delta's system. A piece of the puzzle she hadn't even considered had just fallen into place. "Where do they go to pick up their supplies?"

"The market," Manny answered.

"Take me there."

Bianca looked up at Manny, who shook his head. "It would not be wise to get in their way."

"I just want to see what they're picking up, that's all. Besides, I need a few items of my own before we go."

Manny shook his head again. *"Muy loca."*

"I'll take you," Bianca said, taking Delta's hand. "I'm not afraid of those Colombians."

"It has nothing to do with fear," Manny said defensively. "It just isn't wise to bother those kind of men."

"I won't bother anyone, Manny. Come on." Letting Bianca pull her to the store, Delta looked over her shoulder and found Manny hurrying after them. He said something to Bianca in Spanish, but she did not respond.

"At least let me help you get the supplies you'll need," Manny said as he caught up to them.

Delta nodded. "I'd appreciate that, thanks."

Less than a minute later, Delta was standing in a small store called a *mercado*. It took about thirty seconds to browse because there was only one choice of anything. As she watched Manny and Bianca argue over the wisdom of getting crackers, Delta saw the three Colombians enter the store and look at the packages on the floor while jabbering quickly and intensely to each other. One of the men, apparently disgusted with the other two, grabbed insect repellent, matches, and rubbing alcohol before reaching for one bottle that caught Delta's eye. The last bottle tossed carelessly on the counter sent a red flag to Delta's brain, and she visibly shuddered. Drug smugglers in the rain forest would certainly need bug spray and matches, but that one bottle told Delta everything she needed to know.

Lying on its side next to the bottle of rubbing alcohol was a small bottle of perfume.

# 10——

It was lunch time when they were finally relieved of their burdens. It had been a particularly good morning in the river portion of the cavern, with many nuggets being plucked from both the sides of the cavern and from the silt at the bottom. Megan and Siobhan had a neat little pile of gold waiting to be picked up by the soldier in charge of collections.

When the soldier started down into the cave carrying sandwiches, he smiled down at the mound of gold glittering in the flickering light from the torches. Tossing Siobhan a sandwich, he squatted on his haunches for a better look.

"It has been a good day, no?"

"Where's Megan's food?" Siobhan asked.

Without turning from the gold, the soldier ignored Siobhan. "The general wishes to see her."

Megan gingerly picked her way over to the bank. "Now?"

Looking up from the pile, the soldier stared lasciviously at her rear end and grinned. Several of his teeth were missing. "*Sí. Pronto.*"

As they walked out of the cavern, Megan squinted from the harsh glare of the noon sun. After working all day in the near-dark of the caverns, she found the sun especially unforgiving. "What does he want?"

The guard chuckled. "What he want always?"

Megan sneered at him. "How about good conversation? Oh, I forgot, you and your pals are incapable of intelligent thought."

The soldier whirled around and raised his hand to hit her, but Megan held her ground defiantly. "General Zahn might not appreciate you beating on me, Pedro," she said calmly.

The soldier slowly lowered his hand as he snarled in Megan's face. *"Puta. Me llamo, Hector."* This was followed by a rapid series of curses uttered in Spanish, none of which Megan could, or wanted to, understand.

They walked the rest of the way in silence, until they stood in front of the general's door. As Megan reached for the knob, the soldier grabbed her arm and squeezed it hard. "When he is done with you, *señorita,* you are mine."

Suddenly the door swung open, and General Zahn loomed large in the doorway. *"Basta ya!"* Zahn yelled. Hector immediately came to attention. In the blink of an eye, Zahn pulled his revolver from his holster and jammed it into Hector's neck. *"Estúpido! Puerco!"* were the only words Megan could make out, as Zahn lashed out at Hector in a verbal barrage. Stupid pig. If Megan hadn't been so afraid of Zahn's flashpoint temper, she might have added her own insults to Zahn's litany.

When Zahn finished, he lowered the gun and abruptly ordered Hector out. *"Lárgate!"* he shouted.

Hector opened his mouth to respond, but thought better of it and scurried away.

As he turned to Megan, the frown lines on the general's face were replaced by a charming grin. It was frightening how quickly this man's moods changed. "I am sorry if Hector was...shall we say, rude."

Megan strode past the general into the little trailer and shrugged. "What do you expect from kidnappers? Hospitality?" To her surprise, she saw a large tray of food set out on the coffee table.

"We're not all barbarians, Megan. As you can see, hospitality is what I had in mind." Closing the door behind him, the general looked genuinely pleased to see Megan. "Please, have a seat."

Megan glanced over at the elaborately prepared tray that could have come straight from a caterer. What was this? Was he treating her to lunch? Was this his idea of a date? Or was he just thanking her for a blowjob well done? Suddenly, Delta's words resounded loudly in her mind. *Never underestimate your opponent.*

It was an adage that had kept Delta alive more times than Megan dared count. She had never really understood what Delta meant, until now. The enemy was so close, had such power, that Megan realized the importance of never underestimating him.

No, there was more to this little luncheon than a platter of food. Of that she was sure. Sitting down on the sofa, Megan tried to ignore the rice, beans, fruit, cheese and tortillas teasing her nose with their aroma. They were so appetizing, they almost looked fake. There were also two flutes of champagne sitting at either end of the tray.

"What's this all about?" Megan asked flatly.

"I've grown tired of eating alone in this godforsaken jungle. I thought it would be much nicer to dine with you."

"Oh, I'm sure one of your merry bandits would love to have lunch with you."

This prompted a huge smile from the general. "Women know so little about the military. I cannot eat with my men. That would make them equal to me, and no man in this camp is equal to me."

"How modest of you."

The general continued smiling at Megan as he sat down. "To enforce discipline, the ranks must fear you and your power. As soon as the men believe you are like them, you will no longer be able to control them."

"Is that why officers have their own clubs and their own dining facilities?"

The general smiled even wider. "You are a very bright woman, Megan Osbourne."

Megan stared at the food and felt a knot of anger begin to unravel. On one hand, she wanted desperately to keep her so-recently-earned self-respect, and on the other, she knew that, once again, she needed to do what she needed to do in order to survive.

"Don't you see anything here you like?" the general asked with apparent concern.

"I do," Megan quickly responded. "But, General—"

"Tito. Please, call me Tito."

Megan sighed. "Tito, I appreciate all of this, really I do, but—"

"But you feel like you should be working with your friends."

Megan nodded.

"I imagined you would say as much. There is a nobility about you that the others do not possess. Trust me, Megan, if they could take advantage of my kindness, not one of them would think of you first. It is human nature to put ourselves first. In Colombia, we learn to take care of ourselves first. Our bodies are the temples of Christ, so there is no shame looking out for it first."

Megan looked into his coffee-brown eyes and tried not to laugh in his face. Christ? Temple? Shame? Was he serious? It was no wonder she'd turned her back on her grandmother's Catholic religion all those years ago. The hypocrisy was simply overwhelming, the irony inescapable. "Tito, I've taken care of Number One all my life. Good care. That doesn't mean that I have to turn my back on the others."

General Zahn raised one thick eyebrow. "Others? Are there others waiting for you, Megan? Is there a fortunate man waiting back home for your return?"

Megan leaned forward, picked up one of the tortillas, and bit into it. Well, this was certainly an interesting, if unexpected, question. If she was going to die in this forest, the very least she could do was be true to the one love of her life. When all was said and done, Megan could go down knowing who she was and what she stood for in life. Even the general's quick change in temperament was not enough to keep Megan Osbourne from remaining true to herself. Squaring off, Megan stared deep into his eyes. "No, General, there is no man waiting for me at home."

The general appeared surprised. "No?"

"No. But there is a woman."

The smile dropped off his face like a rock into a pond. "A...woman?"

"I'm a lesbian."

General Zahn looked like he had just been slapped with a wet fish. "A...lesbian? Surely, you joke."

Megan shook her head. "No joke."

A frown fixed itself on his face as he reached for a papaya slice. "You love other women, then?"

"No. I love one woman. And I'll do what I have to to return home to her."

The frown receded from his face and was replaced by a bemused grin. "I like a woman with passion."

"That fire is a passion, a devotion I have only for Delta."

General Zahn said nothing for a moment as he studied Megan's features. "You are a jewel, Megan Osbourne. How is it the American male would let you go to another woman?"

It was now Megan's turn to smile. If there was one thing she'd learned about Latin American men, it was that *machismo* was alive and thriving. "In the United States, men do not dictate where women go or what we do. I'm not a lesbian because I don't like men. I'm a lesbian because I prefer women, and I love this woman because she is the best person I have ever met."

General Zahn leaned back, taking one of the flutes of champagne with him. "Fascinating. You are even more interesting than I initially surmised."

Megan took the last bite of her tortilla before picking up a piece of cheese. As she plucked it from the tray, she glanced around the room, her brain calculating coolly. The fax and computer would be impossible to get her hands on unless she could sneak in here at night. She reasoned there was probably a gun in one of the desk drawers, but she knew getting into the drawers and out again would take more time than she had. As she reached for a slice of banana, a glint of metal caught her eye, and Megan focused on a long carving knife with a serrated edge. The way it was wedged between the plate and the tray, it was possible the general hadn't seen it. Taking the banana slice, she looked up at the general and nodded. "I've led an interesting life."

General Zahn moved closer and lightly touched Megan's face. There was a tenderness in his touch that surprised her. *How much would it take before that tenderness turned to rage?* Megan wondered. And was this a trait she could use against him?

"You took a great chance in telling me the truth," he said, lightly fingering her blonde hair. "I could have recoiled and found you disgusting. I could have spat upon you and had you killed. What made you be honest?"

Megan shrugged. "You have been upfront with me, Tito. You laid out exactly what it is you want and how you want it. You are not a man easily fooled, nor do you want people to tell you what you want to hear. I suspect you have a great distaste for those who do."

The general nodded slightly. "Go on."

"I am not ashamed of being a lesbian, and I'd rather die saying the truth than live a lie."

Lightly taking a strand of her hair between his fingers, the general said softly, "You are such a beautiful creature. Life is important to you, yes?"

"Absolutely. And if I thought I could kill you right now and get free, I would."

The general looked amused. "You are not afraid of me then?"

Megan shook her head. "I stopped being afraid of men a long time ago."

Sipping his champagne, the general continued toying with her hair. "I have never met a man or a woman who was not afraid of me. My name alone strikes fear into the hearts of politicians and murderers alike. What makes you unafraid, Megan? What gives you this strength?"

Megan looked at her hands in her lap. "The women in my life right now have shown me a courage and strength that comes from so deep within, not even the prospect of death can weaken it."

The general released Megan's hair. Gazing into her eyes for protracted seconds, he slowly nodded. "You know that I cannot allow any of you to live."

Megan sighed. "I'm aware of that."

The general picked up a slice of a fruit Megan had never seen before and stared at it for a moment before locking eyes with hers again. "Suppose I could ensure your safety? Would you consider coming to Colombia?"

Megan didn't need to see behind his eyes to know the real question being posed. He was offering her a choice between sexual slavery and death—neither of which was appealing. She hadn't made it this far just to die at the hands of some foreign wannabe dictator. But she had also spent enough time watching Delta and Connie work to have learned a thing or two about playing the odds. If he was willing to buy her time, she wasn't going to look a gift jackass in the mouth.

Taking a bite of her banana, Megan swallowed a large chunk and began choking. As she grabbed her throat, the general slapped her on the back, but could not dislodge it. When Megan's face began turning pink, Zahn stood her up, turned her around and performed the Heimlich maneuver on her. This dislodged the banana and Megan gulped down air.

"Are you all right?" the general asked when she sat back down.

Rubbing her throat, Megan steadied herself. "Thank you. I shouldn't eat so fast. I'm sorry."

"No, I am the sorry one. I should not have blurted out my proposal so soon. It must have been a shock to you."

Megan nodded.

"How are you feeling?"

"I could use a glass of water, if you have some."

*"Uno momento."*

The moment he left the room, Megan quickly grabbed the knife and shoved it up the leg of her jeans, wedging it snugly in her hiking boots. Thank God Augustine had insisted she wear boots.

The general returned almost immediately, and handed her a glass of water before sitting back down. Megan knew he wanted sex; she knew the lesbian conversation had probably excited him, as it seemed to excite most men. If she was going to have sex with him, she would be caught with the knife, and would either have to use it on him or pray for his mercy. She also knew from many, many experiences that there was one thing men loved almost as much as sex, and that was—talking about themselves. If she could get him going on about himself, she just might get out of the trailer alive.

"Are you sure you are feeling okay?" the general repeated.

Megan sipped the water and nodded. "Yes. But enough about me. My life story cannot be nearly as interesting as yours. Tell me about yourself."

# 11——

"**We'll** go with you until the trail ends, but from there, you are on your own. I cannot put Bianca in danger," Manny said sternly.

Delta nodded as she eyed the three Colombians leaving Rivas and heading back toward the jungle.

"Is there a phone I can use?" Delta asked, checking her watch.

Bianca pointed to the house next to the *mercado*. "They have the one with the best sound."

Delta looked over at Manny with questioning eyes.

"Fine. I'll get the horses. You and Bianca finish with supplies and I'll meet you both back here in half an hour."

Half an hour sounded like forever to Delta. "Thank you so much."

Manny grinned, making two deep dimples appear on either side of the smile. "Do not thank me for involving you with the Colombians; you could be cursing me a few hours from now." As Manny jogged away, Bianca took Delta by the arm and led her to the house next to the *mercado*.

When the owner came to the open door, he exchanged greetings with Bianca, who then rattled off a short monologue to him. Halfway through her speech, he motioned for them to come in and pointed toward the phone.

"Señor Monge says it is okay to use his phone. Go ahead."

"*Gracias,*" Delta replied, picking up the phone. Pulling the car-rental agreement out, she found the number to the Gran Hotel and dialed. While she waited for the other end to ring, Delta handed the phone to Bianca.

"*Bueno. El cuarto de señorita Rivera, por favor.*" Handing the phone back to Delta, Bianca grinned.

"Hello?" came Connie's tense voice when Delta put the phone to her ear.

"It's me."

"Where in the hell are you?"

"Didn't you get my message? I came to the little town called Rivas. About two hours outside of San Jose. Did you have any luck at the embassy?"

"Nothing. Apparently this is the place to come if you want to escape. They were perplexed and not very helpful. You?"

"I turned Megan's place upside down, but didn't find anything useful, so I took a shot and came here. Rivas is at one of the openings of La Amistad Park. If that's where Megan went, then that's where we need to go."

There was a pause on the other end. "You're going to go into the rain forest, aren't you?"

"Just to get a feel. I won't do anything until you get here, but I think it's a good idea for one of us to take a look at what we're getting into."

Connie's loud sigh could be heard on the other end. "Good thinking. What do you want me to do?"

"Call Sal and Josh and get them down here. Tell them I'll pay for it. You still have my charge card?"

"Already made the call."

"Great. We're going to need help if someone took Megan into the jungle."

Connie sighed again into the phone. "It's not that easy. You're not in River Valley, Storm."

"I know that. But my gut, Con. It's ringing like a church bell. I at least owe it to myself to do a little investigating."

Connie opened up a map on the bed and studied it. When she located Rivas, she released another loud sigh. "Delta, that part of Costa Rica is huge. You'll never find one person in there."

"Well...that's just it..." Delta hesitated.

"What? What aren't you telling me?"

Delta looked over at Bianca and shrugged. "I'm not looking for just Megan. I'm looking for a bunch of Colombians, who I think may know where she is."

Connie straightened up from looking at the map. "Whoa. You've lost me. Colombians? Could you start over?"

So Delta told her everything she had seen and heard while in Rivas, right up to the bottle of perfume.

"Perfume, huh?" Connie said after listening quietly to the whole tale. "So you're going to go into the rain forest on a hunch, to follow some guys dressed in fatigues with a bottle of perfume?"

"I've acted quicker on less info, Con. Give me one good reason why guys wearing fatigues in the jungle would want to buy a bottle of perfume. If you can drum up a logical explanation in that Mensa head of yours, I'll reconsider."

Connie tucked the phone between her shoulder and ear and folded up the map. "Logical? I'm afraid I'm all out of logic, Del. Who knows? Maybe they're wooing the tribal women."

"Is that your best guess?"

"Yeah. Pretty weak, huh? Guess that means you're going."

"Yup."

"Okay. I'll pick Sal and Josh up at the airport. You scout around the area and see what you can find out, but don't get carried away. I need you to keep your head on straight."

"Uh-huh. Pick them up and I'll meet you in Rivas tomorrow at a little bar called *Los Rancheros*." Moving the mouthpiece from her face, Delta asked Bianca if Señor Monge would be willing to take a call for her. When Bianca relayed Delta's request, the man smiled and nodded. Returning her mouth to the phone, Delta said, "Rivas is the size of a dime, and the people are warm and welcoming. Have you rented a car?"

"A cute Suzuki Sidekick."

"Good. If you get here and I'm not back, just ask around. Someone will know where we are."

"We?"

Delta grinned over at Bianca, who straightened proudly. "Yeah. I met an *amiga* who has been very helpful. Bianca—" Delta looked at Bianca helplessly.

"Decoubertin," Bianca answered.

"Bianca Decoubertin and her brother, Manny. They live at the end of the road here in Rivas."

"Decoubertin? Delta, that's a French name, not a *Tico* name."

"Long story. Anyway, just drive until you come to the end of the gravel road."

"Which road?"

"There's only one."

"Bianca, huh?" The tone of Connie's voice gave her suspicions away.

Delta laughed. "She's sixteen, and reminds me a lot of you."

"Well...good then. I'm glad you're not alone. Tomorrow or tomorrow night, then, in Rivas."

"Right." Delta pinched the bridge of her nose. She needed another Coke or she would suffer a caffeine-withdrawal headache.

"How are you holding up?"

Delta sighed. "As long as I keep *doing*, I'm fine. If I have the chance to think..."

"Just don't do anything rash, Delta. I don't want to have to come looking for you, too."

"Ten-four, Chief. You be careful, yourself." When Delta hung up, she smiled over at Bianca, who smiled broadly back. "My best friend," Delta explained.

"She must be, if she came all the way down here with you."

Delta and Bianca walked outside and continued discussing the possible dangers they'd face in the jungle, until Manny rode up with two saddled horses in tow. "I still cannot believe I agreed to do this," he said, lowering himself off the small horse. "Have you ever ridden one?"

"Sure," Delta said, thinking briefly about the rodeos she went to with her dad. "Cake."

Manny looked to his sister for clarification. Bianca laughed. "She means, no problem."

When the three were on their horses and ready to go, Delta took one last look at the tiny town of Rivas, and hoped like hell she would make it back tomorrow.

☙ ☙ ☙

By the time they came to the end of the trail, some three miles into the rain forest, the horses were drenched with sweat, and Delta understood the term "saddle sore." Few words had been spoken between the three of them as they plodded through the forest. Even if she wanted to chat, Delta had no adequate words to describe the surprise and delight she was experiencing as iguanas lumbered lazily across their path, parrots swooshed noisily onto treetops, and leaf-cutter ants drew long green mobile lines across the forest floor. As the horses clip-clopped along, Delta never knew when some creature would hop, crawl, slither or fly across the overgrown trail.

Manny proved to be an exceptional guide, well-versed in the flora and fauna of this incredibly diverse land. And it was more than just diverse, it was tranquil. The birds and bugs harmonized like a well-rehearsed orchestra playing a symphonic tune to ease the soul. Delta had never heard anything like it—

it was simply mesmerizing. Though her heart was weighed down with thoughts of Megan in trouble, Delta was still captivated by the peacefulness and splendor of the jungle. Oddly enough, it also seemed to captivate her young companions. Manny and Bianca were as delighted as she was when they happened upon raccoon-like creatures playing together like two kittens. They chased each other up and down the trees and dove on each other's tails, until they realized the horses were almost on top of them. Then, with a speed which belied their looks, they scampered off into the bushes.

"What are those?" Delta whispered to Bianca.

"Coatimundis, or Coatis. They're a combination of raccoon, monkey and squirrel. Neat, huh?"

Delta smiled as she heard the animals scurry up another tree trunk. It was at this moment that she felt something stir inside her—probably the same kind of feeling Megan had when she first saw the magnificence unfold around her. This, which lay before her, was Life; not the hustle and bustle of city streets, nor neon billboards and graffiti-covered walls. What boggled Delta most was that this peaceful life was happening at the same time that she was chasing down muggers, robbers, rapists and murderers. This incredible display of nature's splendor was going on while she was stuck in commuter traffic, triple-locking her door at night, or waiting in line at the store. This was Life with a capital L, and she'd almost missed it.

"Why do you look so sad?" Bianca asked when Delta's horse pulled alongside hers.

Looking up, Delta shrugged. "This is some place you have here, Bianca. I just wish I were here under different circumstances, that's all. I just wish..." Delta let her words trail off into the same abyss as her thoughts.

"Maybe when you find your friend, you can see the rest of the country. There's so much more to Costa Rica than the rain forests."

Delta forced a grin and nodded. In silence, they rode on beyond the trail's end into the heart of the jungle. Delta noted the increasing humidity the deeper into the jungle they went. The plants and trees were different from those they had seen at the beginning of their trek. Suddenly, Delta realized she needed to pay attention to these changes. The jungle, like the city, had various personalities, depending on where one went.

"Your friend...could she survive in here by herself?" Bianca asked after twenty minutes more of silent riding.

Delta glanced around. Three years ago, Megan might have crumbled at the prospect of getting herself out of the rain forest. But the past two years had drastically changed her. Now Megan had the strength to do anything Delta could do. Now, Megan was a woman who had a life worth living. Get herself out of the jungle? Delta had no doubt that Megan could.

"Megan lived in a concrete jungle with animals who kill for no reason."

Manny pshawed this and waved her off. "Animals do not kill for no reason."

"She was talking about men, Manny."

Delta glanced over at Bianca and winked.

"We must stop," Manny said suddenly.

Delta looked at the path ahead. "Why?"

"Look at your horse."

Delta leaned over in the saddle and was horrified to see its entire neck painted with blood. "Shit!" she exclaimed, jumping off the horse. "What happened?"

Manny dismounted and pulled a towel out of his backpack. Toweling off his horse first, he replied, *"Zancudos."*

"Mosquitoes?" Delta guessed.

Manny nodded. "*Sí*. We spray them down before we leave, but then the horses sweat and the bugs find places to bite." Wiping down the other horses, Manny sprayed them with repellent and then lifted his horse's front feet. Delta and Bianca double-checked their gear while he examined the feet of the other horses.

"Camp before it gets too dark," Bianca admonished, looking up at the sky. "You have about two hours of light left, but not much more. Don't be tempted to go through the jungle in the dark."

Delta nodded. "The sun sets at what time?"

"Six. No more, no less. Trust me, Delta, don't push it. You should be setting your camp around five-thirty." Bianca's intense features conveyed the seriousness of her words. "And be sure to string the hammock up. If you sleep on the ground, the bugs will be all over you."

"*Sí,*" Manny added. "And spray yourself all over with the spray. *Gringas* are not used to the insects like we are. It will be a horrible night for you if you do not spray yourself."

Delta nodded. "I'll be sure to do that."

When Manny finished with the horses, he walked over and squatted down next to Delta. "We will have to leave you now. My horse had a stone in her shoe, and it would not be wise to push her any further." Manny held up the stone and looked at it before tossing it into the bushes.

Rising, Delta nodded. "My friend Connie Rivera will come looking for me when she reaches Rivas. I'd really appreciate it if you could show her the way."

Bianca reached out and shook Delta's hand. "Good luck to you, then. My friends and I will be looking for Connie. What does she look like?"

Delta reached into her wallet and pulled out a picture of Connie. It was the most recent picture they'd taken together, when the four of them had gone camping. Delta was wearing a baseball cap and had her arm around Connie, who held up a three-inch fish they'd caught.

Bianca took the picture and studied it a moment. "She could be Costa Rican."

Delta smiled, wondering what silly story Connie would have launched into if she'd heard Bianca say that. "Oh, I'll bet some part of her is." Handing the reins of her horse to Bianca, Delta patted the horse's nose one last time.

"We'll be sure she gets your message, won't we, Manny?"

Taking the picture back, Delta reached out to shake Manny's hand. He appeared uncomfortable with this. "Thank you, Manny, for all your help."

"Don't thank us yet, Delta. We may have brought you more trouble than you could ever know."

Delta stood in silence as they remounted. "I'll see you tomorrow."

Bianca waved as she took the reins of Manny's horse and quickly laced them to her saddle. Manny easily lifted himself into the saddle of Delta's horse and grinned as he grabbed the reins. "Be safe."

Bianca nodded. "We'll be waiting!"

When she could no longer see the swishing of the horses' tails, Delta turned to face the gaping mouth of Costa Rica's largest rain forest. Something inside her told her she was doing the right thing. Now all she needed to do was go the right way.

# 12 ——

**When** Megan and Siobhan collapsed in their tent at last, it was almost dark. Megan estimated it was close to sundown, maybe five or five-thirty. It had been a longer day than usual, and they had worked nonstop since lunch, with none of their usual breaks.

"I'm too tired to die," Siobhan said, dropping on her back.

Megan reached down and pulled the long knife from her boot, where it had remained since she'd stuffed it in there hours ago. "Too tired to escape?" Even in the near dark of the tent, the blade was still discernible. Looking at the knife, Siobhan bolted upright as if someone had given her an electrical shock. "What are you doing with that?"

"I told you. I have no intention of working my ass off or blowing that s.o.b. until they kill me. No thanks. I'd rather let a jaguar eat me than continue living under these conditions."

"You're not serious."

"I certainly am."

"But there is no escape. What will they do if they catch you? They might kill you!"

"They'll do that whether or not I try to escape. Siobhan, they are going to kill us when we're through here. Don't you see that? The minute that last flake of gold is packed away,

we're through. Well, I'm sorry, but I have a life that's worth
living, and I'd rather take my chances in the wild than here."

Siobhan's eyes grew wide. "But even if you do escape—"

"The odds of making it out of this rain forest are slim,
I know. But at least I'll go down fighting and not on my back.
What I will not do is go down feeling like a victim."

Siobhan lowered her voice. "When will you go?"

"A couple of days. It would be foolish to go running
into the rain forest without provisions. I'll need a machete,
some food and a water container."

"I wish you'd reconsider, Megan."

"Not a chance. Unless we find more gold, General Zahn
will bury us in that cavern."

"But you'll be alone," Siobhan whispered.

Megan grinned. "If you could have met the women I
hang around with, you'd understand why I believe in the
impossible. I'm going to make it, Siobhan, because I'm smarter
than these assholes, and because I so want to live."

Siobhan bowed her head. "You're so much braver than I."

Tucking the knife under her shirt, Megan lay down and
stared at the tent ceiling. "The goddess creates only a handful
of heroines."

"Then you must be one."

Megan laughed. "Not me. I'm more of a...heroine's
apprentice."

Siobhan cocked her head in question.

"The real heroines are on their way this very instant."

"Here? In Costa Rica?"

Megan shook her head. "Uh-uh. Here, in the rain forest.
You can bet your life on that."

# 13——

Connie paced the airport's small waiting area for nearly an hour. With every new arrival announced over the static P.A. system, she would stop, look up at the monitors, and sigh loudly if it wasn't the flight she was waiting for.

She had spent the night making numerous calls and preparing for her trip into the rain forest. She had managed to buy an "H" frame backpack from a Canadian high school student, who was more than happy to accept the exchange of his raggedy backpack for three hundred dollars. After acquiring the backpack, she shopped for dried fruit, three canteens, nuts and anything else she thought they might need. She tossed in the food she'd packed back in River Valley, along with her compass, flashlight, army knife, change of socks and rope. The completely full backpack was now sitting in the Suzuki in front of the airport, waiting; waiting like Connie was waiting. It was this waiting that was driving her nuts. It seemed that no matter what you were waiting for, there were always unanswered questions that made the wait that much longer. Where was Delta now? Was she safe?

Finally, the awaited-for flight was announced; Connie looked up at the monitor and smiled. Help was finally on the way.

Ten minutes later, following a crowd of returning Costa Ricans, a short, freckle-faced woman wearing army fatigues, black army boots and a camouflaged baseball cap bounced down the hall and into Connie's arms.

"Sal! Thank you so much for coming!" Connie said, hugging the tiny woman tightly.

Pulling away, Sal looked hard into Connie's eyes. "You okay? You look awful."

Connie shrugged. "Didn't get much sleep. There's so much to do."

Sal turned from Connie and addressed a tall, broad-shouldered man sporting a black beard and the very same attire Sal had on. When Connie saw him, she threw her arms around him and let out a gush of air as he squeezed her. "Josh, thanks for coming."

"Where the squirt goes, I go," he growled.

"You need an expert in jungle warfare, Josh is the man." Sal patted him on the back and grinned up at him. Josh returned this gesture with a wink.

This was not the first time Sal and Josh had joined Connie in helping Delta out of a jam. Once, when Delta was almost raped and tortured in the desert, both Sal and Josh had killed in order to save her. From that moment on, Sal had become part of their team. With her knowledge of electronics and all that her Viet Nam buddies had taught her, Sal had proven time and time again to be an invaluable ally. The best part of her connection, though, was that wherever Sal went, so did Josh. It was a package deal. Always had been, always would be. And for this mission, Connie would most definitely need the expertise of both of them.

"You and Delta are part of Sal's family now," Josh said, readjusting his cap. "Besides, she'd have come without me anyway. Too much like her father, this one."

Sal beamed up at him, as their mutual affection tangibly flowed between them. "I'll take that as a compliment."

Connie could only shake her head at the diminutive would-be warrior. From the moment they'd met nearly a decade ago, Connie had liked Sal. She was spunky, smart and full of life. Sal never backed away from a challenge, not even when her father was decapitated in Viet Nam after saving several of his buddies' lives. The friends, these survivors of the horror known as the Viet Nam War, returned home vowing to care for their hero's little girl for the rest of her life. Sal might have lost a father, but she had gained a pack of brothers who would lay their lives down for her without hesitation. Josh, the youngest of them all, was the last one her father had carried through the minefield before being captured. It was also Josh who found this same sergeant's head rammed on a pole for gruesome display. That image still haunted him at night, and he would show up at Sal's doorstep whenever he couldn't shake the nightmares. Such was the nature of their relationship. Simply put, Josh had made it his life's work to watch over her.

Whenever Delta and Connie needed help of any kind from Sal, she had dropped everything to come to their aid. And when she dropped everything and ran, so did Josh. Now, here they were, once again, ready at a moment's notice, to scour the wilderness for a friend. It was crystal clear to Connie that heroism and courage were deeply embedded in Sal's genetic code. Like her father, she would go to enormous lengths for those she cared about, even if it meant risking her own life.

"Got a four-wheel drive?" Josh asked.

Connie nodded.

"Then what are we waiting for? Let's do it!"

14——

The early-morning sounds woke her even before the sunlight had a chance to. The rain forest was really two very separate and distinct worlds: green, well-lit, colorful and somewhat quiet during the days; spooky, dark and full of a thousand different sounds at night. Its nighttime serenade had lulled Delta to sleep, with the most incredible songs she had ever heard. Like some kind of witching-hour chorus, the nocturnal animals and insects seemed to give a special performance just for her. It was no wonder she'd fallen asleep so quickly—she'd had a lullaby played for her by musicians she would never see.

When she first lay down on her hammock, she'd been amazed at the denseness of the forest canopy. Try as she might, she could not find a single star in the night sky. Yet, when she woke at 5:15, the air felt crisper, the sounds were less intense, and the darkness was not as dark or as scary.

As she lay there listening to her personal concert, it suddenly, inexplicably stopped. Just like that, as if the conductor had fallen off her podium. The insects stopped buzzing and the night birds ceased their hooting. Sitting up and leaning on her elbows, Delta held her breath as she strained to hear the cause behind the sudden silence. From the west came the sound of a large animal thrashing its way through thick vegetation.

All the night critters seemed to be listening, too. Whatever it was...it was moving towards her.

As the crashing sound grew louder, Delta quickly ran through her options. It was too dark to see it, which could mean IT might not see her. Given the amount of noise it was making, Delta figured it must be huge. A large monkey? Surely the dreaded jaguar was much quieter when stalking its prey through the jungle. Delta picked up the long knife-like machete she had become so good at swinging. It felt heavy to her aching arm.

Taking the machete, she quickly gathered her gear and pushed it behind a tree trunk. Then she squatted down behind another large trunk and waited. She didn't have to wait long. As the sound grew closer, Delta scrunched down lower. Wiping her sweaty palms on her jeans, Delta regripped the machete handle.

With the machete balanced on her shoulder so she could quickly swing it, Delta squinted through the dark. For a second, she thought she saw...Was that...? No, it couldn't be. Yes, there it was again. A flash of light from the direction of the noise. The animals coming toward her weren't jaguars or monkeys—they were humans.

If she was scared before, she was absolutely petrified now. What if they were the Colombians? Or the poachers? What if they were natives? Delta slowed her breath. Four Spanish-speaking men whispered to each other as they hurried past the tree she was hiding behind. In the semi-darkness, she could not tell if they were Costa Rican or Colombian. But she did know one thing—they moved quickly away from her, hacking the foliage as they went. Frozen, afraid to move, Delta stayed in her crouched position for fifteen minutes before feeling it was safe enough to rise. After massaging her cramped left calf muscle, she prepared to follow them. "Storm," she whispered to herself, "I think you just got your first big break."

She grabbed up her gear quickly and started out after the men, but they had already disappeared into the dense undergrowth. If she didn't hustle, their trail would go cold. Whoever they were, they were experts in the art of jungle travel, and Delta wasn't even a novice. From here on out, she would have to slow down long enough to examine the breaks and cuts of the tree limbs hacked away by the men before her.

Standing back a moment, Delta thought about how she would approach this if she were on her home turf. "I'd take a look at the big picture." In the growing light, she surveyed the bushes. It became clear that there was a pattern to the hack marks the men had made. Certain trees had certain bushes surrounding them, and it was these bushes the men seemed to be pushing through. If she could look for those same shrubs, she might be able to move more quickly than if she looked for hack marks.

Delta looked up at the canopy overhanging the forest. For such a large wilderness, La Amistad sure had its share of human activity. Who were those men moving through the jungle so early in the morning? Locals foraging for plants? The one thing Delta was quickly learning was that there were way too many questions and not nearly enough answers.

When the sweat from her forehead dripped into her eyes, stinging them to the point that she had to stop, Delta leaned against a tree and rested. A quick check of her watch told her she'd been trailing these men for almost two hours. It was almost seven, and even the canopy above could not stop the powerful rays of sun from reaching the forest floor.

The question was, should she continue following them as her only possible lead, or head on back to Rivas to meet Connie?

Wiping her forehead with the back of her hand, Delta made the only decision that felt right to her. She wiped her sweaty palms, gripped her machete, and plunged deeper into the embrace of the jungle.

# 15 ——

The guards came to Megan's tent earlier than usual, and this alarmed her. If the general or someone else had noticed the knife missing, she was finished. For the first time since she'd been captured, Megan was afraid for her life. Sliding the knife into a seam on the inside of the tent wall, Megan glanced over to Siobhan and grinned. "It will be okay. Don't worry."

When the lock on the tent zipper was undone and the zipper quickly zipped open, Megan came face to face with Hector.

"General Zahn wishes to see you," Hector said after thrusting open the tent flap.

"This early? Is something wrong?"

"Now." Hector couldn't even look at Megan, who quickly put her boots on and followed him to the trailer.

Hector stopped Megan halfway to the trailer and rubbed himself up against her, his mouth half an inch from hers. "He will tire of you, *gringa* bitch, and then you regret the day you met me."

"I already do."

"*Puta!*"

Megan pried his hand off her arm. "The general will not be happy to hear of your treatment of me, Hector."

"Tell him, and you are a dead woman."

"I'm a dead woman anyway, you dumb ass."

Suddenly, Hector released her. "You will pay, whore. You will hurt so much, you will wish you were dead."

Opening the door to the trailer, Megan turned to him. "I'll see you in hell first." Entering the trailer, Megan felt her heart race. She hated Hector almost as much as he hated her. If she didn't get out of there, Hector would most assuredly kill her.

"Ah, Megan, *buenos días*. Please...sit down."

Megan sat as the general finished lacing up his boots. He looked up at her and smiled warmly. He did not appear to be angry, but Megan was still wary nonetheless. If he knew about the missing knife, it was all over for her.

"Coffee?"

Megan spied two cups and a carafe of coffee sitting on the table. Oh, how long it had been since she and Delta sat over two steaming cups of coffee in the morning. It had been one of her favorite parts of the day. "I'd love some. Allow me." Megan reached across him and poured the coffee from the carafe. Unless he was very good at hiding anger, General Zahn was not throwing out any vibes to Megan. As a matter of fact, what she was picking up from him was just the opposite. Handing a cup to him, Megan grinned.

"It is a beautiful morning, no?"

Megan nodded and wondered if he really expected a captive to notice whether or not the day was a pretty one. "Very."

"Did you sleep well?"

Looking at him over her cup, Megan wanted to laugh. She was being held hostage in a foreign country, forced to do manual labor with little more than rice and beans to eat, was locked up in a tent with nothing but a blanket, and he wants to know if she slept well? The question was beyond absurd.

"I slept fine, thank you." Gazing into his face, Megan saw a look familiar to her—one she'd seen thousands of times on the faces of her johns. He was staring at her with an unadulterated lust which stripped her bare of her clothes, her self-respect and her self-esteem. As Megan returned his gaze, she knew that, if she ever had the chance, if she ever really needed to, she was quite capable of killing a man like Zahn.

"Good." Reaching for a brown bag on the floor, the general pulled out a small perfume bottle and handed it to her. "I thought you might like something a little...feminine."

Megan stared at the bottle of perfume as if she hadn't seen one before. Was this guy for real? Was he as smitten with her as it appeared?

Taking the bottle from him, Megan opened it and smelled the cheap perfume as if it were the most divine nectar. "Mmmm. Nice. Thank you." Turning the bottle over, she dabbed some behind her ears. If Zahn's weakness was his desire for her, Megan was going to use that to her advantage. "This is very thoughtful."

Zahn nodded curtly, almost embarrassed by her pleasure. "There is something I need to do this morning and I would like you to accompany me."

Megan forced a grin. "Accompany you? Where are we going?"

General Zahn smiled. "You'll see. It is a beautiful place, really. We shall finish our coffee and be on our way."

Setting her cup down, Megan rose and followed General Zahn out the door. Once outside, he gave a few commands in clipped Spanish before strapping on a very sharp, very scary-looking machete.

"We should be gone most of the morning. I will have you back before lunch, when my scouts return." Rising, the general opened the door and motioned for Megan to go out. When he closed the door, he locked it, pocketed the key and said something in Spanish to his guard.

"Your scouts?" Megan asked as they left the camp.

"My men. I have men on the Panamanian side who believe they might have stumbled on another cavern much like these."

"Another cavern? How much is enough, General?"

General Zahn started down a path and spoke over his shoulder as they went. From behind, Megan noticed a knife attached to his boot along with a gun on his belt. If he wasn't truly a general in a bona fide army, he sure looked the part.

"Money buys government help, Megan. And governments who are bought turn their heads away from illegal activity."

"Such as poaching and smuggling?"

The general stopped and turned all the way around. "Drugs are the least of man's problems. We aren't just speaking of cocaine, we're also talking semi-automatic weapons, tanks, nuclear weapons, microchips, software and even large corporations. Everyone is in the business of making money."

"And that's what the gold does for you? Buys businesses?"

Continuing down the path, he nodded. "My wife does not understand, either. It's a man's world, Megan. Violent, corrupt and greedy. If I wasn't doing this and making a great deal of money, somebody else would be. And why not? My children go to the best private schools in the world; my wife lives in a mansion on a thousand acres of beautiful land; and my parents can live the remainder of their lives in luxury. If I was an American businessman crushing smaller companies and ruining competitors, I would be a hero, an idol. My face would be on the cover of magazines."

Megan was surprised by his impassioned words. Surprised, and somewhat taken aback. How was it that this monster had a point?

"But how rich does one man need to be, General?"

General Zahn stopped and turned toward Megan. "Did you know that Colombia supplies over eighty percent of the cocaine throughout the world? Have you any idea, any concept of the kind of money we're talking about? Eighty percent, Megan. Our cartels own more governments than England once did. Like any other wise investors, the cartel bosses have simply diversified their portfolios."

"Is that what you'd call murder, kidnap and rape? Diversifying a portfolio?"

The general turned his back and started walking again. "As I have said, it's a man's world, and international business is no place for women."

"Why? Because we choose not to exploit people for personal gain?"

Again, he stopped. Megan could not tell if she was angering him or if he was enjoying the conversation. "Have you any idea how the so-called honorable Japanese businessmen conduct business, Megan? Americans are so busy looking up to Japanese craftsmanship, they are not paying attention to the fact that those same businessmen are buying up your own country out from under you. It's business, Megan, and the good businessman always plays for keeps. This gold is my way of ensuring my place in that business world."

When the general continued down the path, Megan decided it was time to change the subject. She did not care to hear his warped version of Americans, Japanese or women. "Are we going into a town?"

"No. I no longer go into towns. I may not be in my native land, but my face is quite familiar even in Central America. I have not gotten caught because I do not take unnecessary chances."

"What about when you go home?"

"I am a wealthy landowner in Colombia, and I donate much money to the church, the schools and even the local government. I own ranches, a manufacturing plant and even purebred horses. I have a satellite plate, a telecommunications system and a very secure home. The people of my region do not care how I get my money because they know that I spread it around. People who are given things don't ask questions. Poor people given things ask even less questions. That is a motto that your very own government lives by."

"You think so?"

"I know so. There's a drug problem in your country because your government sleeps with the cartels. For every pound of heroin or cocaine they find, there's a hundred pounds more that make it in. With a success rate like that, someone isn't doing their job."

"Are you saying that our government has an association with your cartels?"

This made him laugh. "You weren't listening. I said eighty percent of the world's cocaine comes from Colombia. With the cocaine trade becoming impossible to stop in your country, why is it Americans have not done something political against Colombia to stop it? You still trade with us, you still put corporations in our country, you even visit it as a tourist destination. If your government wasn't as corrupt as everyone else's, and they were serious about their so-called war on drugs, they would impose embargoes, tariffs, every kind of economic sanction they could."

"But we don't."

"No, you don't."

Megan nodded. "Fascinating. In other words, we're trying to kill the weed by cutting off the top, instead of pulling it out by the roots?"

"In a manner of speaking, yes."

"And you were able to acquire all that you have now through drug money?"

"How else can a poor Colombian boy make that kind of money, experience the kind of power I enjoy? But drugs alone are not enough to keep a man in power. One must expand. Like your Donald Trump or Ted Turner. They are wealthy beyond imagination because they diversified. In my world, I am no less successful than they."

As Megan followed, she tried to take note of as many landmarks as possible—a tree bent in half over here, ivy covering the trunk of another there She was certain she'd not been in this part of the forest. "Have you always been a drug runner?"

The term made General Zahn stop so abruptly, Megan nearly collided with him. "First off, I am a businessman. I buy and sell commodities others can't or don't. Drug runner sounds so...amateurish."

"Let me rephrase the question. What did you do before you became General Zahn?"

"I was in the military many years ago, and I realized we were fighting a losing battle. Drugs are everywhere, and it isn't as bad as you Americans make it out to be. Many tribal people still existing in the rain forest use drugs on a weekly, if not daily, basis. Drugs are one way of connecting to one's spirituality."

"But in developed nations, drugs contribute to violent crime. Even Japan is beginning to suffer the effects," Megan countered.

"But it isn't the drugs that are the problem. It's the people and your attitudes toward drugs. Many of your crimes happen because the drugs are illegal. Drugs are illegal because Europeans fear them. Every single Amazonian tribe uses hallucinogenic drugs of one kind or another. They smoke it, eat it or drink it, and it often accompanies some of their most important rituals. Drugs in those cultures are every bit as essential as food. They are recognized for their role in ritual."

Megan wiped the sweat from her brow. "But if drugs were legalized, you'd be out of business, right?"

General Zahn turned and grinned at her. "Then I would become what you call an 'honest' businessman, and instead of dealing with the black market, I would be dealing with the even more corrupt pharmaceutical companies. Don't you see? It makes no difference to me who I deal with, because as long as there are plants, there will be drugs that someone, somewhere will want."

"What happened to make you turn your back on the military?"

"The military turned its back on me. I realized that we weren't Colombian soldiers fighting to protect our country; we were Colombians being used by the American and Canadian governments to fight for *their* countries."

"I don't understand."

"You Americans blame your drug problem on my people, or on the Mexicans, or on your immigrants—on anyone but who it truly belongs to. Instead of solving the problem in your own home, you come into mine and try to clean my house. We were being used by an American government that wanted to make it look like they were doing something to stop the drug flow out of Colombia. Your government does not understand that its unhappy citizens are turning to drugs because there is nothing else to turn to. Look at your failing educational system, your increasing number of homeless, your rising unemployment rate. Your people are so unhappy about how they live that they would rather be numb. This is not the fault of my people, yet we are using armed soldiers to stop them from growing or cultivating a drug that almost every country uses and wants. Such hypocrisy, really."

"So you switched sides."

"Yes, and I have been a rich man ever since."

"But rich and wanted..."

"Perhaps."

"If you're so rich, why don't you stop so you can enjoy it?"

This made General Zahn laugh. "I did not become a wealthy man on my own. There is always someone we are accountable to. One does not simply walk away from the cartels."

"Oh. So you *owe* someone."

General Zahn turned. "Don't you?"

Megan looked back at him, but didn't respond.

For the next half hour or so, they walked in silence, stopping occasionally to hack away at the underbrush. As they pushed on, Megan heard a faint, rushing sound; a sound they were nearing. The closer they got to it, the louder was the noise. Finally, as they pushed their way past several bushes, Zahn split a bush in two and held it back for Megan. When she stepped over the bush, it was as if she'd stepped into paradise.

Falling majestically was a waterfall about forty feet high. The water flowed smoothly over rock and into a pool, which eventually evened out to a smooth, calm pond-like area which trickled lazily over smooth rocks until it reached a creek. The pond-like area was nestled in a small clearing about the size of a football field, and the water, which rushed down the cliff face, was a clear blue. It was the most beautiful place Megan had ever seen. In the open space, there were no trees to block the brilliant sun, which beamed down on the clear water. The smaller trees surrounding the water were canopied with bright green leaves and yellow trunks. The fresh scent of jasmine wafted through the air, as butterflies hovered about.

Standing next to her, General Zahn rocked back and forth, smiling broadly. "One of my men discovered this place by accident. I come here when I need peace."

"It's beautiful," Megan murmured. "Absolutely amazing."

Moving ahead, the general sat on the soft ground and began unlacing his boots. "There are many, many places such as these in Colombia. I long for those places, for the simplicity of life there."

Joining him on the ground, Megan folded her long legs up and rested her chin on her knees. Although she would kill him if she had the chance, Megan still found some admirable qualities about the man. "You speak of Colombia with such passion."

Taking off one boot, General Zahn paused to look at Megan. "It is where I wish to be. When this...project is completed, I hope to spend my days watching my daughters and their grandchildren grow up. I hope to take time to fish in the lake. There is much I would do." He stopped, then added, "But I have debts to repay, just like any other successful businessman."

Megan watched in silence as he removed his second boot. She knew what was coming next, and steeled her insides against the violations she knew would come. "How did you find the gold? According to legend, this rich coast was believed by Columbus and others to have rich deposits of gold and silver, but no one ever found any of this mythical gold."

General Zahn grinned. "Ah, that would be half right, my dear. You have studied your Central American history well."

Megan nodded. Before beginning her internship, she'd consumed every book she could get her hands on about Costa Rican history, lifestyle, rituals. "I have done some reading."

"And what did you discover?"

"Columbus was treated well by the natives when he got here," she answered.

"And?"

"And he noticed their necklaces of silver and gold. The Spanish tried to conquer the natives, because they thought they'd get all of the gold, but—"

"They never found any," Zahn finished for her.

"Not until an earthquake hit this country. What happened then?"

General Zahn grinned. "In 1991, Costa Rica suffered a devastating earthquake, which disturbed the muck on the river floor. One of my connections, an American, as a matter of fact, was completing a geological survey shortly after, and noticed a change in the water. There were trace elements that had not previously existed. It wasn't long before we followed that trace and ended up here. After that, all we had to do was find the underground water source, and here we are."

"You had an American geologist on your payroll?"

"Of course. I also have several doctors, lawyers, politicians, judges, law-enforcement officers and medical personnel in my employ. I have people all over the globe looking out for special artifacts, museum pieces, microchips, even coins. Diversity is the key to wealth, Megan, and I am as diverse as they come. Did you know that San Jose's Jade Museum has the world's largest collection of pre-Colombian jade?"

Megan shook her head.

"Another area of my portfolio, you see. If the earthquake unearthed gold deposits, what about archeological finds? Priceless artifacts might be unearthed here."

"But they would belong to the *Ticos*."

This made General Zahn laugh. "The jade would belong to the highest bidder, Megan. Surely you are not so naive as to believe that archeologists are also humanitarians? Some of the world's most renowned diggers are on some other country's payroll."

Megan watched as he unbuckled his pants and dropped them to the ground. Pulling his shirt over his head, General Zahn now stood in front of Megan completely naked.

"What about the natives here? Have you had connections with any of them?"

"Such as?"

"The Bribri?" The heat from the morning sun drew perspiration down Megan's back.

General Zahn stretched out and smiled. "You have done your homework."

"It's a rich history." Megan swatted a buzzing insect away.

"Indeed."

"And they could be very wealthy." Unlacing her boots, Megan wriggled her toes once her socks were removed.

"You misjudge the situation. Gold doesn't equal riches to the Bri. It is simply ornamentation for them. They don't understand, nor do they care much for its market value."

"So it's okay to plunder it." Watching the water fall, Megan sighed.

This brought a hearty laugh from the general. "You wouldn't give a priceless heirloom to a child, would you? Of course not."

"But they aren't children."

"They are in terms of economy. They are infants with a fabulous bank account they have no use for," Zahn said, grinning.

Megan shook her head. "I can't believe they aren't even attempting to stop you."

Rolling over on his back, General Zahn spread his arms out and closed his eyes. "They tried once, but I believe they realized the extent of our power. Bows and arrows are no match for automatic weapons."

"Is that what all the armed guards are for?"

"Surely you didn't think we feared the animals? I have stayed alive in this business by not trusting anyone—not even simple natives." General Zahn walked to the edge of the water and gingerly stepped into the pool. His bronze body was fit, and without the usual love-handles of a man his age.

"Is nothing sacred to you?" Megan asked.

"Family and money," he answered, smiling at her. Wading up to his waist, the general climbed onto one of the smooth boulders about twenty feet out. "Enough talk. I have come here to bathe and refill my spirit. I wish for you to wash me."

Megan slowly rose and hesitated before walking to the water's edge. This was one of the moments she had been dreading.

"Take your clothes off," he commanded, leaning back on the rock. "There is a washcloth folded up in my back pocket."

Removing the washcloth from his pants, Megan slowly unbuttoned her blouse. Grimacing at how dirty both she and her clothes were, Megan considered washing them before they started back to the camp.

"Turn toward me. I enjoy watching a woman undress."

The grimace instantly disappeared from her face, replaced now by what she had once called her prostitute's game face. Grinning sincerely, Megan turned toward him until all of her clothes were off. Then she folded them neatly in a pile next to his.

"Come, the water is quite warm."

Stepping into the water, Megan felt the revulsion building inside her. She had to do this, she had to stay alive, but the cost to her own spirit was, quite possibly, too high even for her. "So, the earthquake laid a deposit of gold at your feet that had been hidden for centuries."

"Yes."

Splashing the warm water on her face, Megan looked up at the general, who was eyeing her with appreciation. "I'm curious, General, how did you get that trailer into the forest?"

"Helicopter at night. But enough questions." Lowering himself into the water, General Zahn sent a ripple of small waves toward Megan's ankles. "Come. I desire you."

Megan dipped the washcloth in the water and moved around to his back. She so wished she had the strength to kill this man with her bare hands.

"Ahh, that feels good."

Megan washed his back and dipped the washcloth in the water before running it over his shoulders and neck. "What about the rest of us? What will you do when this is all over?"

"You know the answer to that."

Standing in front of him, Megan washed the front of his neck and shoulders. As she did, he took one of her breasts in his hand and stroked it. "It would be such a waste to kill a woman like you."

Megan forced a grin. A woman like her? What, exactly, was that? An old professional? A survivor? A woman who always knew how to peddle her gifts in order to keep living? What so many men valued about her made Megan shudder. *I might live instead of the others because I'm pretty and knew how to please a man.* The thought was so repulsive she wanted to scream.

Moving to the side, Megan did not attempt to brush off the hands that were groping her.

"But if you agree to come to Colombia with me, you could live on one of my ranches. Granted, they are far away from towns and villages, but you could live a peaceful, satisfying existence."

Still wiping his shoulders and underarms, Megan forced back the bile rising in her throat. As she dipped the washcloth back in the water, she noticed his erection and shivered. He noticed her shiver and mistook it for something altogether different.

*Damn it! Where is Delta?*

"Surely a life in Colombia, versus death out here, must appeal to you?"

Washing his arms, Megan locked eyes with him. "I prefer to live, yes."

"Then consider my offer."

Megan nodded as she wiped. She would stay alive for Delta and her life back home. She would do whatever she had to, promise whatever she must, and deal with Satan himself if necessary, but Megan Osbourne was not going to die. As long as she lived, as long as there was one breath left in her body, Delta Stevens would know she was alive, and she would never, ever give up searching. On that, Megan would bet her life.

"Come," General Zahn said, taking Megan's hands in his and pulling her closer. "I have other needs." Putting his hands on her buttocks, he kissed her hard and bit her neck before sucking on her breast. Then, slowly rising, he pulled her over to a dryer part of the rock, where he lay down. Taking Megan's face in his hands, he guided her mouth to his penis.

Closing her eyes, Megan opened her mouth and transported her soul to another place, another time, before college, before Costa Rica, and long before Delta Stevens.

# 16 ——

**Delta** was drenched in sweat. Every muscle and tendon burned. Her machete was beginning to feel like a hundred-pound baseball bat. She gripped it with two hands and swung it with the same power that had won her a national batting title in college. But that was college, in the safety of a playing field, with many others to help her. Now, she was alone, in the jungle, with arms that felt like she was a ninety-eight-pound weakling.

Stopping to rest, Delta pulled out the last of her water and sipped it. It was difficult to imagine what the heat would feel like by noon, now four hours away, but she knew she'd have to find a cool place to rest or risk heat stroke. She'd managed to follow the bush markers with ease, and was surprised at how her detecting skills had come in handy, even way out here in the wilderness. Twice she had come to obvious forks, where she was unsure which direction to take, and both times, she'd analyzed the floor of the forest for footprints, overturned leaves, or other telltale signs of human beings. Once, a cigarette butt had pointed the way. It was still slower going than she would have liked, but getting irretrievably lost wouldn't do her any good. Megan was in here, somewhere, and Delta was certain these little machete marks and bent twigs would lead her there.

It was a weird feeling knowing that the forest was watching her. She felt like an actress on stage, with all eyes focused upon her, waiting to see how she would react. Once, she had raised her machete to chop a thick hanging vine, and just as the machete was over her head, she realized it wasn't a vine at all, but a snake. It could have been a boa, a python or a cobra, for all she knew. Her initial reaction was to kill it anyway, but then she remembered that she was the trespasser here, the criminal element come to the jungle. The snake probably just wanted a closer look at the animal loudly thrashing her way through his home.

Shafts of light penetrated the canopy above and caressed the green floor as the late-morning sun beat down on leaves and bushes. Delta rested momentarily, then repacked her things. After finishing her water, she took hold of her machete once more.

An hour later, Delta continued to push through vines and other tropical foliage. She was tired, hungry and very, very hot. It took all of her concentration to move swiftly through the jungle without creating a disturbance. Despite this, she was still able to follow the trail of the men she'd come across earlier.

Then, before she realized it, she nearly stumbled right over them. With her machete raised above her head, Delta stopped it in midair. Only twenty yards away sat the group of men who had ambled by her camp earlier that morning. Crouching down, Delta wiped the sweat off her forehead and listened to a conversation she had absolutely no chance in hell of understanding.

As the men chatted back and forth in quick Spanish, Delta strained to glean any word she might recognize. It wasn't long before she heard the word *Colombia*. Peeking out from behind a massive plant with six-foot leaves, Delta watched as the four men shook their heads and pointed to the east. Other words she thought she recognized, like *estupido, narcotico, los militares* and *peligroso,* were tossed about, and Delta stretched her memory to recall where she had seen the word *peligroso* before.

*Peligroso*, she thought. Signs around the canals and electrical poles back home said *peligroso*. Didn't it mean dangerous? Or danger? And what about *los militares*? Had these men seen Colombians dressed in fatigues? Were these men afraid of the Colombians? Were they escaping from the Colombians? And what was in those canvas sacks they were carrying over their shoulders? Squatting back down, Delta knew it was time to make a choice.

These guys did not appear to be part of the Colombian group Manny had warned her about. The sacks suggested to her that they could be poachers, and if that was so, they were probably *Ticos* or Nicaraguans hunting game for profit.

Listening to her intuition, which she had so often relied on in the past, Delta decided she would no longer follow this group, but give them time to move away from their perceived threat from the Colombians.

Ten minutes later, when the group of men started toward the west, Delta moved east. For the next hour, she cut through more jungle until she found a small stream trickling over some smooth rocks. She blew the ground free of leaves and ants, then plopped down for a short rest. After a moment, she turned onto her stomach and dunked her entire head into the water. With a sigh of pleasure, she shook her wet head like a dog after a bath. The cool, clear water refreshed her. She perked up a little, and then felt ready to go. Rolling over on her back, Delta closed her eyes. She was beat. In the middle of heaving a sigh, she heard a strange noise she hadn't ever heard before. It was a low, guttural sound like a bear, or...maybe a jaguar. Quickly sitting up, Delta cocked her head and listened. Some creature was in agony.

Delta grabbed her backpack and machete, then crept carefully through the underbrush. As she moved through the forest, the sound grew louder. It was hard to identify it, for another loud, rushing sound filled the air. Closing her eyes,

she listened intently. Maybe it was a hurt animal. It sounded
strange, but then, most of the sights and sounds she'd
experienced in the last twenty-four hours were foreign to her.
After all, how did a jaguar really sound? What sort of noises
did a howler monkey make? The other sound was more familiar.
*Must be a waterfall,* she thought.

Closer and closer she stalked, until she came to the cliff's
edge where water from a swollen creek flowed over and down.
At least if the animal making the sound was down there, it
might not be interested in eating her. She was safe up here. The
drop to the area below was at least thirty, maybe even fifty feet.
Peering over the edge, Delta caught herself on a tree branch as
her eyes located the source of the unfamiliar sound.

In the middle of a small pool of water, Delta saw a
man...a woman...and then her brain finally acknowledged what
her eyes were seeing.

Delta slapped her hand over her mouth to keep from
vomiting. Scurrying back from the cliff's edge, she plopped
down hard, her hand still firmly clamped over her lips. It
couldn't be. Maybe the heat had gotten to her. Maybe she was
hallucinating. Grabbing her machete, Delta returned to her
place on the cliff and tried to look once more. Sure enough,
there was Megan, sucking some guy's dick in the middle of the
goddamned rain forest!

Delta sprang up and was about to jump off the edge
and into the water below, when suddenly, someone grabbed
her backpack, slapped a hand over her mouth, and pulled her
off the rock, With a sickening thud, she hit the ground.
Wrestling out of the grasp of the hand that held her, Delta
twisted around, grabbed the hand off her mouth, and quickly
employed a wrist lock.

"It's me!" came a hushed, pained voice.

Delta whirled around, still holding the stranger's hand,
and found Manny grimacing in her face. "What in the hell are
you doing here?" Delta demanded as she helped him to his
feet.

"Shh," Manny whispered, holding a finger to his lips. "I followed you...I...Bianca convinced me to chase after you. I must say, for a wo—for a foreigner, you have made good time."

"I found her, Manny. I found Megan."

"That's not all you found, I'm afraid."

Delta turned back to the cliff's edge, but Manny stopped her. "I'm going after her," she insisted.

"Do, and you'll get us all killed." Manny tightened his grip on Delta's arm. She looked down at his hand and locked eyes with him; he quickly released her.

"What are you talking about?"

Manny moved down the path away from the cliff. Then he parted the tree branches and pointed. "Look there...and over there."

When Delta followed his finger, she saw two guards posted on either side of the pool of water, just out of view.

Ducking back behind the rocks comprising the cliff, Manny whispered, "There are many others just like them scattered all over. You are lucky none of them saw either of us, or we would be dead by now."

"Why would they post guards over a naked guy and a woman?" Delta peeked once again over the rocks and saw two more guards on the opposite shore.

"I am afraid your friend is in great danger."

A final grunt from the naked man on the rock, and Delta unsteadily dropped to her knees and let the vomit spill from her mouth. Eyes and mouth watering, she clamped her eyelids shut, trying to erase the horrible sight she had just witnessed.

Manny gently laid a hand on her shoulder and helped her to her feet. "I'm sorry you had to see that."

Wiping her teary eyes with the back of her clean hand, Delta nodded. "Me too. I guess it just...caught me off-guard."

"I will watch their movements. When they get ready to return to their camp, I'll let you know. Their camp must be close by. We're going to have to be very careful to avoid any guards."

"Why would a man getting a blow job be so heavily guarded?"

"Perhaps they are protecting him from the animals. Your friend is the prisoner of someone who knows the jungle well. It is the submerged crocodile that will eat you for lunch. And they move with such swiftness that the man would never know what ate him. The guards are probably there to make sure that does not happen."

Delta studied Manny for a long time, and realized that he did indeed know what he was talking about when it came to the jungle. Just moments ago, Delta had dunked her head into a stream, never thinking about what lurked beneath the calm surface. The very thought of a crocodile watching her gave her goose bumps.

"I'll sit right here, Manny. The moment they move, we move."

Manny nodded. "Right."

Leaning against a rock, Delta put her head back and closed her eyes. She had so many questions and nobody to answer them. Nothing she'd ever learned or experienced before could have gotten her prepared for this. Everything was unfamiliar; all the rules, the stage, the players, the script, even the cosmic director seemed to be from another planet. *Okay, so Megan is a prisoner...she is, isn't she? I mean, she didn't do that willingly, did she?*

The questions flew at her like a swarm of bees, each stinging her every time she could not deflect what she had seen with her eyes.

And what was the truth? What would have happened if Manny hadn't followed her? True to her nature, Delta would have jumped down there only to have her fool head blown off before she could hit the water. She might even have gotten Megan killed. For all her gallantry, Delta still hadn't learned that sometimes the best thing to do is nothing.

"Your friend," Manny whispered over his shoulder, "is smart."

Delta fought off the image of Megan on the rock. "What makes you say that?"

"She has made herself popular with an officer of some sort."

Delta immediately stood up. "Officer?"

Manny nodded, but held up his hand, stopping Delta from coming closer. "The clothes on the ground are an officer's. You can tell from the insignia on the shoulders."

"What about hers?"

"Her clothes?"

"Yeah. How are they arranged?"

Manny frowned before returning his attention to the action below. "They are neatly folded next to his."

A slow grin spread across Delta's face. Not once had Megan stopped to fold her clothes prior to lovemaking. As a matter of fact, Megan liked to fling them all over the room. A truth poked its head from the shadows, swatting several bees from Delta's psyche. "She's using her old life to keep her new one alive."

Manny nodded. "Very wise. Colombians respect those they think useful."

Delta cocked her head at Manny, who was still gazing down at the pond. Had she underestimated him earlier, or was he speaking more clearly now? More directly? Something about him seemed to change once his sister was gone, but Delta couldn't put a finger on it. It was increasingly clear to her that nothing was as it seemed in the rain forest.

"We cannot afford to make any mistakes, Delta. We must give them plenty of room. Your friend is alive. Let's keep it that way."

Nodding, Delta sighed loudly. Megan was alive, and that was all that mattered.

# 17——

"This is the place," Connie announced as they piled out of the Sidekick.

When Connie, Sal and Josh arrived in Rivas, they were greeted by Bianca and Kiki, who sat out in front of *Los Rancheros,* waiting.

"You must be Connie," Bianca said, extending her hand. "I am Bianca. Delta Stevens' friend."

Connie shook Bianca's hand and introduced Sal and Josh to the young woman. "This is Sal and Josh, who are also Delta's friends."

Bianca nodded to them both. "Delta Stevens has many friends, doesn't she?"

"You bet she does," Sal answered, looking around the gravel road. "Is there a place for us to get something to drink?"

Bianca nodded and led them into *Los Rancheros,* where a single fan lazily turned overhead and a soccer game played on the small black-and-white television set in the corner.

When the four of them were seated and two beers and two Cokes ordered, Connie turned to Bianca. "Has Delta returned from La Amistad?"

Bianca shook her head. "My brother, Manny, was worried about her last night, so he followed her into the jungle this morning to help show her the way back."

"Worried? Why was he worried?" Connie asked, watching Josh survey the small, dirty bar.

"We saw the Colombians yesterday just before we took Delta to the trail's end. We rode horses as far as we could, dropped her off and then came home. On our way home, Manny thought he saw poachers or something, and decided he should go back in the morning to find her."

Sal chuckled. "Find her? In a rain forest that size?"

Josh shook his head. "Not unless her brother knows the forest really well."

Bianca nodded. "Manny knows the jungle quite well. He has tracked down lost tourists before. Well...he and Augustine did once. The couple had wandered away from the tour bus and once they got turned around, they became lost. It only took Manny and Augustine two hours to find them, and they were a good mile away from the bus. Believe me, my brother knows the jungle."

Josh appeared edgy. "So he went after her this morning to help show her the way back. When do you think he'll return?"

Bianca shrugged. "When he finds Delta."

Connie shot a worried look over to Josh. "Something or someone out there scared him enough to go after her this morning."

Nodding, Josh turned to Bianca. "Delta is supposed to return by nightfall. If she and your brother aren't here, what would *you* think has happened?"

Bianca thought for a moment. "I know Manny. He won't return without her."

"Then that pretty much sums it up," Sal said, taking her cap off and running her hand through her wet bangs. "We wait until he brings her in."

Connie nodded. "Josh?"

"Agreed. We wait. If neither of them shows up tonight, we get a move on into the jungle at first light. Until then, I say we try not to let our imaginations get the best of us. For all we know, he could be showing her the sights."

Kiki jumped off Bianca's shoulders and climbed up to Connie, who reached up nonchalantly and stroked the capuchin monkey's chest. Kiki let out a sound resembling a purr. "I have a bad feeling about this," Connie said, as Kiki took her hand and examined it curiously.

Josh shrugged. "Not much we can do until tomorrow. I suggest we check our supplies and make sure we have everything we need. I'm going to take a look around and see if there's anything at the entrance to La Amistad that might have sent Manny off."

Connie nodded. "We can also talk to the people here. See if anyone has any information. Once we get in La Amistad, we're on our own."

Bianca sipped her Coke, then shook her head. "Don't worry. There isn't a man for miles who's better at scouting the jungle than Manny. If anyone can find her, he's the one."

Connie cast a look over to Josh, whose face was deadpan. If he was worried, he certainly didn't show it. "I wish I knew what Manny saw that triggered his alarm," Connie said quietly.

Josh shrugged. "Me too, Connie. Me too."

# 18 ——

**When** Megan and the general started toward shore, Delta rose, only to have Manny pull her back down.

"They're leaving," Delta whispered tersely.

"We have to give them some room. Once we see the direction they're moving, following them will be...how did you say it yesterday...cake?"

Delta nodded and grinned. "You sure we won't lose them?"

Manny nodded. "Trust me, Delta. I grew up in this forest. We can give them a five- or ten-minute head start and still be able to follow."

Delta heaved a sigh. Trusting anyone was hard; trusting a man was the hardest. It had taken her a long time to trust her new partner, Tony Carducci, and even now, that trust was still sometimes tested. "Okay, Manny Decoubertin, I am going to trust you, but if you lose them, I'm going to kick your ass."

Manny grinned warmly into Delta's face. "I might enjoy that."

Ten minutes later, Manny signaled for Delta to follow him. For the next half hour, they trailed Megan and the others without incident, when suddenly, out of nowhere, sprang two soldiers, each pointing a rifle in their faces. Manny held his hands up and spoke quickly, while Delta nodded and tried to look innocent. She cursed herself for not knowing Spanish, and promised that if she ever got out of there, she would make it a point to learn.

Manny pointed to the trees, gesticulating wildly, until one of the soldiers barked at him, *"Silencio!"*

The guards looked at Manny, at Delta, and then at each other before chattering away. When they had summed up the situation, one guard motioned with his gun for them to walk ahead.

"What's going on?" Delta asked, her heart pounding and beads of sweat forming above her top lip.

"I told them the truth. That we are from a geographical survey unit checking out the local flora and fauna." Manny laced his hands behind his head as he walked.

"And?"

"And I don't think they believe me."

"What now?" Delta ran her hand through her curly wet hair.

"They're taking us back to their boss."

"I don't like this one bit." Delta cut her eyes over to Manny. "We're in trouble, aren't we?"

Manny nodded.

"They'll kill us, won't they?"

He nodded again.

Delta thought about this for a moment. "I didn't come all this way just to let Megan down. We have to do something."

One guard poked Delta in the back with his rifle and barked something at her.

"Any good ideas?" she asked, seeing Manny's eyes dart about as if looking for a weapon.

"We're as good as dead if we get to their camp," Manny said, through unmoving lips.

"I know a little karate," Delta said, casting a quick glance over her shoulder to gauge the distance between her and the guards.

"I don't think so, Delta."

Again, Manny's American colloquialisms caught her by surprise. He had not sounded so American in Rivas yesterday. "They're macho Latinos, Manny. They'll never expect it from me."

"You can't disarm a soldier that easily."

Delta looked at Manny's profile and grinned. "Wanna bet? You take care of the guy behind you, and let me take care of mine."

"But—"

"No time for buts. Just follow my lead. I know what I'm doing."

"Just say when."

"When we get past that dead tree. As soon as I step over." Delta cast her eyes over at the fallen tree.

Manny nodded.

They walked along for a while longer with neither saying a word. The rain forest was so quiet now, it felt like the creatures were spectators of this bizarre game. Well, there were a few tricks she was sure these Colombians hadn't seen, and Delta reached into the very bottom of the bag to retrieve them.

Stepping over the fallen tree, Delta reached out to steady herself but could not stop her fall. On her back, Delta lifted herself up on one elbow, and in one swift movement swept the guard's legs out from under him. As the surprised guard started to fall back over the dead tree, Delta yanked his gun away from him, hastening his fall back over the tree. He landed on his back with a thud.

Manny immediately leveled his captor with a swift kick to the inside of the kneecap. Grabbing his kneecap, the second guard fell to the ground, writhing in pain. Manny snatched the weapon from the ground and pointed it at the guard's face before barking orders to them in Spanish. Both men rose to their knees and laced their fingers together behind their heads.

"Well done," Manny said.

"My best friend taught me a few moves," Delta replied, checking her weapon for a safety catch. It was a foreign automatic she had never seen before. "Doesn't matter what country you're in, men always underestimate the power of women," she said with a grin.

But before either could say another word, bullets zipped and pinged into the trees around them.

"The others have returned!" Manny cried, shooting his weapon in the direction of the unfriendly fire. "Run!"

Delta looked down at the foreign rifle in her hands and then back up at Manny. "Not without you."

"I know the jungle better than you. Go, and don't stop!"

The guard Delta had downed got up and started running. Manny turned and pulled the trigger, shooting him in the back. Delta stood there, shocked to see that her little *Tico* guide had just killed a man.

"Go, Delta. If they catch you, your fate will be much worse than a simple death. Go! I'll cover you."

Delta hesitated a moment before chucking the automatic at Manny's feet. "Be careful." With that, she took off at a run.

Branches lashed her face as she barreled through the unforgiving jungle. Barbed vines grabbed at her ankles and small bushes slowed her progress, but Delta ran desperately, fired by fear. Hearing only her own labored breathing, she wasn't sure if anyone was following her. When she slowed down long enough to check for pursuers, she saw Manny reach down for the second rifle. As he bent over, a bullet ripped through his thigh, throwing him onto his back.

"Manny!" Delta cried, taking three steps back toward him. Should she leave him here and risk getting caught, or worse? Or should she continue on in hopes that she could live through this to help Megan escape? Before Delta could find an answer, one of her would-be captors stepped in her path about forty feet away. The grin he wore like some perverse voodoo mask reminded her of another man's grin moments before she'd killed him.

So arrogant was this guard that he wasn't even pointing his rifle at her—a grave mistake against a woman of Delta's caliber.

"Run, Delta!" Manny yelled, reaching a bloody hand toward the rifle.

One look into the soldier's eyes told Delta he planned to do more than just kill her. Saying a silent prayer for Manny, Delta wheeled around and began her descent into the darker region of the forest. Bullets thudded into the bark of trees all around her...*Run for your life, Delta. And don't look back.*

"Gunfire," Josh murmured to himself, as the sound of automatic weapons reverberated through the jungle.

Peering through his binoculars, he tried to locate the source of the gunfire, but knew it would be futile—the jungle was too dense. There was only one way to find out.

☙ ☙ ☙

The next morning, as shafts of light peeked through the dense canopy, Delta pushed the large palm frond leaves she'd hidden under off her. They were wet, but had kept her safe and dry. She didn't know how far she had traveled from where she'd left Manny, but she was sure she could make it back. If, of course, he was still there...

Last night, the gunfire that followed her as she escaped had died down shortly after she'd rounded a huge tree that resembled a sycamore—the species found dotting the sidewalks of her hometown. If she could find her way to that tree, she might be able to find Manny.

Taking out her canteen, Delta took a drink of water. *Gotta stay cool. Manny could very well still be alive. I owe it to him to try and find him before the Colombians do. On the other hand, he could very well be dead, and I could be wasting valuable time going back for a corpse.*

The decision was an easy one. Delta Stevens always repaid her debts.

After several false turns, she finally located the sycamore-like tree. Just as she started around its ten-foot base, the guard spotted her. Before she could duck back, he moved toward her. For a second they stared at each other, as if both were unsure of what this moment meant. Then the guard smiled at Delta and raised his automatic rifle.

Darting to her left, Delta plowed through the bushes as bullets ripped through the leaves and thudded into the dirt. The guard was in hot pursuit, cursing and shouting in Spanish as he fired off half a dozen rounds. This time, Delta did not look back. Arms and legs pumping, she could feel the bullets as they whizzed by her. If she didn't get out of the line of fire soon, it was only a matter of seconds before one of those bullets found its mark.

Running blindly through the jungle was like racing through a dark house, not knowing where the furniture was. She didn't know if the drops running down her face were from sweat or blood, but whatever it was, it was making it difficult for her to see.

She was also having a hard time hearing. There was another rushing sound, besides the beating of her heart and the bullets tearing into tree bark, but she was too frightened to identify it. In an attempt to get out of the line of fire, Delta took a sharp right turn, and was greeted by a slap in the face from a huge leaf.

She wiped her eyes and had a hard time focusing on the vegetation ahead. Just as she turned to see if the guard was gaining on her, the ground disappeared from under her feet. Too late, Delta realized that she'd stumbled right into a raging river. The current grabbed her like a rag doll and propelled her downstream. By the time her head surfaced, she was already fifty yards downstream, swept further along with every passing second.

Delta needed to turn herself around before her head crashed into a rock and cracked open like a pumpkin on Halloween, but knowing and doing were two separate things. She had seen it done in the movies, but then, that was the movies.

Fighting the pull of the current and inhaling more water than air, Delta managed to turn herself around so that her feet were facing downstream. White foam slapped her face, forcing its way up her nostrils. With flailing arms, she struggled to keep her head above the raging water. She coughed and gagged as she tried to keep water from pouring down her throat. It seemed she'd escaped one threat of death only to run into the embrace of another. Even in the midst of the roaring rapids, the irony didn't escape her.

How long she traveled, she did not know. What she *did* know was that fatigue was setting in and she was weakening from the effort of repeatedly pushing herself away from oncoming rocks.

Delta craned her neck and saw a bend in the river where the rapids slowed. She was sure it would pick up speed again once it rounded that curve. *Okay, Delta, you have one chance— grab an overhanging branch...pull yourself out. Otherwise, it's all over.*

Pushing off a boulder in the middle of the rapids, Delta propelled herself closer to the left bank, where a large branch loomed over the water. Her timing would have to be exact, or else she risked being knocked out and drowning. As she neared the overhanging branch, Delta used every ounce of energy she possessed to thrust herself up and out of the water. Overestimating the distance, she hit the branch with her forearms, but as her arms scraped down the branch, she managed to hang on.

With the water still tugging at her legs, Delta fought to pull herself up. Her body weighed a ton, and she feared she wouldn't have the strength to pull herself completely out of the water. Hanging on for as long as she could, Delta made one more attempt to hoist her body out of the water, but failed.

"Goddamnit!" she cursed, not relishing the idea of dropping back into the river. As she hung there considering her limited options, she noticed that the water was slightly calmer next to the bank. If she could swing herself over to it, she might be able to grab the roots of a nearby tree and dig in before the current could sweep her downstream. Clenching her teeth, Delta gripped the branch more tightly and lifted her feet out of the water so that her body hung like a backwards L. With a mighty effort, she kicked her legs forward and started swinging her body like a pendulum. Finally, she swung out as far as she could and released the branch. She plunged back into the water...but now she was only a foot from the shore. She dug her hands into the sandy ground, searching for roots to hang on to. *Gotta keep from being dragged back into that treacherous current.*

Finally, her fingers found their target. She held fast to the tree roots. Then, slowly, she pulled and dragged herself, using the last vestiges of her energy to get her body out of the water. Once her feet were clear of the river, Delta collapsed face first into the mud. She had gambled it all and had won. Exhausted, she lay her head on the riverbank and rested.

# 19 ——

"There it is again," Sal said, as the gunfire in the distance echoed through the jungle.

"Then we're right on track," Connie said, picking up the pace. "Where there's trouble, we'll find Delta." More shots rang out as they swiftly moved through the lush undergrowth.

"Wait." Josh reached out and grabbed Connie's shoulder. "That's the same weapon I heard yesterday."

Connie stopped and listened. "You sure?"

"Three years in 'Nam, Connie," Sal answered. "The man knows his stuff."

"But what does it mean?" Connie wiped the sweat from her forehead with the bandanna she wore around her neck.

"That our Colombian boys are either target practicing or they have enemies here in the jungle. Come on." Josh started for the river bank. "In 'Nam, lots of the camps were near a water source. Even in a rain forest, guys gotta drink water. By the sounds of those shots, if we continue following the river like we have been, we have a good chance of running smack dab into whoever's shooting that weapon."

Connie looked at the river contemplatively. "I think it's the best shot we have. You have to have a water supply."

Josh turned to Sal. "Salamander? Got an opinion?"

Sal cocked her head for a moment. "How far away are they?"

Josh closed his eyes and listened. "Could be half a mile, maybe more. Hard to tell, but in this thicket they're not close enough to do us any harm. Bullets don't go very far in a jungle as dense as this one."

Sal took her hat off and shook her head. Drops of sweat flew in every direction. "Umm...I think Connie's right. We go where the trouble is and we'll find Delta."

"Then up the river it is." Picking up his gear, Josh started cautiously around the river's bend.

Connie and Sal followed him. No one said a word.

Suddenly, the shooting stopped.

"Someone must have won," Sal offered.

Connie shuddered. "God, I hope Delta didn't have anything to do with that."

Josh shook his head. "Not unless she was able to get her hands on that Sten. How likely is that?"

Connie narrowed her eyes at him. "You know Delta. What are the odds she was involved in that?"

Josh grinned. "Pretty high."

"Exactly."

ജ ജ ജ

Delta had no idea how long she lay there, but when she came to, the sun had shifted and no longer cast its bright rays on her. Slowly opening her eyes, she expected to see nothing but flora and fauna. Instead, she found herself staring at a very large pair of black combat boots. *Great! I escaped drowning only to be shot,* she thought. Not having the strength to get up, let alone fight, Delta dropped her head back to the ground.

"What have we here?" came a deep male voice in English. "Looks like something my cat spit up."

Delta cracked open one eye. That voice was distinctively American, and there was something oddly familiar about it.

With her cheek still on the ground, Delta peeked out of the one eye as a second pair of combat boots joined the first. *Great!* Delta thought. Closing her eye, she sighed. When she opened it again, a third pair of boots had joined the combat boots, but these were hiking boots—boots she had definitely seen before.

"Tanning, Storm?"

A grin spread across Delta's face. Suddenly she felt two hands grab her waist and haul her to her feet. Finally vertical and on solid ground, Delta smiled at Josh before throwing her arms around Connie's neck and hugging her tightly. She had never been so happy to see Connie in all the years they'd known each other.

"I don't think I've ever been this happy to see your face," Delta said, pulling away so she could put her hands on Connie's face. Connie's eyes were filled with warmth and love.

"I knew you'd be somewhere in the middle of the fracas." Reaching her arms out, Connie pulled Delta to her and hugged her tightly.

"I found her," Delta whispered as she hugged Connie back.

Connie pulled herself from the hug. "What?"

Delta nodded. "I found her."

Connie looked around. "Where?"

Delta explained what had happened prior to her falling in the river. When she finished, she looked over at Josh and Sal. "Thanks for coming, guys."

Sal grinned and her freckles moved. "Umm...*no problemo.* That's *Español* for no problem."

Delta smiled as she turned and hugged the diminutive woman. "You're the best."

"Actually," Sal said, straightening her cap, "Josh is the best. He really moved us through the jungle. We caught up to you sooner than I thought."

"Where's Manny?" Josh asked, his head swiveling from side to side as he surveyed the area.

*Manny.*

Delta suddenly remembered. "Manny—Omigod—he was shot. We have to find him."

Josh reached out and grabbed Delta's shoulder before she could take another step. "Whoa. Don't you think you've had enough for one morning?"

Delta started to respond, but Connie cut her off.

"Besides, you took a beating in that water. You need time to rest."

Sal nodded. "They're right, Del. No use in bringing more gunfire our way."

"But Manny..."

"Point me in the general direction, Del, and I'll see what I can do about finding him," Josh said. Taking Delta by the elbow, Josh helped her to a seat on a log. "By the sounds of it, those yahoos are pretty well armed. We can't just barge in there and demand Megan back, and it sure as hell isn't safe to be traveling during daylight."

Connie sat next to Delta and brushed her dark wet hair from her face. "Let Josh see if he can find Manny. In the meantime, you can rest and we can devise a plan that's going to get Megan out of here alive."

Delta looked into Connie's eyes and nodded. Suddenly, the fatigue from her night under the palm fronds and her "swim" in the river blindsided her. "Okay. But we head to their camp tonight."

Josh knelt in front of Delta and took one of her hands. "You trust me, don't you, Del?"

Delta nodded. Besides Tony, her direction-challenged partner, Josh was the only other man she really trusted.

"Then trust that I'll find your friend and scout out the situation. But you have to promise me one thing."

Delta nodded.

"That you play this jungle operation by my rules. I've done this before, honey, and without a really good plan, it's all over for every one of us. You hear what I'm saying?" Josh looked sternly at Delta.

Delta nodded again.

"Good. Now, whereabouts would you say you fell into the river?"

Once Josh had as much information as he could get from Delta, he started on his way, leaving the three women to set up a makeshift camp.

"Hungry?" Sal asked, offering Delta some beef jerky.

Delta shook her head. "I'm too tired to chew."

Delta looked at the two worried faces staring at her. If they were reflecting the shape she was in, she must really be in trouble. Glancing at her hands and her clothes, Delta sighed. Her black cotton shirt hung in torn strips, as if someone had tried to cut it with dull scissors. Her arms looked like someone had rubbed a cheese grater over them. Her bloody left eyebrow throbbed, and she wasn't sure she could take another step on her wobbly legs.

Connie continued stroking Delta's head. "You sure know how to scare the shit out of me."

Delta barely nodded. "Sorry, Chief."

"Where have I heard that before? And how many more gray hairs are you going to give me?" Connie moved to Delta's feet, pulled her boot off and poured water from it. "You sure you're okay?"

Delta nodded and grinned. "I saw her. Megan is alive."

"Of course she is. Megan is a survivor, Del, and she'll do whatever she needs to do to come home. You have to believe that."

*Whatever she needs to do...Is that what Megan was doing on the rock?*

"Doesn't make it any easier." Delta put her head between her knees and started to cry. Finally, she was safe enough to release the pent-up anger and sadness she'd been feeling ever since she'd seen Megan blowing that guy on the rock.

Connie put her arms around Delta and held her tightly. "Come on. Let's get you out of these clothes so you can rest easier."

"But—"

"But nothing. When Josh gets back, we'll figure out what we need to do to get Megan back, but for the time being, rest."

Dropping her jeans, so she was only in her bra and panties, Delta lay on the soft carpet of leaves covering the ground. Behind closed eyes Delta saw Megan's face float in and out of her mind's eye.

Megan was alive.

And soon, Delta was going after her.

When Delta woke up, Connie was sitting nearby, just staring at her. Josh and Sal were nowhere in sight, and by the looks of the sun, Delta had been asleep for some time.

"How long have I—"

"Three hours. How are you feeling?"

Delta stretched and her muscles and joints screamed at her. "I ache all over."

"I bet. Up to eating?" Connie opened a bag of trail mix and handed it to Delta.

"Thanks. Did Josh find Manny?"

Connie shook her head. "Josh's come and gone a couple of times, but so far no luck."

"Then maybe I should go."

Connie stopped Delta as she tried to stand. "Josh is nervous that those guys might still be looking for you."

Delta sighed. "More than likely. So?"

"So, we're not going anywhere until nightfall, so you might as well relax."

Delta reached into the trail mix and pulled a handful from the bag. "Relax. Yeah, right."

Connie studied Delta for a moment before reaching over and taking her free hand. "I've seen that look in your eyes before, Storm. Something's up. What is it?"

Delta sighed again. Connie was her perpetual mirror, always reflecting the truth about how she truly felt. There had never been a time when she could hide her feelings, fears or frustrations from Connie. "You were right. I'm so far out of my element, I might as well be on Mars."

Connie brushed a hair away from Delta's eyes. "Being out of your element has never stopped you before."

"Yeah, but it feels like I'm playing a game where everyone knows the rules except me."

Connie picked the peanuts out of Delta's palmful of mix. "That's an unfamiliar feeling for you, isn't it?"

Delta grinned. "This place has an eerie effect on me. I don't know what it is, but something in me is changing, something I can't even put a finger on."

"Nature is definitely mysterious."

"Is that it? Is being this close to the heart of life what's making me have all these strange thoughts and feelings?"

"Strange? How so?" Connie asked.

Delta thought about this for a minute before answering. "Even though we're in foreign, if not hostile, territory, there's something oddly peaceful about this place. I can't really describe it, but I feel...connected, I guess. Maybe that's it. Although I've been out here by myself, I never really felt alone. Does that make any sense?"

Connie nodded. "I suppose that's why tribal people deal with nature so much differently than we do."

"What do you mean?"

"Look around you, Del. This is the most alive place on the earth. Life happens here, and we're part of it. We may not belong here, but nature embraces us nonetheless."

Delta reached over and held Connie's hand. "Well, I'm glad we're embracing it together."

Connie grinned warmly at Delta. "Thank God for that."

Delta finished her trail mix and looked into Connie's face. "What do you really think the chances are of getting all of us out of here alive?"

Connie glanced over at the rushing river before answering. "Honestly?"

"Honestly."

"Sixty-forty."

Delta nodded. "Well, that's better than fifty-fifty." Looking around, Delta's raised her left eyebrow in a question. "Where's Sal?"

Connie jerked her head to the left. "On guard duty." Rising, Connie reached out and helped Delta to her feet. "Feel like a little walk?"

"You're kidding, right?"

"There's a family of white-faced monkeys about a few hundred yards from here. I'd like a closer look."

"A little obsessed with learning, aren't we? Don't you ever feel like your brain is full?"

This made Connie laugh. "Never. Come on. We have nothing else to do until nightfall, and we've been hustling through this damn forest so fast, I haven't really been able to get a good look at it. Besides, it'll do your joints good."

Following Connie into the rain forest, Delta suddenly felt her old fighting spirit again. "There's just one more thing."

Connie waited. "Yes?"

"Change those odds to seventy-thirty."

## 20 ——

**When** Megan finally rejoined the others in the cavern three hours later, she noticed how diligently the captives were working. At first, she thought it was because of her, but Siobhan assured her this was not the case.

"What's going on then?" Megan asked, as she stepped into the knee-deep water.

"Two people tried to escape into the forest and were killed." Siobhan did not look up from the screen she was using to sift through the silt. "Didn't you hear the guns?"

Megan nodded slowly. *So, that was what the gunfire was all about.* She'd thought they were target-practicing or shooting monkeys. "Who were they?"

Siobhan shrugged. "It was a man and a woman, but that's all we could find out. The soldiers shot them and left them both to die and be eaten by the animals. Can you believe it?"

Megan inhaled deeply the musky, damp air. The underground stream flowing through the cavern brought a different kind of air to breathe. It tasted old and stale. "Were they from the other cavern?"

Siobhan shrugged. "Must be, because we are all accounted for. I thought at first..."

"That it was me?" Megan lowered her voice as she reached her small trowel to scoop silt up from the bottom of the stream.

"Yes."

"Maybe they were newly captured and escaped," Megan offered.

"Perhaps. How was your...morning?"

A hot blush rose to Megan's cheeks. "Could have been worse, I suppose."

"The guards say he likes you. A lot."

"I guess. I'd rather not discuss it. It's bad enough I have to do it, talking about it only makes it worse." Running her hand through the silt, Megan plucked out a small gold nugget the size of a pea.

"You're going to live through this, aren't you?" Siobhan asked quietly.

Megan nodded. "I sold my body to survive when I was younger. It's taken me three years to find my soul, and I don't intend to live without it again."

"Even if it guarantees your survival?" Siobhan lowered her voice when the guard at the entrance shifted his feet.

Megan brought up the small trowel. "Surviving and living aren't the same thing. I've done both, and if I can't continue living, I'd rather not survive."

Siobhan bowed her head. "Then I suppose that means you will continue with your plan?"

"Especially now. They'll never expect someone to run after the shootings today. It's perfect."

Siobhan's eyes filled with tears. "I'll be scared without you."

Megan touched Siobhan's face with the back of her hand. "Don't be. Know that I'll come back with help. Keep believing, keep hoping, and keep yourself alive."

Nodding, Siobhan started to cry.

"Don't cry, Siobhan. I believe in those two women I told you about. They won't let me down."

# 21——

The morning came with its usual burst of sunlight streaming through the canopy. And with it, the birds and innumerable animals woke to begin another lazy day. Delta checked her watch: almost 6 a.m. She rubbed her eyes before rolling over and saw Sal squatting on her haunches, packing her blanket and sheathing her huge hunting knife.

"Morning, Glory," Sal said, grinning.

Suddenly, Connie appeared out of nowhere, catching Delta off-guard. "How in the hell do you do that?" Delta asked.

"Do what?"

"Creep up on us?"

Smiling widely, Connie joined them at the river bank. "My Native American ancestry. You white folks might say that moving quietly is in our genes."

"Along with bullshitting and telling tall tales. You know, when your daughter is born, you're going to have to stop with all this hoo-ha or you'll confuse her."

Sal and Connie both cocked their heads questioningly. "Hoo-ha?"

Bowing her head to hide her grin, Delta barely managed a nod. "Gina asked me to start watching my language so when the baby comes, we're not talking like truck drivers."

Connie straightened up. "She said the same thing to me, goddamnit!"

The three women laughed as they checked their gear and refilled their canteens.

"You know, you two were crazy to come down here without me and the big guy."

Delta looked around and realized Josh was not around. "Speaking of which, where is Josh?"

"He wanted to make sure the morning bathing between Megan and that guy isn't a daily occurrence." Sal thrust her arms into the straps of her backpack, then cinched it around her waist.

"And if it is?"

"We'll fall back and wait for Josh to follow them to camp," Connie responded.

"You know I have to go with him." Delta ran both hands through her hair.

"That would be stupid, Del." Sal's voice was matter-of-fact as she stared up at Delta. "Josh can get there and back without being detected. As good as you may be, you're...umm... not good enough to accompany him. You'll only put us all at risk."

"Sal's right. Let Josh find it first before we go in there with guns blazing. We still don't know exactly what we're up against."

Delta hated to admit it, but they were right. They needed a good plan—needed to know what the numbers were, what weapons they had, and how many others, beside Megan, there were. There was still a great deal of information they needed, and getting caught wouldn't get any of it.

"Josh is used to being outnumbered, Del. He and his four buddies snuck into a village where the Cong had set up base. In less than three hours, Josh's men had killed over fifty soldiers. Trust me. He's very good at this."

Looking down into Sal's eyes, Delta recognized the admiration and devotion Sal held for the man who must have truly loved her father.

"Sal, is there more to your relationship with Josh than what you let on?" Connie asked.

Grinning at Connie, Sal answered, "He's my family. We're tight. I guess you could say we're like you and Delta."

Delta shook her head. "What Connie is delicately trying to say is, are you two doing each other?"

"Hell no! I love him and all, but there's no sexual chemistry, if you know what I mean. Besides, Josh likes...fru-fru women."

Connie and Delta laughed. "Not 'fru-fru' women!"

"Josh and I are friends, you guys, come off it!"

Connie put her arms around Sal and hugged her. "You are too cute for words."

"Could you gals keep your voices down?" came Josh's voice from behind the foliage. "I think even the Panamanians probably heard you. Jesus! Trying to get us all killed?"

"Damn it!" Delta said, whirling around at the sound of his voice. "How do you two do that?"

Josh grinned, displaying white teeth against his black beard. "Connie was born with it. Me, I practiced." Josh checked Sal and Connie's backpacks before continuing, "Sal's old man was like a wild creature, just like Connie and me. I watched that man wade through quicksand like it was water. I followed his lead as he moved through the jungle as silently as a shark cuts its way through the ocean. He could go where others couldn't because he became part of the earth."

"Wade through quicksand? How does someone do that?" Delta asked.

"People who are not of the earth will try to fight it, and that is what drags them down. If you are part of the earth, you know how to be so that it actually buoys you up."

Delta looked over at Connie, who smiled, but said nothing.

"Umm...*anyway*, did you find the waterfall?" Sal interrupted.

Josh leveled his gaze at Sal before looking at Delta. "You fell in much farther upriver than you thought. I found the waterfall, but I'm afraid Manny is dead, hiding or captured."

"And the Colombians?" Connie asked.

Josh shook his head. "Nothing. We'll just have to travel up the riverbank until we reach the point where you fell in."

"Anything else we need?" Connie asked.

"Just luck. And lots of it."

# 22——

Delta hadn't realized how far the river had taken her. It was after nine and they still hadn't reached the area where she'd fallen in. Of course, hurtling downstream like a human torpedo was much speedier than hacking their way through dense foliage. Even with the four of them taking turns, it was slow going. By ten, they were exhausted, but finally managed to make it to the waterfall where Delta had found Megan.

Collapsing on the cliff rocks where Manny had found Delta, the three women sat quietly while Josh disappeared on another reconnaissance of the area. Sitting with their backs to each other, they were able to scope out three hundred and sixty degrees.

"I can't believe you made it past some of those huge rocks, Del," Sal whispered, wiping the sweat off her forehead with a bandanna.

Suddenly, Josh reappeared. "No one down there still."

"Is that good or bad?"

"Good. Do you remember which way they escorted you out?"

Delta pointed in the direction the guards had taken her and Manny. "That way. They took us that way."

"Let's go." Josh led the way, using his powerful arms to swing the machete. After a while, the trail became passable, as they made their way over paths already cut by the soldiers. About three hundred yards in, he held up his hand, signaling everyone to stop.

"What is it?" Sal whimpered.

Squatting down, Josh examined some leaves. "Blood. You're sure they hit Manny yesterday?"

Delta nodded.

"I think he may still be alive. Well, he or someone else. This blood is fairly fresh. Someone out here is bleeding."

For a moment, no one said a word. When Delta looked at the blood, she glanced up at Connie and motioned for her to take a look as well. "Remember that blood-splatter class we took?"

Connie knelt next to Delta and studied the patch of blood. "You mean the class I took while you doodled and flirted with Jill Hodges?"

"Can you tell which direction the bleeder is moving?"

Connie took a side view of the blood before looking around. "He's moving in that direction," she said, pointing south.

"Then it isn't one of the soldiers," Josh said. "They'd have headed back to camp."

"Manny," Delta said to no one in particular.

"I'd be very surprised if he escaped the soldiers for this long, but it's sure worth a look. Stay here." Before anyone could reply, Josh silently vanished.

"How in the hell did he even see that blood?"

"I told you," Sal replied, "he's very good."

Five minutes later, Josh returned, carrying Manny in his arms. Manny's head bobbed against Josh's meaty shoulder; his face was sweaty and pale. There was a tourniquet tied around his right thigh.

"Manny!" Delta cried, running over to them.

"I take it this is the right guy?" Josh carefully set Manny on the forest floor.

"Is he still alive?" Sal asked, watching their backside.

"Yeah. He has some kind of herbal wrap on the wound, so I can't tell how bad it is; but it looks like he's lost a lot of blood."

Delta knelt next to Manny and held his hand. If it was possible, he looked younger than ever, and it broke Delta's heart to see him so lifeless.

"Manny? It's me, Delta. Can you hear me?"

Manny's eyelids fluttered a moment before slowly opening. "Del-ta?"

"It's okay, Manny. Don't talk. You're...safe now. My friends are here to help us."

Manny rolled his eyes over to Connie, Sal and Josh, and nodded his understanding. "Lost a lot...of blood. Leave me."

Delta reached over and brushed his wet hair off his forehead. "Sorry, no can do. You saved my life. I owe you one, and Delta Stevens always pays up."

"You won't get out carrying me."

Delta looked up at Josh, who nodded. "Still underestimating women, eh, Manny?" Smiling warmly, Delta rose and joined Connie and Josh. "We can't just leave him here."

"He'll slow us down, Del," Josh said. "This guy needs a doctor."

Delta looked at Manny, who lay with his eyes closed. He already looked dead, but that didn't mean she was going to treat him like a corpse. "Then he goes back."

"What?"

"He saved my life, Con. I'm going to return the favor. One way or the other, we have to get him some help."

"It would take us too long to get him out," Sal replied from her position.

"Too long for the three of us, but not for Josh." Delta tipped her head in Josh's direction. "Josh can carry him out of here in no time."

"No way," Josh said, shaking his head. "You're not facing those bastards alone. Uh-uh. No way."

Delta shot a look over to Sal, who caught the pass. "Delta's right, big guy. He'll die if we don't get him help, and you're the only one who can do it. We've come too far to turn back, but you can go. You had to split up in 'Nam, didn't you?"

"Yeah, but—"

"But nothing," Sal said. "We have to go with the flow here, and this man needs help. If he were in another platoon other than yours, what would you have done?"

Josh thought about it for a minute before nodding slowly. "I'd save him."

Delta threw her arms around Josh's neck and hugged him. "Thank you."

"Thank me over a brew in San Jose, Delta. Make that a dozen brews."

Josh looked at Manny, at Delta, and, finally, at Sal. His facial features softened when his eyes landed on her. "This is against my better judgment, Squirt."

Sal stood on tiptoe and hugged him tightly. "I know. But we came to help."

Josh released himself from Sal's grasp and bent down to take a closer look at the dressing on the wound. After examining it for several seconds, he glanced over his shoulder at Delta. "How much do you know about this guy?"

Delta frowned and shrugged. "Not much. I met his little sister in town first. He's a tour guide in the rain forest for a local tour company. Why?"

Josh merely shook his head and returned his attention to Manny. "Carrying him will take too much out of me. I'll make a sling to go over his shoulders so I can drag him behind. I'll go back the way we came so I shouldn't have to do so much hacking." Rising, Josh stood over Sal. "Don't do anything I wouldn't do, Salamander. You got that?"

Sal grinned and saluted. "Got it."

Josh then turned to Delta. "Here's what you do. Get as close to the camp as you can tonight. No matter how much you want to go now, wait until nightfall. It will be easier to see how large the camp is and how many men they've got. Spend a few hours counting and recounting. Check their routine, see where they come and go. Find out where they're keeping Megan, but don't do anything. Wait until tomorrow night to make your move.

Patience is the key to every successful attack. As much as it pains you, Delta, hold off. Don't do what you've always done. Take it from an experienced soldier; if you go barging in there, you'll get everyone killed. You understand me?" His face was stern.

Delta nodded. "Yes."

"And remember, there will be guards all around the camp, so don't get too close. Just remember the standard perimeter back home and apply it here."

"Okay," Delta said, nodding.

"One more thing," Josh added.

"Yeah?"

"Don't let anything happen to Sal."

"Gotcha," Connie and Delta said in unison.

Connie touched Josh's shoulder. "We'd rather eat glass than make you mad."

This brought a grin to Josh's face. "Just take good care of her, Connie."

Sal hugged Josh one last time. "You will come back, right?"

"Hell, yes! The second I get this guy to a doctor, I'll be high-tailing it right back here. You can count on that."

"What if you can't find us? What if we...umm...get separated or something?" Sal asked.

"Then we'll meet up in Panama City. No matter what happens in here, you guys have to get to Panama. The border is closer than San Jose and you should be able to get some help there. Check with the American Embassy in Panama in case I don't get back to you. That's where I'll be if anything gets hinkey."

Delta hugged Josh before walking over and kneeling next to Manny. His breathing was shallow, and she was beginning to wonder if he would survive. "Manny?"

Manny cracked open one eye. "*Sí.*"

"Thank you for coming back for me. You saved my life. Now I need you to do me one more favor."

"I'll...try."

Leaning over, Delta whispered. "I need you to stay alive. There's a little girl back home who wouldn't know what to do without her big brother, okay?"

Nodding, Manny reached out and took Delta's hand. "You don't understand what you're...up against, Delta. In the jungle, nothing...is as it...seems."

"Shhh. Save your strength, and remember what I said."

"But—"

Delta placed a finger over his lips. "Later. Right now, conserve your energy."

After everyone said their good-byes, Sal, Delta and Connie trekked back down the path already established by Delta's desperate flight to the river. They were finally getting closer to saving Megan.

# 23——

"**What** are you waiting for?" Siobhan asked, as Megan counted quietly to herself.

"The last two nights, I've counted how many minutes pass before the guards come back in this direction. So far, the quickest is seven minutes."

"So?"

"That gives me seven minutes to cut open this tent and get into the rain forest before they have a chance to notice I'm gone. With any luck, they won't know I'm gone until morning."

"Gone where?"

Megan tied her long blonde hair in a knot behind her head. "Panama. It's the safest route I can think of."

"Do you even know which way Panama is?"

Megan nodded. "Before these bastards shot Augustine, he told me to get to Panama if I could and that it's southwest, over there." Megan pointed to her right. "If I go in a straight line from here and connect with the Rio Chirripo and follow it south, I'll be in Panama in no time."

"And then you'll send help?"

Megan nodded. "Of course."

"Promise?"

Megan nodded, reaching for the knife under her blanket. "I promise."

"What about me? When they see the hole, they'll know I knew and they'll kill me, too."

Megan smiled softly at her. "Already thought of that. If they discover I'm gone during the night, claim you slept through it. If they don't catch on at night, when you wake up, start calling for the guards and tell them I escaped."

Siobhan nodded. "Good thinking."

"I know. Delta's a good teacher."

"You speak of her with such adoration."

"You would, too, if you met her. Delta Stevens is one of a kind."

"Will it be tonight then?"

Megan shrugged. "I don't know yet. We'll just have to wait and see."

# 24——

**When** the sun had completely set and darkness reigned, Delta raised her head from their hiding place on the cliff's edge and was astounded by the number of torches lighting the campground. This was a much larger operation than she had initially suspected. Green pup tents were strategically placed, and torches burned every twenty feet or so. Perched atop a small knoll was also something that looked like a mobile home.

"What's your count, Chief?" Delta asked Connie, after the first hour of silence.

"Somewhere between twenty-five and thirty-five." Connie did not take the binoculars from her eyes. "Hard to say. There's a lot of commotion. Like they're partying or something."

"Jesus," Sal hissed, shaking her head. "What's really going on here?"

Connie stopped her counting and turned to Delta, who was lying on her stomach peering through a second set of infrared binoculars. "This isn't just some drug-smuggling operation, Del. Smugglers are much more mobile than this. Something else is going on here."

Delta observed the movement in camp. "Maybe that's what Manny was trying to tell me. What could be bigger than drugs?"

Connie and Sal looked to each other for an answer neither of them had.

"Then that's the first thing we need to find out. What are these guys up to?" Connie peered through her binoculars and followed the booted steps of a guard who paced across the compound.

"Any suggestions?" Sal asked, lowering herself back to the ground cover. Drunken laughter from the men pierced the otherwise melodic sounds of the night insects.

"I say we grab ourselves a man or two, get their weapons and some information before we introduce ourselves."

Delta nodded. "Agreed."

Delta and Connie both crawled behind some large ferns, joining Sal. "If we take a guard, we'll have to move more swiftly because by morning, they'll know their boy is missing." Delta looked across at Sal; she hadn't realized how dark it had become. Sal's features were barely discernible.

"Del's right," Connie said. "If we take one of them, we're committed. We'll have to get Megan tonight."

"Then let's wait until they're good and drunk."

Delta thought about this a second before shaking her head. "We don't have time."

Sal looked at both of them before shaking her head. "What do you suggest?"

Connie sighed loudly as she retied her ponytail. "Before we do anything, we need more information and a few of their automatics. One of us will have to get as close to the camp as possible and find out how many men there are, what kind of weapons they have, and how many other captives besides Megan there are."

Sal nodded. "That means you."

Connie nodded. "Right. You two couldn't sneak up on a corpse. Besides, I speak Spanish."

Delta pinched the bridge of her nose. She felt so isolated and trapped here in the jungle that issues like language differences seemed to escape her. Fatigue and exhaustion must be setting in, or she would be able to think more clearly. Suddenly, she was feeling very, very unsure of herself.

Connie studied the layout of the camp from their cliff position. The tents were set up in a rectangle, with the trailer at one end. A torch flickered, occasionally revealing a man and a woman embraced in a bizarre little dance. On the other side of the ring, men were drinking and laughing in a circle. Connie lowered her binoculars. "There are two tent sizes."

Delta peered through her binoculars in time to see a man pull a woman out of one of the smaller tents and press his body up to hers. Dropping the binoculars so they fell hard against her chest, Delta rubbed her temples. "Megan's not alone down there. There are other women. The small tents are probably for them."

Connie raised the binoculars to her face and caught a glimpse of what Delta had just seen. Lowering the binoculars once more, Connie reached out and touched Delta's arm. "We'll wait a little longer before I go down there. Don't worry, Storm, we're going to get her out of there."

Delta continued rubbing her temples, trying to press the image of Megan on the rock out of her memory bank. "And we have to do it tonight."

Delta moved next to Connie and gazed down at the torches below. Megan was down there, a prisoner of someone she'd never met, forced to do things they both thought she had left behind a lifetime ago. "Con?"

"Yeah?"

"What then? I mean, realistically, what do we do once we find her?"

"We haul ass outta here," came Sal's answer for Connie, as she joined the two women at the rock. "We run like the wind until we get to Panama."

Connie looked over at Sal. "What about the others?"

Sal looked at Connie hard and shrugged. "Casualties of war, then. We didn't come here to save them. Hell, it's going to be hard enough to get Megan out."

Connie stepped next to Delta and laced her fingers inside Delta's large hand. "Well?"

Reflecting back on all the times she'd left Megan stranded, the times she chose to save people she never knew, Delta was determined that this time, she would not make that same mistake. "Sal's right. Casualties of war. We came to get Megan and only Megan."

"Del—"

"I'm sorry, Chief," Delta interrupted, shaking her head. "For once, I am putting my love for Megan before any other real or imagined obligation. This time, I won't let her down."


An hour later, Connie crept past a sleeping guard, passed out against a tree. She had gleaned bits and pieces of information as she moved stealthily around the perimeter of the camp, listening to the men's conversations. So far, she'd discovered that the tents to her left were filled with "workers" and the tents to her right with "soldiers." The smaller tents' flaps were completely zipped up and secured with padlocks. The larger tents, where she supposed the soldiers slept, were unzipped and wide open. Light from the campfire allowed her to see inside some of the tents, and what she saw turned her stomach. In one tent, there were two women and one soldier engaged in sex acts she'd only seen in porno flicks. In another, one naked soldier was riding the back of a whimpering woman on her hands and knees. Gazing up at the sky, Connie noticed the crescent moon peeking out from behind a group of trees, and didn't know whether to be thankful or not for the extra light.

Sneaking behind the left row of a dozen or so tents, Connie listened to two women speaking German, one of five languages she herself was fluent in.

"I cannot do this any longer. My fingers ache, my wrists hurt, and I cannot bend down into the cold water one more day," came the tiny voice of the first woman.

"You will. They will kill you if you don't. Just one more day."

"They will kill us even if we do. You think they'll let any of us live? Hardly."

The first woman started crying, so Connie moved to the next couple of tents. She was somewhat puzzled by the woman's reference to standing in water. What did this mean? Squatting behind another tent, Connie listened to a French conversation, and though her French was somewhat rusty, she could make out most of what they said.

"Our side of the cavern mine is nearly finished. We have two, maybe three days of work left."

"How much is enough for those bastards? Our section came up with almost three kilos today."

"I've heard there may be another cavern to the south. I'll bet they take us there."

"Aren't you scared?"

"Of course, but I am happy those warthogs leave me alone. I've heard stories about what they do to the other women."

Other women.

Megan was probably one of them. But what were these women doing when not satisfying the male flesh? What "job" were they talking about? There were too many questions and not enough answers, so Connie moved on. How would she find out where Megan was without hearing Megan's voice? Her pulse banging loudly in her head, Connie pressed on, hoping and praying Megan was not in one of the larger tents.

Stopping in a low crouch, Connie made her way back to the two French women. "Psst," Connie hissed, tossing a rock against the back of the tent. Both women became silent. "Don't be scared. I'm from the other side of the camp, and I'm looking for my sister, Megan. She's a very pretty blonde. Tall. Would you know which tent she is in?"

Neither women responded.

"Please. I need to see her," Connie pleaded. "I don't know if I can hold on much longer if I don't see her."

Connie could hear them whispering now, but could not make out what they were saying. Their suspiciousness was a good sign. If they were suspicious, maybe they wouldn't tell anyone anything and she could get out of there undetected.

"She's two tents over to the left, one of them whispered, but she's not there now. She's...with the general."

"Thank you so much. I appreciate it."

Creeping back into the bushes, Connie's heart raced. Suddenly, the picture took on a whole new meaning. There were other women who needed their help. How could they possibly just take Megan and leave the rest in the hands of these animals? Didn't that go against everything she and Delta stood for? And what would Megan want them to do? Connie heaved a sigh, then started back up to the cliff. Somehow, some way, they had to figure a way to get everyone out of the grasp of these bastards.

Quietly maneuvering around the still-passed-out guard, Connie stopped in front of him and contemplated taking his weapon. When he snored and twitched, she thought better of it and hurried quickly back up to the cliff.

❧ ❧ ❧

"Gold?" Delta asked when Connie relayed her story.

"Unless my French has taken a serious nosedive, I'm almost sure the women were talking about gold. Five pounds of gold."

"Do you know how much pure cold, hard cash that is?" Sal asked, adjusting her cap.

Connie nodded. "Enough to bankroll quite a few drug operations. Whoever these guys are, they're definitely not penny-ante drug dealers."

"Then who are they?" Delta asked, crossing her arms, her patience wearing thin.

"I don't know," Connie said, uncapping the canteen and taking a sip. "But at least we now know why all the guard posts and secrecy. Somehow, these yahoos found caverns filled with gold, and I think they've kidnapped their work force."

"You're sure these women worked in the caverns?" Sal asked.

Connie nodded. "I heard them."

"Then why—" Delta could not finish the sentence. She didn't want to know why Megan had done what Delta saw her doing. "Did they tell you Megan had a tent?"

Connie nodded. "Two tents down from them. You can't see it from here because of that boulder."

Delta put the binoculars to her eyes and looked down at the camp. "I don't understand."

Connie glanced over at Delta, who lowered the binoculars and returned her gaze. Even in the crescent moonlight, a flash of understanding flew between them.

"No way, Consuela. I know what you're thinking, and I'm not going to do it."

Connie stepped closer to Delta. "We can't just pull Megan out of there, Del. There are—"

Delta waved Connie's words away with her hand. "No way."

"But Del—"

"But nothing!" Delta growled. "I've spent my entire career putting it all on the line at the cost of my own life. Not this time. We came for Megan and that's it. I'm not going to put our lives in jeopardy for people we don't know." Crossing her arms over the dangling binoculars, Delta continued shaking her head.

"We've never turned our backs on anyone, Storm," Connie said quietly.

"There's a first for everything," Delta spat.

"You don't mean that."

Delta pulled her hand away. "The hell I don't. I will not put Megan's life in danger out of some skewed sense of saving the universe. I don't care how many people need saving, they can count on someone else. Damn it, Con, haven't I given enough? Don't ask me to risk Megan's life. I won't do it."

"Risk is risk."

Delta shook her head. "What do you want from me? I'm nobody's heroine, I just want my lover back. I just want the chance to make things right with her, with my life, with my job." Delta bowed her head and squeezed her eyes shut. "I just want to be back home with Megan."

"We're going to get her back," Connie said quietly. "You believe that, don't you?"

Delta slowly looked up and nodded. "And the others? Do you agree to leave them?"

Connie sighed and brushed a stray hair from Delta's face. "We'll think of something."

Two hours later, Connie led the way to Megan's tent, with Sal and Delta close behind. The guard had shifted positions, but it was clear by the booze smell coming from his open mouth that he wouldn't be waking up anytime soon.

Connie motioned to Sal to stay with the guard, so Sal tucked herself away behind a large palm frond and nodded for Connie and Delta to continue.

As they moved around the rear of the tents, being careful to stay in the shadows, Connie and Delta maneuvered over to the tent Megan was supposed to be in. To their surprise, they found the back of the tent cut open. The gaping hole revealed a frightened woman, who scurried to the opposite side of the small tent when she saw them.

"Where's Megan?" Delta whispered, struggling to keep her voice down.

Stammering, Siobhan shrugged. "I...I don't know. I was sleeping and—"

Delta reached in, grabbed her arm, and slapped her hand over Siobhan's mouth. "Listen to me. Don't be afraid. We came here to help. Do you understand?"

Nodding slowly, Siobhan's eyes grew wide as Delta pulled her hand away. "You! Megan said you two would come for her."

"Where did she go?"

"She...escaped...," Siobhan stammered, tears coming to her eyes.

"Escaped? What do you mean, escaped? She cut this hole in the tent wall and took off?"

Siobhan nodded. "To Panama."

"How long ago?"

"Two, maybe three hours ago. I...I couldn't really say." Delta's heart sank.

"She stole a carving knife and was determined to cut her way out. She's in the rain forest trying to get help."

Delta released Siobhan's arm and stared helplessly at Connie, who motioned for her to hurry up.

"Did she say anything else?" Connie asked, glancing out to the camp. Time was running out.

"She said you would come, and that you would bring help."

"How many of you are there?"

"About twenty or so. Are you going to help us?"

Delta opened her mouth to answer, but Connie spoke first. "Yes. But we have more to do before we can help. Do not mention our visit to anyone, or you could get us all killed." Connie checked her watch. Fifteen more seconds and the guard would be rounding the corner.

Siobhan nodded. "You must hurry, though. Once they find out Megan is missing, they could take their anger out on the rest of us."

"We'll do whatever we can." Connie pulled away from the tent and grabbed Delta with her. "Remember, tell no one," she said over her shoulder.

Siobhan nodded.

"Go!" Connie whispered, pushing Delta to the rear of the tent. In a matter of minutes they made their way back up to the cliff, where Sal waited anxiously.

"Where is she?" Sal murmured when she stepped out from her guard post amidst the palm fronds.

"Escaped."

Sal's eyes bugged. "Into the jungle? Megan is wandering out here in the dark all by herself?"

Delta and Connie could only nod.

"How could we have missed her?"

"The back of the tent faces away from us. She cut herself out of there about three hours ago."

Sal shook her head. "And then did what?"

Connie looked out into the darkness of the jungle. "My guess is she took off from the back of the tent."

"Umm...so, now what?" Sal asked, jamming her hands on her hips.

Unsheathing her machete, Delta leapt into the darkness. "We go after her."

# 25 ——

**Her** heart pounded, her legs ached, and her clothes were shredded, but Megan was determined to put as much distance between herself and the camp as she could. It was important for her to maintain a straight line, otherwise she could end up back where she started. She did this by following the crescent moon hanging overhead. Her survival now depended on her ability to keep a clear head, keep moving and keep believing in herself.

Megan made her way through the rain forest with more speed than she thought possible. As long as she moved forward, as long as she was free, nothing else mattered except the distance she could put between herself and the general. Thank God Professor Juan Carlos had made her study the geography of Central America, not just of Costa Rica. She silently thanked Augustine for imparting crucial knowledge of the flora and fauna before his death at the hands of the general's men.

Stopping to rest, Megan couldn't help but smile. She was free, and freedom had never tasted so sweet. Even if she didn't make it out of here, she would at least die a free woman, in possession of her soul, once again.

Megan wiped her face with the front of her shirt and paused when she heard a familiar sound. Plucking the knife from her belt loop, she held it fast in her hand. There it was again—that sickening hissing sound a snake makes when it slithers over dead leaves. Augustine had told her that La Amistad was full of poisonous snakes, but they were seldom seen because they waited until it cooled off to move about. Megan held her breath and listened. Whatever kind of snake it was, it was huge. The dead leaves crunched beneath its weight, and Megan was sure it was just a foot or two away.

Megan didn't know how long she stood there, motionless and barely breathing. Finally, she took off, and ran faster than she ever had before. As she pushed through the jungle, she suddenly felt a presence. She was not alone. Something lurked out here...and it was watching her. Whatever it was, she hoped it was one of the friendly animals in La Amistad.

Megan knew La Amistad Park had very few ranger stations, and that the park itself crossed over into Panama. That was where it got its name—"The Friendship Park." If she could continue to move toward Panama, she just might get to a village before the Colombians could find her. Megan was certain that her death at the hands of the Colombians would be horrible, ugly and very, very painful. It was not something she wanted to think about. It would frighten her too much to think of Zahn making an example of her. Instead, she focused on staying free and finding a way to safety.

She had watched the soldiers' movements enough to know that only a few of them were adept at getting through the jungle with any sort of speed. They were overly cautious, loud and lazy, taking breaks at every opportunity. These men were not men of the jungle, and it showed. This she would use to her advantage.

With less than three days' worth of work remaining, it was a matter of seventy-two small hours before the soldiers shot the slave laborers. After the gold was successfully removed, the Colombians would destroy any witnesses to their crimes, then leave much richer than when they had arrived. Of course, there was always the possibility that the second set of caverns also had deposits. If so, the workers would be moved there. Either way, time was Megan's greatest concern. She felt the weight of dozens of lives sitting on her shoulders. On one hand, the enormity of the responsibility frightened her, while on the other hand, it exhilarated and excited her. No doubt this was the same sort of emotional seesaw Delta experienced every time she pulled someone to safety or prepared to save someone's life. It was the first time since they had met that Megan fully understood what it meant to be Delta Stevens. Delta was a saver of lives, a giver of gifts. She did what she did because she was obligated to do it, just as Megan was somehow obligated to go back to help the others once she found help. There was no other decision to be made, yet it was a decision she had questioned every time Delta went to work. Megan understood, at last, why Delta did what she did; it only made her love Delta that much more.

*Delta! Poor Delta's probably sick with worry, tearing around Costa Rica trying to track me down.*

Megan had no doubt that Delta and Connie were in the country somewhere. She simply *knew* Delta was here. She could feel it as easily as she felt her own heart beating. Megan also knew that she was the proverbial needle in the haystack deep within the rain forest. They were, after all, city women, whose idea of the forest was something out of Kipling's *Jungle Book*. But bless their hearts, Megan knew they would try. They would turn this country on its ear trying to find her, and they would not stop until they either found her or got some answers. Just knowing that Delta was in Costa Rica made her heart swell. Was it even possible to love Delta Stevens any more than she already did? Megan laughed for the first time in a week. Of course she loved Delta more now than when she'd left; the time away had done that.

*Just stay alive so you can tell her that yourself.*

꾸 꾸 꾸

It was almost dawn when Megan paused long enough to look at herself. When she did, she got a real good dose of just how dangerous the jungle was. Her arms were bloody and long scratch marks and bug bites dotted her fair skin. Her hair was wet and plastered to her head, her clothes were torn, but her legs, although trembling, still managed to hold her upright.

Still, the smell of freedom, the feeling of independence pushed all of the pain aside. Today, she would not be working her fingers to the bone, nor would she be forced to give any blow jobs, hand jobs, or quick, rear-entry fucks that so many men demanded. She had found her way to freedom, and nothing, not even the fear of getting caught, could dampen her spirits. She had made it through the night in the jungle. All she needed now was to get somewhere where there were decent people who could help her.

Megan knew that if she could make it to the river, she could follow it to the Caribbean side of the country. From there, she would follow the coast and head south until she reached Panama. No doubt General Zahn's tentacles extended far and wide; there would be men on the lookout for her. But Megan hoped that once she described to the Panamanian authorities just what the Colombians were doing, they would act swiftly to save the lives of the remaining captives.

Now, if only she could get there.

Breathing hard, she pushed forward and formulated a plan. What would she do when the sun was at its peak? Should she slow down? Rest? Stop? What would she eat? She must think ahead—prepare for the unexpected. She should play this like a chess game against Delta. Look beyond the next move. She knew enough to stay hydrated, and was aware of the possibility of heat stroke. Around every corner lurked some kind of danger. She had managed to avoid the snake last night, but she still had an eerie feeling she was being followed.

She parted two huge fig leaves, spotting a small stream tumbling into an area where the water swirled silently around three large rocks before continuing on its way. It was an inviting place to rest, and beckoned her weary limbs to sit for a moment. As she sat on a smooth, flat rock, Megan dipped her hands in the cool water and splashed it on her face. The water felt refreshing as it ran down her neck and into her cleavage. Augustine would have been angry with her for not checking for snakes, but she was just too tired to care.

Stretching her legs out, Megan needed to drink a little water, take a short a nap, and collect her thoughts. After that, she would continue on, aware that Zahn's men might be closing in on her. She was trying so hard not to be scared. After all, what could possibly scare her now? She'd made it through the jungle in the dark. What could be scarier than that?

Lowering her hands and her head for a drink, Megan jumped back. The answer to her unspoken question was staring back at her in the reflection from the water.

Whirling around, Megan realized, too late, that she was not alone.

# 26——

They'd been moving all night, and when dawn came, it took everything Connie and Sal had to convince Delta they needed to rest and eat. When Delta finally agreed, the three of them sat down heavily on the forest floor and munched on granola bars.

"I wish Manny and Josh were with us," Delta sighed, resting her head against a tree. Closing her eyes, Delta thought about Rikki, the beautiful blue-and-gold macaw she'd wanted to give Megan as a welcome-home gift. It was Delta's small way of getting involved in the important things in Megan's life, to let Megan know that her passions and interests were important to Delta as well.

Opening her eyes, Delta blurted out, "I sure as hell hope Megan learned a lot about the rain forest and the macaws' habitat. Maybe that Augustine guy taught her enough about the jungle to keep her alive."

"She'll be okay," Sal said quietly, relacing her boots.

Connie nodded. "She's a bright woman, Del, with a good, sharp head on her shoulders. She'll find her way to safety."

"I sure hope so." Delta scratched a big bite on her elbow.

Connie reached over and took Delta's hand. "Don't worry. A week from now, we're all going to be sitting in the

Leather and Lace, toasting Megan's return and Gina's pregnancy. You'll see."

Delta squeezed Connie's hand. "I'd sure like that a lot."

It was nearly dusk when they stopped again, each too tired to talk about their thoughts and fears. Having found a second river, they hiked during the hottest part of the afternoon, following it as it wound its way through the jungle, the humidity suffocating them. The terrain was rough and unstable, but not nearly as dense as the area they had covered in the morning. Delta had allowed only one rest stop during the day, so when they came upon a smooth beach area of the river, Connie held up a hand for them to stop.

"This is it. We'll camp here."

"Camp?" Delta snapped.

"Del, we've been going nonstop. We're hungry and beat. I, for one, am not about to do another night hike through this jungle mess." Flopping on the beach, Connie started to unlace her boots. "We need a break, and I'm taking one."

Standing on her tiptoes to put her arms across Delta's shoulders, Sal hugged her and nodded. "Connie's right, pal. Josh would say that we got lucky once in the night. Let's not push it. We need a rest, Del. All of us."

Delta looked at both of them before acquiescing reluctantly. "I suppose."

"I'll take first watch," Sal said, climbing up a small cashew tree and sitting in the crook of it.

Plunking her backpack down, Connie lay on the soft moss. Delta quickly joined her. It was only a matter of minutes before they were sound asleep.

Delta wasn't sure what woke her, but she knew something wasn't right. She rolled over ever-so slowly, and carefully reached for her machete. Taking the handle, she slowly slid the long blade from the sheath and brought the knife to her body. Whatever it was was staring at her. Letting her eyes adjust to the semi-darkness of a half-moon, Delta squinted through the blackness of the forest. Focusing her eyes, she suddenly saw the cause of her apprehension: two glowing red eyes stared back at her from about forty feet away. Whatever belonged to those eyes was bigger than the white-faced monkeys or sloths she had seen.

Keeping her eyes riveted on the glowing red orbs, Delta didn't have a clue as to what to do.

"Don't do anything," came Connie's soft voice next to her.

"What?" Delta said, startled at Connie's nearness. *How did she do that?*

"Umm...what are you two doing?" Sal asked in a whisper from her perch.

"We have company," Connie responded quietly.

Sal slid out of the tree and ripped her machete from its sheath. "What is it?"

"With any luck," Connie whispered, "we'll never find out."

Sal joined them. "I don't really believe in luck, Connie."

For the next ten minutes, the three women looked at the unblinking eyes that glared back at them. When the eyes slowly rose in the darkness, the slight crunching of the creature's movements echoed through the jungle.

"Oh, God, it's coming," Delta whispered, taking her machete in both hands.

"I say we kill it before it kills us," Sal offered. Delta nodded her silent agreement.

"We're the trespassers here," Connie whispered. "We can't just cruise in here and kill it because *we're* afraid."

As if on cue, a beefy jaguar slowly walked out of the shadows. It was the size of a large rottweiler dog, with massive paws and legs. When its entire body emerged from the dark, it stood in the partial moonlight staring at them

Sal grabbed her machete in both hands. "I say we kill it before it attacks."

Connie stepped next to Sal and Delta, both of whom were now holding their machetes like baseball bats. "If we kill that cat for no reason, I guarantee we'll never get out of here alive."

"What're you talkin' about?" Sal asked.

"Don't go out on that mystical limb now, Con. Save that Indian folklore shit for someone who believes. We're in trouble here." Delta swallowed the lump in her throat and looked for an escape route.

"Think about it, Del. We don't belong here. We've invaded its home and it probably just wants some water. More than likely it has never seen humans before."

"Suppose it attacks us?"

"Then we defend ourselves. But I swear to God, if either of you two attack that animal, we'll all die here. Trust me on this."

Sal lowered her machete. When she did, the cat took a step closer, and both Sal and Delta raised their knives again.

"Con, I know you're the smartest person in the world, and I know you believe all that ancient Indian mythology, but I'm not so sure you're right this time."

"When, in our years together, have I ever let you down?" Stepping in front of Delta, Connie turned toward the cat. "It *is* an Indian thing, Storm, and if I have to explain it to you, you really wouldn't understand. Do you trust me?"

Delta nodded. "Unconditionally," she said, and lowered her knife.

Connie leveled her gaze at the jaguar. She held its gaze for three of the longest minutes in Delta's life. It was like the time she was playing chicken with her mom's car. Those headlights bore down on her and seemed to glare in her window for hours. Now, as Connie communed on some mystical ancient level with an animal that could surely kill them all, Delta counted the minutes as they dragged by. As the fourth minute started, the jaguar slowly turned around and walked back into the jungle shadows.

Delta and Sal sighed loudly. Delta's hands were frozen in a viselike grip around the machete's handle.

"You can put those away now."

Neither moved. Connie shook her head and grinned. "What a couple of city geeks you two are. You're embarrassing."

Slowly putting her machete away, Delta stammered, "How in the hell did you do that?"

Laying her hands on Delta's shoulders, Connie gave them a squeeze. "I've been sharing bits and pieces of my ancestral heritage for years, my friend, and all you've ever managed to do was make fun of it."

"Well, now you have my undivided attention."

Connie's grin widened. "Promise? No tricks?"

Delta crossed her heart. "Swear."

Connie walked over to Sal, took the machete from her and sheathed it herself. "My grandmother was a Navajo Indian, and when I was little, she used to tell us stories of our people's old ways and our rich past. Like many elders, she was well-versed in the old stories, the ones which haven't been corrupted by the white man's retelling of them."

"Old ways?"

Connie nodded. "The ways of the shaman, the way Indians lived before the white man changed their future forever." Connie paused and waited for some sign that Delta was going to joke or question her.

But Delta nodded. "Go on." It was the first time in their relationship that Delta hadn't cut one of Connie's stories short.

"When I was eight, Grandmother took me into the desert to teach me about life. Not life as we know it, but a different kind of life, a life that the Indian nation still struggles to find and keep alive."

"What happened?" Delta asked.

"We came upon a coyote. It was the first time I had seen the mystical beast. I had heard many coyote tales, mostly about him as the trickster, so I was afraid. Grandmother told me I had nothing to be afraid of because the coyote was only there to make sure we respected his home. The Chippewas call him Shawnodese, or Keeper of the South. I won't go into all of the details about the different symbols of the coyote in Indian lore, but I will tell you that I watched Grandmother talk to that coyote just as you saw me do with the jaguar. It was out there that I learned the power of nature and how important it is to respect it."

"Talk?" Sal asked, shaking her head. "I couldn't hear anything except my own heart pounding in my ears."

Connie grinned. "She was just checking us out, much like you do when someone odd-looking cruises through your neighborhood."

Delta nodded slowly, as if, for the first time, understanding Connie's ability to speak the language of life. "Then you're implying some kind of ESP between you and that jaguar."

Shrugging, Connie sighed. "I wouldn't call it ESP."

"What would you call it?"

"It has no name, but I think 'instinct' would be a better word. She was able to look in my eyes and sense the truth of our visit. The Chippewa would tell you that she was reading my spirit. That's all instinct really is—the ability to read another's spirit in order to connect to the greater life force."

"That's what the Native Americans believe," Sal said, "but what do *you* believe?"

Connie turned and gazed in the direction the cat had walked. "I believe we underestimate animal intelligence. I know we communicated; she found us to be harmless, and left."

"Maybe she just got bored," Sal said, starting back up the tree.

Delta stood silently next to Connie for a moment. "I would have killed her," Delta whispered sadly.

Connie reached over and touched Delta's shoulder. "No you wouldn't have." Turning to face Delta, Connie took her by the shoulders and stared deep into her eyes. "No matter what you think about the lives you've had to take, Storm, you're not a killer."

Delta averted her gaze from Connie's. This time, Connie was wrong. *I've killed two men, and regardless of the reasons, that makes me a killer, no matter what you say, Connie.*

"It's time to stop beating yourself up, Del. You did what you had to do. Let it go."

Let it go? Let it go? How many times had Delta lain awake at night replaying those two deaths? Like bad movie reruns, she saw them over and over again, with the same result every time. How many times had she tried to "let it go," only to dream of the bullet that penetrated the perp's forehead, blowing his brains out the back of his skull?

Connie reached up and ran her hand through Delta's hair. "Listen to me. Right here and now, I want you to cut that baggage loose."

"I...I don't know how."

"Sure you do. If you would look in your heart like I do, like Megan does, you would see what we see. This is an incredibly mystical place, Del. Maybe it has the power to heal your heart."

Delta bowed her head, tears running down her cheeks. "I didn't know it was that obvious."

Connie took Delta in her arms and lightly stroked her back. "Everything you feel and think is obvious to me, silly. And if there is anyplace in the world that can heal someone's spirit, the rain forest is it. Am I the smartest woman you know?"

Delta nodded.

"And you trust me more than anyone?"

Delta nodded again.

"Then let it go."

Wrapping her arms around Connie, Delta quietly released the fear, the anger, the guilt, and the sadness that had built up in her since she'd blown the back of that man's head off six months ago. As the tears flowed freely for the first time since Megan's abduction, Delta began to feel stronger.

"Thanks, Chief."

Connie pulled away and wiped Delta's eyes. "Now get some rest."

## 27——

**Before** the sun was completely awake, the three women were back at it, pushing and hacking at the jungle ferns and vines. The nagging fear which had plagued them was gone now, replaced by the knowledge that they'd faced the forest's queen and survived. Each, in her own way, began to have a growing understanding of the natural order of the rain forest. Delta grasped the fact that they were visitors, guests in a world that didn't need them, didn't want them, and was certainly better off without them.

Watching Connie make her way through the jungle, Delta's respect for her friend grew, and Delta's only regret was that in the past, she hadn't listened with an open heart when Connie shared her fantastic stories. Thinking of some of those stories now made Delta smile. Who could blame her for not believing that Connie's uncle was Juan Valdez, the Colombian coffee-grower on TV? Or how about the story of Connie's family being Hungarian gypsies? Delta doubted anyone would blame her for her skepticism. Until now, that is. Now, everything had changed.

Suddenly, Sal stopped in front of an orange bromeliad, pulled out her binoculars and started a three-hundred-and-sixty-degree check of their surroundings.

Catching up to Connie, Delta grabbed her arm and turned her around. A band of sweat surrounded her face and dripped onto her shirt. "You need a rest?"

Delta shook her head. "No. I just wanted to say thanks."

"What for?"

"In all the years we've been friends, you've never, not once, let me down. You've always been there for me. I don't say it enough, but I want you to know if there's one person on this planet I can't live without, it's you."

Connie wiped the sweat from her forehead and grinned. "Ditto."

"Thanks for coming here with me," Delta said, genuinely.

Connie lightly touched Delta's face. There were too many experiences, too many emotions flowing between them to ever truly say how they felt about each other, so Connie kept it simple. "I wouldn't have missed it for the world. You're the most fun a girl can have."

"I love you a lot."

Connie smiled warmly into Delta's face. "It's one of the few things in life I can always count on."

Sal suddenly stepped up to them and cleared her throat. "Umm, guys?"

"Yeah?" they said in unison.

"This is really touching and all, but we've got company, and I have no idea if they're friendly." Handing the binoculars to Connie, Sal pulled her machete from its sheath; when Delta saw this, she unsheathed hers as well.

"Shit!" Connie hissed, handing the binoculars back to Sal.

"What?" Delta asked, squinting in the direction Connie and Sal had looked.

"Natives," Sal said, looking over at Connie. "What now?"

Connie took the binoculars and when she peered through them, saw the men in their breechcloths holding long spears and waving their arms about. "Uh-oh."

"What?" Sal asked.

Connie watched the men gesture to each other. One was pointing in their direction, and started running toward them. "Here they come."

"Fuck!" Sal bellowed. "What in the hell are we gonna do?"

Delta sheathed her machete. "We have to run for it."

"We can't outrun these guys," Connie reasoned.

Sal looked through the binoculars and shook her head. "Then we're screwed. These guys don't look like they're the Welcome Wagon." It was only a matter of half a minute before the men would be on top of them. "Umm...Con's right. This is it."

Delta looked over at Connie, who was shrugging her shoulders. She grinned at Delta helplessly. There was no chance for escape this time, and they both knew it.

"Who knows?" Connie said, "Maybe they're friendly."

"Umm...Connie, not a chance. These guys look like they're on some kinda warpath."

Delta stood next to Connie and regripped her machete in both hands.

"No, Storm," Connie said, gently placing her hand on the machete handle and lowering it. "Our only hope is to surrender."

Inhaling her fear, Delta nodded once and dropped her machete at her feet. Connie was right, she was no killer. It was time she recognized that. She slid her hand over to Connie's and held it firmly in her own.

Connie grinned and nodded. "We'll be okay."

"Here they come!" Sal announced, tossing her machete next to Delta's.

The natives moved deftly through the vegetation, seemingly without touching the leaves. Eight long-haired men in tan breechcloths with spears raised high above their heads were upon them at once. Delta watched with almost detached fascination as the natives flung their spears at them. *This isn't how I thought I'd die.* If someone had told her she would end up being run through by a tribal spear, she would have laughed and called for the men in little white suits.

But wait...the spears didn't appear to be directed at them. High over their heads the spears flew, and all three women turned to see where these weapons of death would land.

"Holy shit," Sal murmured as one spear pierced the chest of a white man perched high in a tree, holding a rifle. With a sickening thud, the spear tore through his chest, forcing its way out his back. Like a lead weight, the man fell to the ground, his khaki shirt shorn away and soaked in blood.

A second spear found its bull's-eye in the stomach of a black man, also holding a rifle, also wearing a khaki shirt. The rifle went off as he hit the ground, pinned there by the spear.

"What in the hell—"

Delta looked at Connie, who shrugged. "I wish I knew."

Delta watched quietly as all but one of the men retrieved their spears. "Poachers?"

Connie nodded. "That's as good a guess as any. I think these natives just saved our lives."

Sal scooted closer to Connie and eyed her machete. "Yeah, but saved it for what?"

# 28——

**Connie** stepped in front of Delta and Sal and quickly spoke Spanish to the small group of natives. They looked at her oddly, as if trying to decipher what she was trying to say.

"Umm, Con?" Sal said, as the men slowly encircled them. "Think your jaguar trick will work with humans?"

"I don't think so."

Delta started for her machete, but thought better of it. These men were like a photo she'd seen on the cover of *National Geographic*. They were a cross between Zulu warriors and Native American Indians.

"Con, who are these guys?" Sal asked softly.

"There are a few indigenous preserves in La Amistad, Sal. These people could be from the Bribri tribe or the Cabecar tribe."

"Tribal people?" Delta asked, as the men started talking to each other and pointing.

"You're kidding, right?" Sal asked when one of the men pointed to her boots.

"Meet the natives of Costa Rica," Connie said, opening her hands to show she was weaponless and harmless.

"I sure hope they're friendly," Sal said, slowly moving next to Connie. "What should we do?"

"Do?" Connie asked, looking askance. "The 'doing' is up to these people."

"Maybe they'll just go away," Sal offered.

"I don't think that's likely," Connie answered. "They didn't happen to show up. They've probably been trailing us for some time."

Suddenly, one man stepped out and pointed his spear at Sal's boots. The others started talking at once, looking down at Sal's feet. Something about Sal was making them anxious.

"This doesn't look so good," Delta said, resisting the urge to go for her machete. She didn't need to know anything about tribal cultures to know these men were agitated, and Sal's appearance appeared to be the cause.

Connie attempted Spanish again, but still to no avail. Whatever language they spoke, it wasn't Spanish.

"Well, we can't outrun them, and we can't outfight them, so what now?" Sal looked around for a way to escape.

Connie watched the men talk to each other. Sal was clearly the focus of their interest. "I think the fatigues or the boots scare them."

"Well, it's too late to do anything about that," Sal said bitterly. "I'm not taking them off."

The man next to Sal shouted something at her, as the rest of the men opened the circle up and pointed in the direction from which they'd come.

"I think he wants us to go that way," Connie said, slowly reaching for her backpack. Before her hand could reach it, a spear landed right in the middle of it, pinning it to the ground.

"Guess that means it stays here," Delta said.

Two men grabbed Sal and pushed her up front.

"Hey, take it easy! What did I do?"

"Just do what they want," Connie said, watching Sal escorted away by two of the natives.

"Con, in all of your reading, you didn't happen to see if these guys are vegetarians, did you?" Sal asked over her shoulder.

"Relax, Sal. I don't think they mean us any harm."

"That's a relief."

Walking next to Connie, Delta tried to read her face. "Con, are we in big trouble here?"

Connie looked around at the stern faces of the men. "To be honest, Del, I really don't know. But I imagine we're about to find out.

They had hiked a little over an hour in relative silence, following the leaders of the small band of warriors, when they suddenly came upon a clearing. Dotted around this open space were thatched roof huts and various lean-tos. Women and children were occupied with assorted tasks; the women were working over open fires, while the children were making something with bright red and yellow feathers. When the bare-breasted women looked up and saw them, they rose up from their duties and calmly walked into their huts.

"Remarkable," Connie muttered.

"What?" Delta asked.

"They've brought us to their village."

"This is a village?" Delta glanced around. Other than the huts and the fire, there was little to indicate to Delta that this was a village.

"Del, there are four remaining tribes that they know of left in Costa Rica. We've just been brought to the village of one of those tribes. Few, if any, Westerners get the opportunity to see this. What luck."

"Luck? Did you say luck? We don't even know what they're going to do to us!" Sal said, and was immediately nudged by one of the men.

Connie glanced around and shook her head. "These people seem to be most interested in your boots, Sal."

"Well, they can't have them!" Sal replied defiantly.

"Sal—"

One of the men motioned for Sal to sit against a tree.

"If we could tell them we're not hostile, maybe they can help us get out of here."

"And how are we going to do that? They don't appear interested in being friendly," Sal said.

Three men spoke to each other before pointing to a tree and motioning for Connie and Delta to sit there. When they sat down, two men stood guard with six-foot spears while the others disappeared into the huts.

Delta said, "Listen, they have no idea who we are, what we want, or if we mean any harm to them. We're wandering around in their backyard; I can see why they'd be suspicious."

Before Connie could comment, a man wearing a number of necklaces emerged from the hut and approached them. Connie and Delta both stood up, but the slender, older man strode confidently over to Sal and spoke to his men, who took each of her arms and pulled her to her feet.

"Umm, Con?" Sal whimpered.

Connie stepped forward, but the men guarding her would not let her through.

"Do something, will you?" Sal pleaded, keeping her eyes on the larger of the two men.

In one swift movement, the two men holding Sal's arms practically lifted her off the ground and whisked her away. Delta stepped forward as well. Like the proverbial fish out of water, she hadn't a clue as to what to do next. Where were they taking Sal?

"What do we do now?" Delta whispered to Connie.

Connie shrugged. "Even if we could escape, they'd spear us in the back as easily as we throw paper in the trash can."

"But Sal—"

"Isn't in any danger that we know of."

"Why doesn't that make me feel any better?" Delta glanced around the tiny village. Where were the women she'd seen when they first arrived?

Less than five minutes later, Connie grinned and pointed to the hut. "Look, they're bringing her out already."

Delta looked up to see Sal smiling. "What happened? Are you okay?"

Sal just shook her head, the grin still deeply entrenched on her face. "You're not going to believe this. I mean, you are not *even* going to believe this."

Delta and Connie glanced at each other and then back at Sal, who was still shaking her head.

"What? What is it?" Delta asked, looking over Sal's shoulder.

Sal hooked her thumb behind her. "You'll see."

Delta sighed as she stared beyond Sal's right shoulder, in the direction of the hut Sal had just left. The sun was hot against her face, so Delta shielded her eyes with her hand. "What? I don't see anything."

"Just wait."

Delta squinted against the sun's rays and wondered what could possibly have made Sal grin so broadly. "Sal?"

"There." Pointing to the hut's entrance, Sal continued beaming. "You were right, Con. These guys aren't barbarians. They're...well...you'll see."

Delta and Connie exchanged curious glances.

"At least we're not in any harm," Connie whispered before returning her attention to the hut.

Suddenly, from out of the hut came a woman; a white woman, wearing jeans and a dirty pink, torn tee-shirt. As the woman ran toward them, it took Delta a fraction of a second before she realized who the woman was.

"Megan?" Pushing the spears away, Delta ran as fast as her legs could carry her until she swept Megan up in her arms. Crushing her lover to her chest, Delta held on with every bit of energy she possessed. "It *is* you!"

"My love!" Megan said, embracing Delta so hard, Delta could barely breathe herself. "I knew you'd come! I knew!"

Finally putting Megan on the ground, Delta took Megan's face in her hands and gazed into the blue eyes she had missed so much. The same sparkle and warmth shone from them just as it always had whenever Megan looked into Delta's face. "Are you okay?"

Megan's smile lit up the forest. "I'm fine, sweetheart." She stepped back and looked at Delta. "But what about you? Are you all right? How in the world did you get here?"

Delta pulled Megan back into an embrace and closed her eyes tightly. Nothing she could say or do could keep the tears from rolling down her face. Suddenly, all the fear of losing Megan, all the anxiety she had experienced over the last few days, flooded her. "Oh, God, Megan, I thought..."

"Shh, my love, I'm here. I'm here." Megan held Delta for a minute while she cried. When Delta finally raised her head, Megan wiped her tears and smiled warmly. "I knew you'd come. I knew you were in Costa Rica." Releasing Delta, Megan reached over for Connie, who had slowly ambled over for her own reunion. Embracing Connie, Megan did not let go of Delta's hand. "Thank you for keeping her safe."

Connie grinned. "It's my job."

Megan pulled away and smiled. "You're an expert at it by now."

Connie reached out and lightly touched Megan's face. Both women had tears brimming in their eyes. "You're a sight for sore eyes, Meg." Wrapping her arms around Megan's neck once more, Connie hugged her tightly. "God, is it good to see you."

Kissing Connie's cheek, Megan pulled Delta to her and held her again. "I just knew it." Megan reached over and draped her arm around each of their necks. "If anyone could find me, you two would."

"We three," Sal said, joining them. As Sal moved toward the huddle, the men backed away from her.

"What is it with these guys, anyway?" Sal asked, hugging Megan tightly.

Megan grinned down at the little woman. "It's good to see you, Sal. How on earth did Josh let you come here without him?"

Sal took her cap off and tucked her hair behind her ears. "Umm...long story."

"Speaking of stories," Delta said quietly, "who in the hell are those guys holding you captive? And what is this about gold? And where in the hell is that Augustine guy who was supposed to be taking care of you?"

Megan grinned warmly as she pressed a finger to Delta's lips. "There's plenty of time for answers, my love. But we have an obligation to the people who reunited us."

"But—"

"But later," Megan said breathily.

Delta thought she might fall down.

"Megan's right, Del," Connie said. "There are certain customs we would be wise to follow. Megan, Sal thought we were going to be prisoners here."

Kissing Delta's cheek, Megan smiled warmly. "The Bribri aren't holding us prisoners, Con. They're my friends."

"Friends?" all three women said in unison.

Megan nodded as she slipped her hand into Delta's. "Good friends, right, Tamar?"

As Megan spoke, a young man dressed only in jeans walked out of the hut accompanied by a rather old man nearly a foot shorter. The two men walked up to Megan and Delta. "Yes. Good friends," the younger man said as he turned to the older man and translated.

Tamar and the older man began talking in a language that sounded to Delta more like a song than a language. When they finished talking, Tamar turned to Megan and translated. "Itka thought these were the soldiers you told us about."

Everyone turned to look at Sal, who blushed. "And here I thought they were admiring my attire."

Megan took Tamar's hand and held it in both of hers. "Please thank Itka for all of his help and explain to him that these are my friends. They have come from far away to find me."

Tamar translated for the elder Itka, who pointed to Sal as he spoke. Itka listened for a long time, looked over at Sal, and laughed. After saying a few more words to Tamar, Itka spoke to the other men, who slowly strode off in various directions. The old man with the necklaces nodded solemnly as Tamar continued with his explanations. Whenever Itka spoke, Tamar listened like a college student, respectful and engrossed in the old man's words.

"Itka says your friends should be more careful. Foreign women should not go in a forest they know nothing about."

"Hear, hear," Sal added.

Megan released Tamar's hand and stood in front of Itka. She towered over the diminutive old man, so she bowed her head in deference. It was an odd picture, and Delta wasn't quite sure what to make of it. "Please tell Itka that I will forever owe him for finding my dearest friends."

The two men chatted back and forth before Itka nodded and walked back to his hut.

"What's going on?" Delta asked, standing next to Megan just to be near her.

"Explanations will have to wait, sweetheart," Megan answered. "Right now, we must be respectful to our host and join Itka and his family for a meal. That is the custom here."

"Come on guys, I'm starved," Sal said, rubbing her hands together as she walked toward the hut.

Joining Sal, Connie turned to Megan and grinned. "You have no idea how hard it was keeping your friend out of trouble while you were gone."

Megan cut her eyes over to Delta and shook her head. "No, I don't, but I suspect you'll fill me in later." With that, Connie and Sal entered Itka's hut.

"I have so much I need to say to you," Delta said softly from behind Megan.

Megan turned and kissed Delta's forehead. "I know. But there are certain...rituals we need to follow. As much as I'd love to throw myself on you, we have an obligation to these wonderful people. They've brought us together, Del. The very least we can do is honor their home, their traditions."

Delta grinned and sighed. Megan had grown up so much. "Later?"

Her blue eyes twinkling, Megan nodded. "Try and stop me."

As Delta turned, she saw an odd expression on Tamar's face; it was a look Delta had seen many times before. "He knows, doesn't he?"

Megan nodded. "He knows enough."

"So, what do you think, Tamar?"

Starting down the path, Tamar shook his head. "I think you are crazy for coming into the jungle."

Delta's grin grew. "Crazy?"

Tamar did not turn around. "Or something else. Only Itka knows for sure." With that, Tamar disappeared into the hut.

"Something else? What did he mean by that?"

Standing at the opening of the hut, Megan motioned for Delta to enter. "I'm sure we're about to find out."

# 29——

**Once** inside the hut, Delta watched curiously as Itka spoke to an older woman, who nodded before scurrying past them. Then Itka spoke quickly to Tamar, before also leaving the hut.

"Itka is going to select the best food in the village, and has asked that you sit down and rest a while. He knows you must be tired from your journey."

Megan nodded and motioned for the others to sit. "These people seldom have enough food to offer anyone outside the tribe, so no matter how bad it might look or taste, it would be rude and wasteful not to eat it."

"Oh, no," Sal moaned. "Monkey brains, here we come."

This made Tamar laugh. "Not monkey brains, little one."

Sal sighed. "That's a relief."

"We eat the entire monkey."

All three women looked to Megan for confirmation. A slight smile told them that Tamar was joking. "Relax. As long as you don't know what you're eating, you'll be fine."

Tamar grinned. "Monkey is good. Better than turkey. Don't be afraid. You may like it."

Megan turned and reached a hand out to Tamar. "This is Delta, Connie and Sal."

Tamar looked at Delta and nodded. "This is the warrior woman of your stories."

Megan smiled at Delta and beamed. "Yes, she is."

Squatting so he could shake Delta's hand, Tamar appeared awestruck. "It is an honor."

Taking Tamar's hand, Delta blushed. "Thank you, but I'm not rea—"

"I must tell the others. This is wonderful news! Megan, if you need anything, send someone to the river. This is the hand sign for river. The women will know what to do." With that, Tamar exited the hut.

Nodding, Megan watched in silence as he left. When she turned back around, there were so many questions on the three faces looking at her that she had to laugh. "One at a time."

Delta shook her head as she addressed Connie. "I have so many questions, I don't even know where to begin. You start, Chief."

"Perhaps Megan ought to begin at the beginning, and we can ask our questions after."

"Yeah," Sal chimed in. "What in the hell is going on here? You been leading an alternate life, or what? Who the hell is this Tamar guy, and how come he speaks English?"

Megan chuckled as she held Delta's hand. "God, it's so good to see you all." Megan picked up what looked like a strip of jerky and chewed it. "Augustine and I were tracking international poachers when General Zahn, a Colombian drug runner in cahoots with the cartel, snatched me right from camp."

"Snatched you? What happened to Augustine?" Connie asked.

Megan sighed and looked down at the hut floor. "They killed him."

Delta nodded, resisting the temptation to reach out and stroke Megan's cut cheek.

"When I got back to Zahn's camp, I realized that he had done the same thing to others who had ventured too deep into the jungle. He had managed to kidnap quite a handful of tourists and students from all over the globe."

Connie nodded. "Brilliant maneuver. That leaves each embassy dealing separately with its own missing persons report, so it could take weeks or months before anyone put two and two together."

Megan smiled over at Connie. "Exactly. He's managed to abduct women who were planning on spending some time in the jungle. He isn't grabbing tourists off the streets because that would bring too much unwanted police interest. Instead, his men cruise around the various rain and cloud forests, searching for people who planned on being incommunicado for a while."

Delta couldn't stand it a second longer, and reached out to caress Megan's cheek. "Like biology students, environmentalists, etcetera."

Megan nodded. "Yep. When Zahn's men came to the camp, they said they were lost, and engaged Augustine in a conversation which eventually led to his death. When they knew we were searching for poachers, they killed Augustine and carted me off to that bastard's camp. They forced about two dozen of us women to work in the caverns. We've been panning and scraping the walls of an underground cavern for gold to back the cartels." Megan shook her head. "Can you believe it? Anything to make a buck."

Delta set her palm on Megan's cheek and stared sadly into Megan's exhausted eyes. Her face was gaunt and she had lost a good deal of weight, but she was still the most beautiful woman Delta had ever seen.

"To make a long story short, I managed to steal a knife and cut my way out, and the Bri eventually found me and brought me back here."

Connie released Megan's hand and rose to examine the interior of the hut. There were five hammocks strung from one pole to another. The floor of the hut was dirt covered with straw, and there was a makeshift window on one side. Turning from her examination of the hut, Connie said, "We knew we'd find you, Meg, but even *I'm* confused. How is it you came to know these people?"

Sitting next to Delta and snuggling close to her, Megan continued. "These people are part of the Bribri tribe—one of the last indigenous people in Costa Rica. Tamar is Bri. I met him when Augustine and I were preparing to come here the second time."

"You met him in the jungle?" Delta asked.

"Heavens, no. Tamar and Augustine were friends at the university. See, the Costa Rican government sponsors a program for tribals who wish to go to school. It's all part of a program to actually save the indigenous cultures. Tamar learned Spanish and English from an ethnobotonist back in—"

Sal held up her hand. "An ethno-what?"

"Ethnobotonist. Someone who studies how indigenous people know and use the plants around them. Tamar learned much of his English from the scientist."

"So he came back to the rain forest to do what?" Delta asked.

"Because of his schooling, and the massive rain-forest destruction in Central and South America, Tamar is attempting to catalogue the plants his people use for specific ailments."

"Fascinating," Connie mused under her breath. "Civilization isn't for everybody."

"I guess not. Tamar said he felt closed in, missed the greenery and the tranquility. So he finished his botany degree and came home. He is an apprentice to the tribal shaman now, trying to record all of the old ways so that the tribal knowledge doesn't die out."

Connie nodded. "We actually have programs like that back home. Both non-native and Cherokee students are learning Cherokee and then teaching it to the Cherokee children."

Delta released Megan's hand and stroked her cheek with the back of her hand. "But how did you get here? How did you know how to find them?"

"I didn't. They found me. I'd been running all night long and was resting when they found me. They saw this necklace and recognized it." Megan showed them the necklace she was wearing. Tamar gave it to me after one of our trips. Thank God I was still wearing it. They brought me back here, and there was Tamar."

"That necklace saved your life," Sal said, leaning forward to get a better look at it.

"In a way, yes. The Bribri are a peaceful people, and might have simply passed me by, but they saw the necklace and my condition, and knew I needed help. All I had to do was say Tamar's name with a smile and they were more than happy to bring me here."

"Incredible," Delta said, shaking her head in wonder. "Even the rain forest is a small world."

Megan took Delta's hand and kissed it. "Apparently so. When we got here, Tamar told Itka and his men of my dilemma, so they went out looking to see if the General's men were coming. Apparently, while they were out there, they spotted a pair of poachers getting ready to make sport out of the three of you, so they killed them. The Bri hate poachers."

"Okay, but why the ever-so-chilly reception?" Sal asked.

"When they saw Sal's uniform, they thought she might be one of Zahn's soldiers. They were a little confused about you being women, however."

"So that's why they kept staring at me and pointing to my boots."

Megan nodded. "The Bri were just protecting their home from the poachers and someone they care about from Zahn. See, they know I care about them and their culture. Tamar told them of my interest in preserving the macaws and other rain-forest birds, so the Bri respect what Augustine and I were doing."

Connie rubbed her chin. "But don't these people also hunt the macaw?"

Megan nodded. "Some tribes do, when the food supply is low. In the ecosystem of the rain forest, the tribal people are simply another strand of the food web. Macaws aren't their first choice, but in here, you eat whatever you can catch. That's the beauty of it. The Bri are part of the ecosystem, not above it."

"But how did you make it through the rain forest alone at night?" Delta asked.

Megan took Delta's face in her hands and peered into her green eyes. "I was never alone, honey. Not so long as you live will I ever be alone. Your love gave me courage. I knew if I could just get out of there, I would come home to you. I didn't know how long or when, but I knew I would."

"You're incredible," Delta said, lightly kissing Megan.

Megan reached for Connie and Sal and pulled them closer so the four women formed a tight circle. "The question remains, how did you even know where to begin looking for me?"

Linking arms, the three weary travelers recounted their tale of adventure, beginning with the alarming phone call from Liz.

# 30 ——

**When** Delta finished telling of their trials in the rain forest, Tamar and Itka returned, bearing platters of colorful fruits, roots, various meats and nuts—all laid out artistically.

"It is our custom to offer guests our finest food. You will insult Itka and the tribe if you do not eat."

"What is it?" Sal asked, pointing to the meat.

Tamar grinned at her. "Just pretend it is the beef you Americans are so overly fond of."

Megan reached for a piece of meat and put it in her mouth. The others waited for an expression that did not come. Instead of making a face, she smiled at Itka and nodded. "Tastes like chicken."

"Frogs' legs," Sal muttered under her breath. "I bet they're frogs' legs."

Connie looked down at the platter. "Cassava."

Tamar smiled at her. "We have cassava beer, but women do not drink it."

"That's fine. This meal will more than suffice, thank you." Connie plucked what looked like a large kiwi from the platter and ate it. "It's certainly fresher than we get at the supermarket."

For the next fifteen minutes, the small group ate quietly, but Delta could hardly focus on eating; all she wanted to do was take Megan in her arms and kiss her until morning. Megan was thinner than when she'd boarded the plane, but her beauty was as captivating as ever. Whatever fate had befallen her at the camp had put a wisdom in those blue eyes. As Delta gazed at her, she realized that the prostitute she'd fallen in love with was long, long gone. Sitting beside her now was a worldly woman with more poise, more confidence, more self-assurance than the lady of the night Delta had first met.

As she finished the last of a yellow fruit, Megan caught Delta's stare and returned it. "Later," she mouthed, grinning warmly at her lover. Delta nodded shyly and returned her attention to a strip of meat she was sure was not beef.

When the platter was completely empty, Itka spoke to Tamar, who listened carefully, occasionally nodding. When Itka rose, he nodded to everyone, but placed his hands on Megan's head and mumbled a few words before leaving.

"Itka says it is an honor to have you here, but he senses your weariness. He has offered you his home for as long as you care to stay."

Megan nodded and took Tamar's hand in hers. "Please tell him we are grateful for his kindness, but to stay would put his people in jeopardy. If we can sleep here tonight, we will be on our way in the morning."

When Tamar rose and started to leave, Megan called him back. "Tamar?"

"Yes?"

"I don't know how we can ever repay you or your people for your kindness and hospitality."

Tamar stepped back in the hut. His face was a mask of seriousness. "Helping to save our home is thanks enough, Megan Osbourne." With that, Tamar left.

"Someone pinch me," Connie whispered. "This is...this is incredible."

"Isn't it amazing how we view the quality of our lives by how much we have, yet there are still hunters and gatherers who understand that the quality isn't in possessions but in the people you surround yourself with?" Megan fingered her necklace as she spoke. "No freeways, no televisions, no punching a time card. They really know how to live. It's amazing."

Delta slid her arm around Megan's waist. "So are you."

Megan blushed and looked down. "Why? Because I was able to stay alive?"

"Among other things."

Looking up at Delta, Megan's lips curled up in a smile. "You would have been disappointed if I had acted like the rest of the women at the camp. I couldn't let you down by waiting to be butchered."

"Let us down?" Connie interrupted. "You did this all on your own. I mean, you escaped from some paramilitary criminal in the middle of the jungle."

Sal yawned again and stretched. "Yeah, man. Who does that asshole think he is, anyway?"

He's a very bright, very successful crook, Sal. The amount of gold we've pulled from the water would blow you away."

Connie's eyebrows shot up. "What do you mean, water?"

"There's an underground river flowing through some caverns which opened during the earthquake of 1991. Zahn will use the gold to back the drug cartels as well as strengthen his own empire."

"Then, they really aren't drug runners?"

"Not right now. Gold is the only thing they're after here. Once they get it, they'll be off to plunder some other country of some other resource. Believe me, I've learned more than I care to about the diversity of the Colombian cartels."

"How are they going to get it out of the rain forest?"

Shrugging, Megan laid her head on Delta's shoulder. "I'm not sure. I heard something about a boat offshore in the Caribbean, but my Spanish isn't very good yet. That was about all I could make out."

"They're carrying it out of the jungle?" Connie asked.

Megan shrugged again. "All I know is about a half a dozen men leave every other day with their backpacks filled with as much gold as they can carry. They return by nightfall with empty backpacks, so they're leaving it somewhere."

Delta studied Megan's eyes for a minute before pulling her closer. You must be exhausted."

Megan closed her eyes and nodded. "I am."

Connie kicked Sal's foot before standing up and pulling her to her feet. "Come on."

"Where we goin'? I was just gettin' comfy," Sal muttered.

Connie looked at Delta and Megan before glaring at Sal, who slowly understood what Connie was getting at.

"Oh. I bet you two would like some alone time, huh?" Sal asked, grinning sheepishly.

Delta smiled warmly at the would-be soldier. "A little. If you don't mind."

"Mind? Hell, she's the reason we just ate monkey guts. Besides, the resident genius over here can't wait to have a chat with the natives. Her eyes haven't stopped bugging out since we arrived."

Pushing Sal out the hut entrance, Connie knelt down and held Megan's hands.

Megan brought Connie's hand to her lips and kissed it. "Thank you. Thank you for not letting her come alone."

Connie looked at Delta and nodded. "Not in a million years. You two take your time. God knows, you deserve it."

After Connie left, Delta turned to Megan and kissed her long and deep. It was the kind of kiss only two impassioned women could experience together—a soul-binding exchange that said more than a dictionary full of words. It was the kind of kiss women dream of sharing once in a lifetime. As Delta's lips slowly pulled away from Megan's, Delta knew that although they were in the middle of a rain forest, they were home.

As their lips melted together again, Delta thought of home. She'd learned so much about what this word meant. It wasn't where her job was, or the street her house was on. Home was wherever Megan was, and in this tiny hut in a village so far removed from River Valley, Delta was home.

"I have missed you so much, I ache," Delta whispered, lightly touching Megan's cheek. "There are so many things I need to share with you—so many feelings I never knew I could feel, but I don't even know where to begin."

Megan's fingers lightly danced across Delta's shirt buttons, until her shirt was completely undone. "Then show me, my love. We don't need words to express what we have been feeling for the past three months. Take me in your arms and show me." Sliding Delta's shirt off, Megan began kissing her neck, as her hands found their way to Delta's belt and unbuckled it.

Delta closed her eyes and could hardly breathe. She had imagined their reunion so differently than this, yet this was somehow far better than her mind could create. Megan's lips nuzzled her neck, her delicate hands reaching for Delta's breasts, with only the sounds from the jungle to accompany them. Delta was in paradise.

"Take your pants off," Megan whispered as she gently bit Delta's ear.

Chills ran down Delta's arms and her nipples immediately reacted. "God, I have missed you so very much." Taking her shoes and then her torn jeans off, Delta lay back while Megan slipped carefully between her legs. They fit together so perfectly, it felt as if they had only been apart three days, not three months. Delta ran her hands through the long blonde hair she loved so much and didn't take her eyes off Megan's face. "You are everything I need," Delta whispered, kissing her softly. Megan's weight felt so good on her body, as they kissed with rising passion.

"I'll never leave home without you again," Megan said, gazing intently into Delta's face. Locked in an embrace that nothing but death could pull apart, Megan slowly lowered her mouth to Delta's and kissed her with more passion and more power than either had ever experienced together. With her lips gliding over Delta's, Megan lightly ran her hand over her lover's body, eliciting goose bumps on those long arms and legs.

"Trying to drive me mad?" Delta said softly.

"You're already there, my love." Megan ran her hands over Delta's breasts, down her stomach, and over her patch of brown curls, pausing for a moment with her hand resting solidly on Delta's fleshy mound.

Delta reached out and laid her hand on top of Megan's. Tears suddenly sprang into her eyes as Megan's face now blurred before her. "I thought..."

"Shhh. None of that matters now. Nothing matters, Delta Stevens, except that we are here together in this beautiful, magical place."

Delta thought she might explode before Megan even touched her. Every nerve ending was alive and on fire.

Megan grinned down into Delta's eyes before tossing her long hair over her shoulder and out of Delta's face. "It's true. Nothing but death can stand in our way. Where we were, who we've been, doesn't matter anymore. Our lives begin here and now, Delta." Kissing Delta softly at first, and then with more passion, Megan slid to the side and began stroking Delta's breast with one hand. Delta's body came to life, her nipples hardened, and she ached to be touched all over.

Slipping down from Delta's mouth to her neck and then to her other breast, Megan's hands didn't stop moving over Delta's body. It was as if she was trying to memorize every inch of her.

"Oh...God...," Delta moaned.

"She can't help you now, my sweet. "Megan played with Delta's coarse dark hair, then slowly moved her hand lower and lower, until her hand rested on top of Delta's vagina. The heat coming off Delta's body was nearly palpable.

Megan moved up so they were face-to-face. That was how Delta enjoyed lovemaking with Megan: looking in her eyes as their hearts beat in unison. But their hearts weren't beating now. They were racing, and Delta could barely tolerate the tension building up in her body.

"Love me, Megan. Love me forever."

With that, Megan slowly, lovingly slid her fingers into Delta, as Delta arched her back to take them as far as she could. If it was possible, she would have engulfed Megan's entire arm, maybe even her whole body—that was how connected she felt to her beautiful lover. She wanted it all; she wanted to know everything Megan felt. She wanted to feel the love she knew existed between them. Delta wanted this purest of emotions to flow through her like the blood in her veins.

"Hold on, sweetheart," Megan whispered in her ear.

Delta put her arms around Megan and held on tightly, as Megan's fingers worked magic inside Delta's body. It was as if the love Megan felt pulsated from her fingertips and into Delta's soul. She had never loved like this before, and she knew, no matter what happened in her life, Megan Osbourne was her one true love.

"Oh...shit..." Delta said, as her heart pounded and the muscles in her body began contracting and expanding. It was coming, like a runaway train: fast, furious, out of control, and she was powerless to do anything but lie there and feel it. All she could do was feel the energy and emotions pouring into her. And like a dry sponge, Delta took it all in. Together, she and Megan moved in a rhythm born out of knowledge of each other's bodies. Megan knew when to slow down, when to apply more pressure, when to tease and when to give in. And as the train picked up speed, Delta stared into the luminous blue eyes she loved so desperately. She could never imagine her life without this woman.

"I love you," Delta barely managed to say.

Megan stopped everything she was doing and lightly touched Delta's face. "I knew you would come." With that, Megan pulled Delta to her and held onto her with everything she had as her fingers massaged parts of Delta only Megan knew about.

"Oh...no..."

Megan smiled into Delta's face. "Oh, yes."

As the train zoomed over a crest and hurtled on its way, Delta felt her eyes well up with tears. There were simply too many emotions for her heart and body to take in. But still, the train sped on, and Delta's body felt as if it were being lifted magically in the air. She no longer felt Megan's fingers, or her body, or the breath on her face. All Delta could feel was this intense, pulsing rhythm at the base of her neck as it traveled down her spine. Her back arched, her eyes closed, Delta envisioned this barreling train as it passed through her stomach and her legs. Rising almost completely off the floor of the hut, Delta was on another plane, in some other universe, experiencing the most intense emotional feelings of her life.

"Oh..."

Holding on to Megan for fear of becoming that ball of fire and shooting out the top of the hut, Delta squeezed her eyes closed and felt the hot tears run down her face. Every muscle in her body felt the passion, the unabashed love Megan had unselfishly given to her. After several minutes, when she could catch her breath once again, Delta felt her body return to the floor of the hut.

There were, at once, no words and too many words to express what she felt. For the first time in a long time, Delta knew what it was to be full—to be in harmony with herself. As Megan gently touched Delta's cheek with the tips of her fingers, Delta let the tears come.

"Shh, my love," Megan whispered softly, wiping the tears away.

Delta pulled Megan to her and clung to her tightly. "I have never been so afraid in my life. I thought...I didn't know what to think. I guess...I thought...we'd run out of time."

Megan wiped a lingering tear from Delta's eyelash. "I had that thought once or twice myself, but I refused to listen to it. There's too much for us to experience in this life together. As long as my heart beats, my love, it belongs with you. I had a dream that kept me going."

Delta wiped her eyes and sat up, still holding Megan. "A dream?"

Megan nodded. "Of the life I want to live with you back home. I came here looking for something that was standing beside me the entire time. I wasn't about to let some filthy drug dealers take that dream away from me."

Delta kissed her softly. "I've had that same dream."

Smiling, Megan shook her head. "I've always known you were a remarkable woman, Delta Stevens, but how on earth did you make it through the rain forest? You don't even like going to the park on Sundays."

"I would have gone to Hell if you needed me to. I didn't think about the jungle. I just kept my sights on finding you."

"I knew if anyone could do it, you and Connie were the ones. Seeing Sal was also a nice surprise."

Delta nodded. "She arrived right after we did. We needed someone with jungle-warfare experience, and Josh was the ticket."

"And where is Josh?"

Delta replayed the scenario when Manny got shot and Josh carried him out of the jungle on a sling-type stretcher.

"I sure hope Josh manages to get that poor man some help," Megan said, kissing Delta's bruised cheek. "Enough people have died over drug money." She paused, then continued, "If we don't get the others out of Zahn's camp, they'll be killed."

Delta held both her hands up. "No way. We're getting the hell out of here and going home."

Incredulous, Megan said, "You can't mean that."

"I most certainly do. My days of saving the world are over. We came to get you, and now we're going home. We don't owe anybody anything."

Megan was clearly taken aback. "This isn't like you at all."

"It is now, honey. For three years, I've put our life together on the back burner for everybody and everything else. It took almost losing you for me to figure out that that was a really bad plan. I'm through being everybody's hero. I'm through jumping through hoops for people who don't even know me. Enough is enough."

"But good people are going to get killed."

Delta shrugged. "Good people die all the time. I learned that hard lesson the night Miles was killed."

"I can't believe you're going to turn your back on people who need your help." Megan tossed her hair over her shoulder and leaned closer to Delta. "This isn't like you," she repeated.

"I'm sorry, Meg, but for once in my life, I'm going to take care of me and mine, above everything else."

Megan took Delta's hands and held them to her chest. "My sweet, sweet Storm. I've come to understand an awful lot during these months away from you, and one thing I've finally figured out is that being a heroine is your place in life. It's what you're meant to be. Not everyone in the world is as gifted as you are. Saving lives is your destiny."

"Not anymore it isn't. My destiny is with you."

Megan's grin broadened. "Lord knows I've whined enough about your commitment to your job and the people you've sworn to protect, but those days are over. I've grown up, Del, and I recognize how very lucky I am to be in love with one of life's true warriors."

Delta looked hard and deep into Megan's eyes. Yes, she had certainly grown up, that much was clear. But to go back—to take that chance—there wasn't anything in the world that could make Delta put them at risk again. There wasn't anything worth losing Megan for again. "I won't risk your life by going back to that camp, Megan. I'm sorry. I just can't do it."

Megan smiled gently and touched Delta's cheek. "That choice isn't yours to make, sweetie."

Delta cocked her head. "What does that mean?"

Megan's eyes narrowed as she held Delta's gaze. "It means I'm going back with or without you."

# 31——

"Shaman?" Delta asked, as she and Megan stepped from the hut. It was dark now, and a fire blazed in the center of the clearing. "Wants me?"

Sal nodded. "Uh-huh. The shaman wants to meet you."

Delta smiled over at Connie. "Okay, let's go."

"Does this have anything to do with voodoo?" Sal asked, quickly adding, "And I ask sincerely."

"Of course not," Connie answered. "Shamans are a tribe's spiritual leader and physical healer. They're responsible for the spiritual safety and health of the tribe. In the past, shamans have been the ones who both started and ended tribal wars. They are the most powerful men in the tribe because of their wisdom and knowledge. Many shamans mix a variety of plants to heal certain illnesses. Often, there's a ritual or ceremony involved, especially if the sickness has been caused by a spirit or outside source, but that's not voodoo."

"Sounds like voodoo to me," Sal said, keeping a watchful eye on the warrior standing nearby.

"Sal, don't make me have to kill you," Connie replied, putting her arm across the shorter woman's shoulders. "Tamar is an apprentice to the shaman. He is trying to—here he comes now. He can answer any of your..." Connie hesitated and stared at Sal, "...intelligent questions."

Tamar strode up to them. He no longer wore jeans, but donned the simple breechcloth worn by the other men. "Shaman will see you now."

As the four women followed Tamar through the tiny village, Connie shook her head. It reminded her of back home, in Mexico, when it was too hot to be indoors, and everyone sat on their porch. Some people sat in hammocks talking or singing. One much older man rocked back and forth smoking something that resembled a huge joint. Children sat with their mothers or sisters and laughed at something the women were saying. It was so much like a little neighborhood ringed around the fire. "I knew tribes like the Bribri existed, but I had no idea how developed they were."

"Don't you mean primitive?" Sal asked, looking at a man sound asleep in a hammock.

Tamar suddenly came to a dead stop. "Primitive compared to what? Your nine-to-five overworked, underpaid, destructive culture? Primitive compared to drunk drivers, teenage suicides, violent crime rates and unwanted children? I've been in your culture, and believe me, it is *your* people who act primitive and barbaric."

Sal started to respond, but Connie cut her off. "I think she means that your people appear so happy and healthy and she can't understand how anyone could be happy without electricity, cable television or microwave ovens."

Tamar continued walking. They were moving out of the village now and into the fringes of the jungle. "Just as I cannot understand how anyone can be happy or healthy surrounded by cement, air pollution, paying for what should be free."

"Tamar has a point, Sal," Delta added. "It's all a matter of perspective."

Tamar explained why they were going into the forest. "Shaman believes the spirits are more comfortable coming to him when they are in their natural environment. Too many people around drives the spirits away."

"Spirits?" Sal quipped. "I'm telling you guys, this sounds a lot like voodoo to me."

Connie, Tamar and Megan all shook their heads. "No more primitive than giving ten percent of your income away to the church, and believing that wine and bread are the blood and body of Christ," Connie answered.

Tamar came to a sudden stop again. "It is those Christian missionaries who come here with their religion and their medicines who are aiding in the extinction of tribes like mine. I would rather believe in Shaman's spirits than in a religion which endangers our ancient ways."

"But everything evolves, Tamar," Delta stated.

"That does not mean that change is good. Once our shaman dies, all his knowledge will die with him unless he passes it on. The younger boys are not interested in the old ways. They know there are pills you can take instead of Shaman's medicine, and they would rather do that than learn. They do not understand that Western civilization means the end of us. That is why I returned to the village to study as much as I can. Everything our tribe knows, it knows through oral tradition. Once that tradition dies, it will be as if we never existed." Tamar rubbed his brow in frustration.

"Well, what does he want with us?" Sal asked, watching an iguana slowly crawl down a branch.

"Itka says Shaman felt an energy when you arrived."

"Energy?" Delta asked, averting her eyes from two bare-breasted women carrying palm fronds from outside the village. For a split second, she wondered if tribal people had lesbians.

Tamar slowed as they rounded a large, sweet cedar tree. There, in a smaller clearing away from the opening to the village, was a single hut with a fire burning just outside it. An incredibly old-looking, shriveled man squatted by the fire, poking a stick at the burning embers. He appeared trancelike, and only looked up when they all rounded the tree and entered the clearing. Tamar waited for the shaman to greet him first. In a language that sounded much like Hawaiian, Shaman rose and greeted

Tamar, whose singular response was to point to the group of women standing behind him. The shaman then walked over and stood in front of Megan. His small brown eyes looked hard into her face as he held his hands out in front, palms facing outward. Then he closed his eyes. When he opened them, he placed his face inches from Megan's and peered even harder, as if looking for something. After that, he stood in front of Connie and did the same thing. Only when he opened his eyes, he smiled at Connie and nodded once. The expression on his face was different somehow, as if they had met before. Connie smiled knowingly and nodded back.

When he came to Delta, the ritual suddenly changed. When he put his palms out, he started to close his eyes, but quickly opened them, as if hearing a sound. Then, for a full minute, he did nothing else but stare in her face. When he was through staring, he walked slowly around her until he returned to stand in front of her. Taking her hands in his, he stood, eyes locked on her eyes. At last he nodded. Releasing her hands, the shaman stepped back and said a few words to no one in particular. Then he finally looked over at Tamar and spoke to him in their clicking language.

"Shaman requests that I send for Itka," Tamar translated, before motioning for all but Delta to sit. "The energy he felt when you arrived is coming from Delta."

As they waited, Delta stared at the shaman's face which was home to many deep wrinkles etched across it. With shoulder-length graying hair that smelled of vanilla, and a short, skinny body, the man staring at her did not appear to be powerful. He reminded Delta of her favorite crazy homeless guy who lived behind the dumpster off Hemingway Street back home. His fingernails were dirty, he was missing some front teeth, and he looked like he hadn't slept in days. Delta shuddered to think he was the tribal source of wisdom.

Five minutes later, Tamar returned with Itka in tow. When the two older men met, they exchanged greetings and spoke quietly to each other. Then, Itka approached Delta, closed his eyes, and nodded. When he opened them, he nodded again before speaking to Shaman. Then Shaman entered his hut, while Itka and Tamar conversed in that beautiful flowing language.

"They seem awfully interested in you, Del," Sal whispered.

"Shaman says he recognizes your energy now," Tamar translated. Itka stood motionless, staring hard at Delta.

"And?" Delta said, raising her left eyebrow.

"And that energy is the spirit of a warrior."

"Hell," Sal interrupted, "I could have told you that."

Tamar ignored Sal. "Shaman and Itka believe it would be a great honor to join your spirit with the spirits of our tribe."

Delta looked over to Connie and raised her left eyebrow.

"What does she need to do?" Connie asked.

"She must be prepared for the ceremony," Tamar said.

Delta glanced helplessly at Connie, who nodded. "Why not? We're here for the night, and this is an incredible opportunity for you, Storm."

"I say go for it," Sal cheered, whipping her hat off and swinging it over her head.

Turning to Tamar, Delta nodded and said quietly, "Tell him I would be honored."

゜⚶゜ ⚶ ゜⚶゜

"This tribal ritual stuff is too much voodoo for me," Sal moaned, watching three of the Bri women wash Delta, who turned and smiled at Sal. A single torch flickered outside the hut's opening, sending in a small shaft of light.

Megan reached over and messed up Sal's cap. "What do you mean?"

Sal thought for a moment before answering. "How come the shaman called Delta's spirit an 'it'? Aren't warriors in these places always men?"

All three heads turned to Connie, who shook her head. "For many tribal people, including our own Native Americans, positions of spiritual leadership are often accorded to people with two spirits."

"You mean bisexuals?" Sal asked.

"No. Sexuality has nothing to do with it," Connie replied. "This ceremony has nothing to do with Delta's gender. It is about the warrior spirit the shaman saw in her. He must have seen two spirits in Delta or he wouldn't think she, as a woman, is capable of being a warrior. Having two spirits could account for the energy he said he felt when we arrived."

"So, you're saying he saw a male and a female spirit in Delta," Sal said.

Connie nodded. "That's my best guess. My people call such individuals *two-spirits* and they are valued in many tribes because two-spirits are considered to be whole people—people who know more and have experienced more than one path. Shaman knows Delta's spirit will strengthen the tribe as a whole, and that's basically what his job is all about. The stronger the collective tribal spirit, the less other spirits can threaten them."

"And you believe all this hooey?" Sal asked.

"I do. I've seen Delta get out of too many tight spots not to believe there isn't something remarkable about the path she is on."

"On that, we can agree, but how much of it is spiritual, and how much of it is just dumb luck?" Sal asked.

"I don't know the answer to that question," Connie said, brushing a yellow-and-green insect off her arm. "Do you?"

Sal opened her mouth to respond, but shook her head. "No, I don't."

"Well, there you have it. If you don't have proof that a thing does *not* exist, then it's quite possible that it *does* exist."

Sal shook her head as she straightened her cap. "Are you sure the sun hasn't baked your brains?"

Turning from Sal, the three other women could only smile to each other.

# 32 ——

**When** the women finished drying Delta's lean, muscular body, they ground up something in a small bowl and sprinkled it on her back, shoulders and arms. Then they poured water into a separate bowl and mixed in something that resembled ashes. One of the women rubbed her thumb into the mixture and smeared a line across Delta's forehead and down the sides of her cheeks. A second woman approached with a bowl containing a bluish liquid, and this she dotted across Delta's collar bone and down the middle of her stomach. The dots were nearly exact in both spacing and size. The women still did not speak as the third women dropped a necklace of flowers, leaves and berries over Delta's head and around her neck. Their silence was eerie as they draped a cloth over one shoulder, covering only one of her breasts.

With their task completed, the women motioned for Connie, Sal and Megan to leave with them. The six women filed out of the hut, leaving Delta standing there alone. *I wonder what Mom would have said about all this. Could she appreciate the beauty of this ceremony, being a Christian? To think...her daughter, a warrior! What did the Bible say about that?*

Suddenly, Itka appeared at the hut opening and motioned for Delta to follow. When she stepped from the hut, she froze. Before her stood more than thirty men circled around a blazing fire. The men bore the same markings on their chests as Delta, and they stood tall and erect, staring at Itka and her. Kneeling next to the fire was the shaman, who sprinkled something into a bowl and swirled it around. While all eyes were on Delta, Shaman was absorbed in the contents of the bowl. Delta looked for her compatriots, but did not see them. Was this a male-only ritual? Would they miss the chance of seeing a tribe induct a spirit into their world? Gazing into the darkness of the surrounding forest, Delta somehow knew they wouldn't.

Itka motioned for Delta to join the circle. As she did, Shaman rose slowly and extended the bowl toward her with both hands. Taking the bowl the same way it was handed to her, Delta stared down at the dark liquid before looking back at Shaman. She had no idea what to do next, and wondered why Tamar wasn't translating all of this for her. Not knowing what to do, Delta did nothing.

Shaman walked around her now, chanting words she so wished she could understand. After circling her once, he held both hands over the bowl, chanted a few more lines and then motioned for Delta to drink it. As she brought the bowl to her lips, Delta thought she smelled jasmine, roses, garlic and other familiar scents. She wondered if those plants grew in the rain forest. There was so little she knew of this world. How had she gotten all the way through college without learning anything about nature?

Gulping the mixture down in three large swallows, Delta tasted a slightly bitter aftertaste. Shaman then took the bowl, dipped his finger in it and pressed the wet finger on her forehead. Delta closed her eyes as he did this, and concentrated on the loud crackling of the fire. After this, he placed both hands over her heart. They stood like this a long time until he started a low, rhythmic chant. The men around the fire joined in. It was so very beautiful. And the song seemed to go on for a long time, as Delta kept her eyes closed and listened to the chanting. Slowly, the chanting died down, and Delta opened her eyes, expecting to see the shaman still standing before her. Not so.

Delta had no idea how long the song had gone on, but when she finally opened her eyes and looked around, she realized she was completely alone. Even the fire had nearly died out.

"Where'd everybody go?" Delta asked, looking around the empty clearing. A single spear stuck out from the ground near the fire, and Delta plucked it out and balanced it in her hand. It was weighted perfectly. Poking her head into the nearby hut, Delta found it empty. "That's odd," she muttered, backing out of the hut. She started to leave the clearing, but stopped when she spotted a jaguar standing at the edge of the forest.

"Shit," she snapped, facing it squarely. "Con," she whispered in a low voice, "where are you?"

The large cat made a sound somewhere between a growl and a snort. Then it turned from her and started back into the rain forest. It stopped at the edge of the clearing, looked over its shoulder at Delta, and made the chuffing sound once again.

"What?" Delta asked, shrugging. The cat seemed to answer by taking two more steps and then looking at her again. "Like I'm going to follow you into the jungle," Delta said. The jaguar sat down facing her. Delta looked at the huge animal and grinned. The cat sat just like her cats did at home whenever they were waiting for her to do their bidding. The only difference was that this cat could kill her in an instant.

In an instant.

Delta supposed if it really wanted to kill her, it already would have done so. She was alone, with only a single spear at her disposal, and she sure as hell wasn't going to be able to outrun it. Maybe it really wasn't going to hurt her. "Fine. So, you want me to follow you, or what?"

Coming off its haunches, the cat turned to the jungle, looked back at Delta, chuffed again and waited. Only when Delta took a step forward did the jaguar enter the dark forest.

"I've done some crazy things in my life, but this..."
Following the jaguar into the darkness, Delta stopped at the
edge of the rain forest and cast a final glance back at the village
clearing. How had everyone managed to slip away from the
ceremony without her hearing them? And where was Megan?

Cocking her head to the side, Delta listened. In the
distance she heard beating drums. Was there another village
nearby?

"Shaman?" Delta called out, as she ran swiftly behind
the powerful animal. She was amazed that she didn't stumble
on roots or lash her face on thorny vines as she had when she
first entered the rain forest. She seemed to know the jungle
now, able to move like one of the inhabitants.

When the jaguar came to a stop, Delta stopped also.
Across from a small stream burbling over smooth rocks, Delta
saw Megan kneeling by the water and filling her canteen. Delta
started to call her name, when she saw the raised ridges of a
crocodile's back floating toward her.

"Megan!" Delta shouted, sprinting toward the stream.
Holding the spear up, Delta considered throwing it, but knew
that would be futile. She had never thrown a spear, and would
merely waste the only weapon she had. As the crocodile neared,
Megan looked up and waved to Delta.

"There's a crocodile in the wat—"

But it was too late. The crocodile sprang up at Megan,
and as she jumped away, Megan fell backwards, hitting her head
on one of the rocks. Having missed its intended prey, the
crocodile splashed back in the water and floated downstream

"No!" Delta cried, as she splashed through the waist-
high water. At the sounds of her splashing, the crocodile
submerged with one powerful beat of its tail.

When Delta reached Megan, she pulled her away from
the stream bank and checked for a pulse. "Megan? Can you
hear me?" Megan was alive, but not conscious. "Shit!"

Suddenly, the yellow eyes of the croc resurfaced, gliding
its way slowly toward the bank Delta and Megan were on.

"Connie! Shaman!" Delta screamed out, but there was no answer from either of them.

The crocodile, which Delta estimated to be about twenty feet in length, slowly lumbered out of the water a little way downstream, never taking its ugly, beady eyes off Delta's eyes. Delta frantically looked for an escape route, but she knew she would never be able to get both of them away from the crocodile before those huge, yellow teeth chomped down on one of them.

"I can't do this alone," Delta muttered, staring into the open mouth of the crocodile, which paused about ten feet away from them. Raising the spear, Delta locked eyes with the crocodile. One well-placed spear and she could end this. Delta chuckled sardonically. Who did she think she was? She-ra, Queen of the Jungle? Lowering the spear, Delta shook her head. "I don't know what to do."

"Yes, you do, Storm."

Looking back across the stream, Delta saw Connie coming from the village.

"There you are! Where the hell have you been? Forget that. Help me get Megan out of here."

Connie shook her head. "Can't. I'm not even supposed to be here."

Delta eyed the crocodile, remembering the devastating attack at the Tarcoles bridge near Rivas. "What does that mean?"

Grinning warmly, Connie said, "You'll see."

The crocodile, which appeared to be ignoring everyone but Delta, took another step towards her. "You get Megan, Con, and I'll distract the croc."

"I can't help you, Del. It's against the rules."

"Fuck the rules, Chief!"

Connie nodded, still grinning. "Exactly." With that, Connie disappeared into the darkness.

"Con! Don't go! I need you!"

"It's your journey," came Connie's voice from the darkness.

"Connie!"

Connie didn't answer.

"God damn her. How could she leave me like that?"

When the crocodile slammed its long mouth closed, Delta turned to it.

There had to be something she could kill it with. She could wait till it got closer...or....Shit, what the hell kind of test was this, anyway?

Delta inhaled a deep breath and calmed herself. In her mind's eye, she saw herself graduating from the Academy. She remembered the isolated feeling she had in that warehouse; saw the faces of the two armed men who were getting ready to torture her. She recalled being alone in that burning house, with no way out. In every case, she had broken the rules to survive. In every instance, Delta had gone out on a limb, and just simply gone for it, regardless of the consequences. She was an expert at breaking rules. Is that what Connie meant by "exactly"? Was it because someday, breaking the rules would cost her her life? Was she supposed to learn how to live *within* the system? Was it time to discover how to be a part of the bigger picture?

Delta glanced over at the other side of the stream and saw the jaguar lying there, watching her. Oddly enough, it felt as if there were others watching her as well.

When the crocodile slithered forward again, Delta lowered the head of the spear and held it about two feet from the crocodile's nose. When the crocodile continued coming at her, Delta jabbed his snout with the tip of the spear. This stopped the croc, and he dropped back and eyed her.

"We can do this all night if we have to, but you're not getting us," Delta said calmly. The crocodile responded by trying it two more times. Both times, Delta poked it in the nose. With the fourth jab to his nose, the crocodile turned away, suddenly disinterested, and waddled downstream.

"Hang in there, baby," Delta mumbled as she hefted Megan's lifeless body over her shoulder and started out of the jungle. About fifteen feet from the bank, something inexplicable happened: Delta stepped into a thick, boggy swamp, glubbing around her ankles like a huge bowl of oatmeal.

Already in up to her waist before she realized she was sinking deeper, Delta cried out, "No!" Hefting Megan to the edge of the swamp and pushing her as far away from danger as she could, Delta dropped her spear. It sank in the oozing mess.

"Connie!" Delta yelled, trying to pull the spear from the mire; but it was impossible.

"Delta?" Megan said, sitting up, disoriented and shaken. "I have to get you out of there."

"Don't come any closer. I think it's quicksand or something."

Megan stared over Delta's shoulder, her eyes suddenly fearful.

Following Megan's gaze, Delta saw that the crocodile had returned and was coming straight for her.

"Oh, God, Del, what should we do?"

"You can't get me out of here by yourself. Go get help, and tell Connie this little test is over. I don't give a shit if they want my spirit anymore."

Megan rose on shaky legs and ran in the direction of the drumbeats. Delta watched as she disappeared, and wondered if Megan hadn't suffered a concussion. Her voice had sounded hollow and stilted.

Delta looked around for a vine or stick she could use to pull herself out. *I sure as hell didn't fight all this way just to sink to the bottom of some godforsaken swamp.* She had never given up before, and wasn't going to start now. While she considered her options, she stayed still. To her relief, she discovered that she hadn't sunk much since she'd stopped wriggling. Josh was right about quicksand—struggle and die; be still, and there was a chance.

This wasn't so different from being trapped in a fire or dragged out to the desert to be shot. Delta had seen her share of sticky situations—some, she wasn't sure how she'd escaped from unscathed. Each time, she had thought about getting out of the mess to return to Megan. Megan's love had helped pull her through many a rough spot. But this time it was different. This was about Delta's love; her love of life, her love of herself. This time, she was in this because she needed, once and for all, to discover just who Delta Stevens really was.

The crocodile looked at her with its beady reptilian eyes, but it was a very different look from the stare-down they'd exchanged earlier. The creature moved slowly to the edge of the swamp, stood parallel to it, and swished its powerful tail back and forth. One gigantic swipe knocked everything out of the way.

Delta studied the tail for a half a moment before looking back into the crocodile's face. It was at this moment that Shaman's words, Connie's words, Delta's thoughts and feelings all started to make sense.

The next time the crocodile swished its tail, Delta lunged for it and held on with every muscle in her aching body. Once she grabbed it, the crocodile started walking away, each thick, short leg sinking slightly into the earth as it slowly dragged Delta from the goo. When her feet were clear of the oatmeal, the crocodile turned, looked at her with that same toothy expression, and then blinked before disappearing into the darkness.

Slowly rising on shaky legs, Delta tried to regain her composure. What had just happened here? This wasn't about becoming one with nature. This experience, this journey, was about becoming one with herself. It was about facing the demons that had been eating her alive ever since she pulled the trigger and shot a man between the eyes. It was about letting go, as Connie had said, and starting afresh. It was about Delta Stevens proving to herself that she wasn't a killer. Sure, her first reaction had been to kill the crocodile. She was going to kill it because of fear. Had she killed that croc out of fear, she would have destroyed herself as well. That's what had happened with those men she had killed. Delta was afraid they would harm her or someone else, so she killed them before they could kill.

But it wasn't that simple. Their deaths had stolen pieces of her humanity. They had taken part of her with them to Hell. And that's what scared Delta the most—that she'd become an executioner of life, instead of its protector—someone whose first instinct was to shoot first, think later. She'd lived with those deaths by believing she had simply done her job.

But she had lost her way if she believed that. After her first partner's death, Delta had fallen off the path because she didn't believe the rules applied to her, so she broke them. And in doing so, she almost destroyed herself. The truth was, the rules of any system she was in *did* apply to her. Here, now, in the middle of a jungle, Delta started to cry. Her spirit had never recovered from the wound of Miles's death, and she had spent the better part of five years risking everything in order to avenge it. But cutting corners, killing bad guys and acting like a vigilante would never bring Miles back.

"Very good," came Shaman's voice from behind her.

Delta stood before him, not the least bit surprised by his sudden appearance, but quite surprised when he spoke English.

"You speak English?"

The shaman grinned for the first time since Delta had seen him. "Nature is a universal language, Delta Stevens."

"Did Megan make it back to camp?"

The shaman nodded. "You have done well."

"I almost killed that crocodile," she said quietly.

"But you didn't."

"No, I didn't."

"And why not?"

"Because..." Delta struggled with all of the new ideas in her head. "It would have been wrong. I would have killed him out of fear."

"Why did you fear him?"

"I...guess because I thought he would kill us. I didn't know what he would do."

"So you would have killed him before finding out what he would do."

"And I would have drowned in the quicksand," Delta said thoughtfully.

"You were never in any real danger."

Delta laughed. "Real danger? Where I come from, drowning in quicksand constitutes real danger."

Shaman smiled. "Were you afraid of dying?"

Delta cocked her head. "Actually, I never thought of it."

"Why do you suppose?"

"I'm not afraid of death."

"But didn't we just say we are afraid of that which we do not know?" the shaman prodded.

"Yes."

"Do you know death?"

The question puzzled her. "Do I know death?" Delta thought of Miles's blood oozing over her hands as she sat holding him on a dark, cold street. "Yes. I do know death only too well."

"And you have let it rule your life. Join the living world, Delta Stevens, and release those whose deaths haunt you. Come. Close your eyes. Listen to the sounds of your breath as it joins with the rhythm of the universe. Breathe in as the land and the trees breathe. Feel your spirit touch the moon, the roots, the water, the air. Feel yourself become."

Delta nodded as Shaman's voice traveled into her ears, to her very being. And, as she let herself go, the drums she'd heard in the distance were now beating all about her. Opening her eyes, Delta found herself back in the clearing with Connie holding one arm, and Megan, the other.

"How'd he do that?" Delta asked, glancing across the fire at Shaman, who nodded once to her. All around the fire, men were beating drums while others danced. Shaman and Itka solemnly watched as the men performed their dance.

Eyeing Connie to her left and Megan on her right, Delta asked, "And what in the hell are you two doing?"

Connie and Megan frowned at each other and both women released their grips on Delta.

"Shaman said you had had enough and asked us to take you back to Itka's hut," Connie explained.

"Actually...I'm exhausted," Delta said with a long sigh.

Megan laughed quietly. "I don't doubt it. I don't think I've ever seen you dance like that."

Delta froze. "Dance? What are you talking about?"

"Call it whatever you want, honey, but you were absolutely hypnotic. You danced with those men as if you'd—"

"I'm telling you, I wasn't dancing! I wasn't even here!"

"Of course you were here, silly. We've been watching the most incred—"

"Look, I don't know what *you* were watching, but I wasn't here, and I never danced. I've been out in the jungle. So have you."

Connie shot Megan a scowl that Delta didn't miss. "What? What's the matter with you two?" Delta snapped.

Megan took Delta's hand in hers. "Honey, you've been carrying on for almost two hours. You're tired, and you drank way too much of Shaman's brew they kept pouring."

Delta took a step back and shook her head. "I don't know what you were doing for the past few hours, but I wasn't here. Shaman and I were in the forest with a jaguar and..."

Connie placed her fingers on Delta's mouth. "You are part of their tribe now," Connie said quietly. "You drank some of the shaman's brew, Itka gave you a ceremonial blessing, and you spent the last two hours on a journey that only you will ever truly understand."

Delta did not take her eyes off Connie. She hadn't merely heard Connie's words, she'd felt them. Every syllable shook Delta to the core. "But I did dance?" Delta asked, incredulously.

Connie nodded. "Your body reacted to the brew, but your spirit was someplace else."

Delta nodded and pulled away from Connie. "What do you mean my spirit? How could I not know what my body was doing for over two hours?"

"You know the answer, Delta, only it's a little scary to believe."

Delta nodded, still slightly dazed. "Where's Sal?"

"Shaman sent her back to the hut because he sensed that she was a disbeliever. She's probably asleep by now."

"Megan—"

"Shh. We'll talk about it in the morning, honey. Right now, I think you should rest. It's been a really long night and we have to start out early tomorrow."

As Delta looked over at Connie, her dear friend smiled and winked before entering the hut.

Later, lying between Megan and Connie on a huge hammock strung between two walls of the hut, Delta kissed them both good night and stared up at the dried palm frond ceiling. It was a matter of seconds before she felt Megan's body twitch beside her.

With her eyes still open, Delta listened to everyone's breathing and knew that Connie was still awake.

"Con?"

"Yeah?"

"You can explain this to me, can't you?"

"Yes."

"I'm not talking about the dancing."

"I know."

Delta's eyebrows knitted together as she listened to the insects of the night. "I don't think I'll ever be the same."

Connie rolled over and spooned Delta. "I know."

Holding Connie's hand to her chest, Delta closed her eyes. She was almost afraid to sleep. "Con?"

"Shh. Go to sleep."

"How come I don't feel like a warrior?"

Connie held Delta tighter. "You should."

"Why?"

"Because you didn't kill the crocodile, did you?"

Delta didn't know what to say. "How'd—"

"Shh. We'll talk about it later. We need to be fresh for tomorrow."

Delta closed her eyes and let her body slide into Connie's embrace. "Just one more question, Chief, and I'll go to sleep."

"Fine. Just one."

"You were there, weren't you?"

"Yes, Storm, I was."

## 33 ——

The four women and Tamar set out the next morning around 5:30, before the sun had completely risen. After saying their good-byes to the shaman, Delta was given a jaguar-tooth necklace from Itka as a symbol of the joining of her spirit to that of the tribe.

They had been hiking for three hours when Tamar squatted next to the river and cupped his hand for a drink. The river branched off in two directions, and a large cypress tree sat isolated on an islet at the river fork. "Following this section of the river will get you to Panama before nightfall. It is easy to cross at many places."

Delta turned and shook his hand. "Thanks for accompanying us this far."

"I would go further with you, but I must stay with my people in case those soldiers should come to the village."

"You've been very helpful, Tamar," Connie said, shaking his hand. "We couldn't ask for more."

"Will you return for the others?" Tamar asked.

Megan nodded. "Once we're in Panama, we'll be able to get the help we need to get back to the others."

Sal nodded. "It would be foolish to go back alone, without weapons, without provisions."

Connie agreed. "Doing that once was enough. I imagine the Panamanian authorities would love to bust a man with Zahn's reputation."

Delta wiped the sweat from her forehead with the front of her shirt. "Don't worry, though, Tamar. We won't be bothering your people."

Tamar grinned. "But you are one of us, Delta. Our village is your village. It would never...Suddenly, the crack of gunfire filled the air, sending Tamar stumbling forward; he landed face first in the water.

"Watch out!" Delta yelled, pushing Megan and Sal behind a tree before she and Connie grabbed Tamar's arms and dragged him from the water and lay him behind a manni tree.

"He's hit!" Connie yelled, as more automatic gunfire filled the air. Connie turned Tamar over and pressed her hands against the bleeding hole in his lower back. "Oh, shit. Meg, help me with him."

As Connie and Megan attempted to stem the bleeding, Delta and Sal peered out from behind a tree. "See anything?" Delta asked.

Sal squinted, but shook her head. "I'm gonna run over to that tree and see if I can draw fire. If we don't know where they are soon, we're screwed."

Delta looked over at Sal and nodded.

Grinning, Sal nodded back. "Here goes." Scampering through the bushes, Sal leapt behind a tree just as more shots rang out. Delta estimated the shooter to be a hundred and fifty feet away. "Over there," she mouthed to Sal, pointing in the direction of a cashew tree.

Delta waited for Sal to acknowledge that she saw him, before squatting down with Connie and Megan. Their hands were painted with blood as they applied direct pressure to the wound.

"Con?"

Connie looked up, her face bathed in sweat. She shook her head sadly. "He's lost too much blood."

"No," Megan said softly, wiping the wet hair away from Tamar's face.

"I'm sorry, Meg. The best we can do for him is to make him comfortable."

"You two stay with Tamar," Delta barked.

"Delta—"

Delta held up her hand to silence Megan's protests. "We'll end up like him if we don't do something."

"Such as?" Megan asked.

Delta smiled reassuringly. "I'm a warrior now, hon. And right now, this warrior needs a gun." Slowly inching her head around a tree, Delta realized that Sal was no longer where she'd last seen her. "Sal?" Delta hissed, but there was no answer. "Damn it."

"What?" Connie asked, joining Delta while Megan applied pressure to Tamar's wound with a large leaf.

"Sal took off. She was there a second ago, and now, she's not," Delta whispered.

"Sounds like someone else I know. Now what?"

"Gotta go after her," Delta said.

Connie glanced down at Megan. "What about Tamar?"

"I'll stay with him," Megan answered.

"Think they got her?" Connie whispered to Delta.

Delta shrugged. "I don't even know who *they* are. Do you think Zahn's men could have caught up to us so quickly?"

Connie thought for a moment. "Maybe. It's possible he has men all over the jungle with communication capabilities."

"If that's the case—"

"We're screwed," Delta said.

Delta looked at Connie's intense brown eyes burning the truth into her. "I'm going after Sal. We are *not* going to die in this jungle!" As Delta rose, she heard a rustle behind her and whipped around to find Sal crouched down.

"Where you guys going?" Sal whispered, winking.

"Sal! Where in the hell did—" Delta stopped mid-sentence when she saw a rifle slung over Sal's shoulder. In her right hand was a bloody combat knife.

"We don't have time to sit around contemplating our navels, ladies. This game is for keeps."

"You killed him?" Connie asked.

Sal nodded. "Had to. He was sneaking up on you from behind. Don't worry, he didn't feel a thing."

Delta could only stare in amazement. She didn't know whether to be in awe or aghast. "Weird thing was, this guy wasn't even wearing a uniform, and the rifle doesn't look like anything a decent mercenary would lend to his neighbor."

Delta and Connie exchanged looks. "Poachers," Delta murmured.

"How is he?" Sal asked, jerking her head in Tamar's direction.

Delta shook her head. "Even if we could get him to a doctor right away, he's lost too much blood. The best we can do is take him back to his people."

Sal's eyebrows shot up. "Carry a corpse back through the jungle? I don't think so."

"Sal's right, Del," Connie agreed. "We have to leave him here."

"Besides," Sal continued, "that shooter wasn't alone. I saw at least three others, and we need to find the rest of them before they find us."

Everyone turned to Connie, who nodded slowly. "We'd better go on the offensive. Take them out. If we don't, we're dead."

Sal held up the automatic. "At least the odds are a bit more even."

"Who stays with Megan?" Sal asked.

"No one stays with Megan," Megan said, joining the group. "I'm a big girl who made it through this rain forest by myself. I'll stay with Tamar because I don't want him to die alone, but no one needs to baby-sit me."

Delta grinned. Megan Osbourne had really come into her own down here. Here, in the rain forest, they'd both discovered their own inner strength.

"Then you take the rifle. I won't leave you here weaponless," Sal said.

She held the rifle out to Megan and showed her how to hold it and fire it. "It's probably got some kick, so keep it on your shoulder, or it could really hurt you."

Taking the rifle, Megan inhaled slowly. "Get going. I'll be fine."

Delta looked into her eyes and searched for something to say.

"Come on," Sal said, tugging Delta's arm. "Tell her later."

Delta nodded and turned away, feeling her heart constrict at the thought of leaving Megan again. "I love you," she said over her shoulder.

As the three of them crept through the brush, Delta stopped Sal. "I need to see the guy you killed."

Sal and Connie stared at her. "Why?" Sal asked.

"A hunch."

When they reached the dead man, whose head was slumped on his chest, Delta realized Sal had cut his throat from ear to ear. Delta grimly looked over at Sal, who regarded the body impassively.

"Christ, Sal," Connie uttered, staring at the knife wound running from earlobe to earlobe.

"Hadda keep him from crying out and alerting the others," Sal said matter-of-factly. "It's war, Connie. Nothing more, nothing less. Get to them before they get us. That's the only rule you live by now. Kill or be killed."

Squatting down, Delta studied the corpse for a second. There was something strangely familiar about him. He wasn't wearing army fatigues; instead, he wore khaki pants and matching shirt. Searching her memory, Delta waited for the lights to go on. She had seen this outfit recently. "I think I've seen this guy before."

"Where?"

"My first night here, some guys walked through my camp. They were carrying two canvas bags."

"How many guys?"

"Four. Maybe five."

A loud screeching sound suddenly filled the air, causing all three to look around. The noise came again, like someone burning rubber in a speedy getaway.

"God, that's a horrible sound," Sal whispered.

"Sounds like something being tortured," Connie said softly.

Delta grabbed her machete and started toward the noise. "Come on."

"Where are you going?" Sal asked.

"I know what that noise is."

Following behind her, Connie and Sal could barely keep up. "What is it?"

The screech filled the air again. "Those are macaws."

"How do you know?"

Delta paused and cocked her head. "I...don't know how. That's weird...I just...know." Delta cast her gaze up at the sky. "That guy you killed back there might be one of the poachers Megan and Augustine were after."

"Well, it won't be long before they know their pal's missing. We better fan out, locate them and get their weapons. It's best if we don't stay bunched together."

They walked another hundred yards or so before coming upon the poachers. Camping next to a small river were four men with two canvas bags. Delta gave a signal to the others, as they took a triangular approach toward the camp. As Sal and Connie quietly made their way through the underbrush, Delta wondered if they would ever escape this tropical nightmare.

She looked across the small camp, at the four men napping in the shade, and watched as one of them stood up. Making eye contact with Sal, who peered at her from behind a naranja tree, Delta pointed to the man who was unbuckling his belt and starting right toward Sal. Delta could do nothing but watch the poacher disappear into the bushes where Sal was hiding.

"Shit," Delta uttered quietly to herself.

When she grabbed her machete in both hands, Delta was only fifteen feet away from the back of one of the men. That's when she spotted Sal holding up her bloody knife. *Guess that guy won't be returning to his camp*, Delta thought grimly.

Delta waited and watched to see if the other men had noticed that their friend hadn't returned. When five minutes crawled by, Delta pointed to the gun leaning up against a tree one of the men had been sitting next to, and signaled Sal to go for the gun. What they needed now was a diversion. Quickly stripping off her jeans and long tee-shirt, Delta grabbed a handful of bright red berries and pressed them on her stomach. Then, picking up her machete, she inhaled once before signaling to Sal and Connie that she was going to go in.

Delta ran into the camp screaming like a wild woman, and the three men were immediately roused out of their naps. Her presence was so disarming, they froze long enough for Sal to reach the rifle and point it at them before they could even move. When one man went for his gun, Connie swung her machete inches from his outstretched fingers, which he drew protectively to his chest.

"Over there, Paco," Sal said, indicating for the one man to join the other two.

Connie quickly swept up the remaining rifles and dumped one at Delta's feet, before issuing orders to the men in Spanish.

"We'll talk about this later," Connie said, grinning.

"Got something to tie them up with?" Sal asked.

Connie rummaged through their things before finding a roll of duct tape. "This oughtta do the trick." Before Connie could get the tape, one of the men lunged for her legs, and got a good taste of how much damage a black belt in karate can inflict with one well-placed blow. With incredible speed, Connie kicked him so hard, the crack of his jaw sounded like a walnut in a nutcracker.

Writhing in pain, the poacher grabbed his jaw and looked to his cohorts, who turned their eyes away.

Ten minutes later, the three men were tightly bound together and secured to a tree. Their hands taped behind their backs and their legs securely bound, there was no movement from any of them. When Connie was satisfied, she stepped back to examine her work. "Like pigs in a blanket," she said, tying her hair in a knot behind her head. Turning from them, she smiled when she saw that Delta had gotten dressed. "Let me guess. Was that the diversion?"

Delta shrugged as she turned her face. "It was all I could think of."

"It was brilliant."

"Thanks." Moving over to the canvas bags, Delta started to untie them, afraid of what she would find inside. With trembling fingers, Delta undid the knot and opened the bag. Immediately, there was a rustling of live animals struggling inside the bag. Slowly turning it over, Delta poured out seven bound and gagged scarlet macaw parrots.

"Oh my God," Delta uttered, seeing the beautiful birds with duct tape around their beaks and feet. Their wings were bound with ropes, and many had lost feathers. Tears came to Delta's eyes as the eighth macaw thumped to the ground—dead.

"Help me get this tape off," Delta said, quickly opening her Swiss Army knife and cutting the tape and rope.

"Del," Connie said quietly. "Do the feet first. Then you and I can cut the tape from the beaks and wings at once. If you do the wings first, they may take flight with tape on their beaks and they'd die."

Nodding, Delta held back the inexplicable emotions raging inside her. She felt so violated, so torn. Who could do this to such beautiful creatures? And for what?

After cutting the rope, Sal held one of the birds while Delta and Connie worked to free its legs from the stubborn tape. When the tape was almost completely off the beak, Delta looked over at Connie, who nodded.

"Let her go."

Releasing the big bird, Delta watched as it immediately took flight, squawking loudly the entire way. It flew up to a large branch and then just sat there looking down at them.

"What's it doing?"

"Probably waiting for its mate," Connie answered. "They mate for life, you know. One of these other birds is probably its partner."

"Yeah? Well, I hope that one didn't have a mate," Sal said, pointing to the dead macaw laying on the ground before returning her attention to the jungle. "Hurry up, guys. Zahn's men could be anywhere."

In the next half hour they released over two dozen macaws. When they came upon the last one, Delta looked down into its face and saw that one of its eyes had been destroyed.

"This one must have really put up a fight," Delta said, tenderly touching the soft white skin on either side of its blushing face. Unlike the others, this bird did not struggle under Delta and Connie's grasp. It merely blinked its good eye up at Delta, who, for a wrinkle in time, thought this bird was communicating with her. And in that split second, Delta knew, beyond all else, that something of mythical proportions had happened to her in the rain forest—something she was only beginning to comprehend.

"That dead one is her mate," Delta said, jerking her head over at the dead bird.

Sal and Connie stopped cutting and stared at her.

Looking up from the macaw, Delta smiled softly at their befuddled expressions. "Don't ask. You wouldn't believe me anyway."

Delta cut the tape from its feet first, then gingerly cut the tape off its beak. The bird shook her head a few times before squawking loudly. With a final snip, Delta cut the rope from her wings. When it was completely free of tape and rope the bird blinked its one eye as it cocked its head to see better. After looking at Delta, the bird hopped over to its mate and made a moaning sound like a sigh, before looking back at Delta. Then, with a few strong beats of her great wings, she joined the other birds on the limb.

All three women looked up in awe as the group of macaws fluffed their feathers and checked each other out. When One-Eye landed, they all began squawking just before taking flight. Their three-foot-long tails waving like red flags in the wind, the flock of birds flew up and out of sight.

"What was that all about?" Connie wondered aloud.

"Ask Delta. She thinks she knows."

Delta shrugged at Sal's continued skepticism, folded her knife and put it away. "Instinct."

"Instinct?" Sal asked. "Well, now that we've done our good Samaritan deed for the year, what does your instinct say we should do now?"

"It says we should go get Megan and get the hell out of here."

When they reached Megan, she was still holding Tamar's head in her lap. "He's dead," Megan said softly when the others came out of the bushes to find her hiding place.

Delta knelt down and took Megan in her arms. "I am so sorry."

Sal nodded. "It may not be much of a consolation, but we did save some birds."

Megan started to cry. "How many?"

"Over two dozen. Actually, we were able to save all but one. Your Augustine was quite a tracker, Meg. You two were on the right trail."

Hugging Delta tightly, Megan pulled back. "Thank you. Thank you so much. Tamar and Augustine would be so pleased."

Delta reached over and wiped the tears from Megan's cheeks. "It may not be a fair trade for the lives lost, but it's better than nothing."

"Did you find the other men?" Megan asked.

Delta nodded. "Left them tied to a tree, took their weapons and hacked up their equipment. If they can get themselves free, they'll live. If not—"

"Then they'll get the fate they deserve."

Megan glanced over at Tamar's lifeless body. Her clothes and arms were stained with his blood. "We have to leave him, don't we?"

Everyone nodded.

"I wish it were different, but I know we'll never make it out with him."

"As it stands now," Connie offered, "we still have a ways to go before reaching the border. When we get to safety, we'll send someone back to the village to let them know."

Nodding, Megan lightly touched Tamar's hair. "He was an incredible person. Now who will learn the shaman's secrets?"

As they started back toward the river, no one looked back. If they had, they would have seen Shaman staring down at Tamar from high above the canopy.

34 ——

The delay caused them to put up camp among a group of trees that seemed to touch the sky. All four women dropped wearily to the ground when they decided it was time to stop for the day. They had hiked nonstop all afternoon, hoping to make up for lost time, but the going had been slow and the rain was merciless. Raindrops as big as silver dollars dropped from the clouds. When it finally stopped raining, they were exhausted, muddy and wet.

"Anyone want something to eat?" Megan asked.

"I'm going to sleep," was Sal's answer, as she climbed down from her watch. "It's someone else's turn to post guard."

"It's my turn," Delta offered, moving to the base of the tree and climbing in the crook Sal had vacated.

For the next half hour, Delta sat there, thinking about her experience with the Bribri tribe, trying to make some sense out of a ritual few would believe. Rolling on her side, Delta gazed into the surrounding area. It was odd. The rain forest wasn't as dark and ominous now. The nocturnal sounds, which were peaceful before, were comforting now, as the night symphony played on. After listening to the individual players of this harmony for a while, Delta finally got up. Strangely, the sounds were familiar to her now, as she stood at the edge of the camp and peered into the darkness. Somehow, the majesty of this place, the sheer grandeur of it all, seemed to put everything in her life in perspective. She had been so busy chasing bad guys, Delta had stopped growing—stopped experiencing the fullness of life. She had trapped herself in her city life. She sensed that her life would never be the same after this.

"Want to talk about it now?" Connie asked, climbing up beside Delta. It was uncanny how Connie could sneak around without being heard.

The two sat silently side by side for a few minutes as Delta collected her scattered thoughts. Sal and Megan dozed sleepily beneath a six-foot palm leaf, as the rains slowly subsided to barely a mist.

"What happened back there, Con?"

"When?"

Delta chuckled. "You know what I'm talking about."

Connie slipped her hand in Delta's and gave it a quick squeeze. "A month ago, you would never have been able to hear the answer."

"A month ago, I thought I knew it all. A month ago, my life, its direction, my feelings and instincts, had some sort of order."

"And now?"

Delta shrugged. "Now, I haven't a clue."

"Want one?"

Delta nodded. "Please. What happened when I drank the shaman's brew?"

"Western civilization has made hallucinogenic drugs illegal, but for many tribal cultures drugs are a way of life."

"I hallucinated all of that?"

"Hardly. You drank a drug the Bribri use in ceremonies when your spirit needs to go forth into the astral plane. Modern scientists would call it 'being under the influence,' but tribal people know there's much more to it than that. It goes far deeper than hallucinations."

"Then I wasn't hallucinating?"

Connie shook her head. "No, you weren't. You were on another plane of existence." Connie's voice was quiet, almost reverent.

"Then none of that really happened? That's what Shaman meant when he said I was never in any danger?"

"That depends on what you perceive reality to be. Did it feel real to you?"

Delta nodded again. "Very."

"Then if you experienced it as a reality, it must have really happened."

"I guess so...but some dreams are like that, and yet, I know it's not a reality."

"Dreams have to do with our state of consciousness. This ritual wasn't about your mind, it was about your spirit. Your spirit was on a different plane, experiencing the reality of that plane. If you try to explain this intellectually, you'll miss out on what was truly an incredible experience for you."

"It was real, Con. I felt feelings, I thought thoughts. It was as real as right now."

Connie released Delta's hand. "Shaman guided you on a spiritual journey while your physical being danced the night away. Dancing, drinking, chanting and drumming are all part of the ceremony."

"That's why I kept hearing drums beating in the distance."

Nodding, Connie continued. "Remember, it isn't your physical being that makes you a warrior. It's your spirit. Your spirit took the journey."

"With Shaman."

"Yes."

"And you."

Connie was quiet a long time before responding. "I poked my head in just to make sure you were okay. You're pretty hard-headed sometimes."

"But how—"

"I'm part Navajo, Del. All these years together and you still don't really know what that means."

Delta looked into Connie's dark brown eyes and sighed. "I'm beginning to see what it means."

Connie smiled. "Remember when Shaman looked inside each of our eyes?"

"Yeah."

"When he looked in my eyes, he nodded, because he saw that I already belonged to a tribe of warriors."

Delta turned. "You mean—"

"I've been through a similar ceremony, yes."

"Then, you're a warrior too?"

Connie shook her head. "No, I'm not. My spirit is more like Shaman's. He recognized a kindred spirit when he looked at me."

"Wow."

Sitting in silence for a long time, Delta finally put her arm across Connie's shoulders. "Thanks for joining me in there."

Connie turned and hugged Delta tightly. "I wouldn't be anywhere else. I know how weird those rituals can be the first time out."

"You've done that more than once?"

Connie nodded. "That's why I was able to get to you."

Delta released Connie and looked at her in the moonlight. "And all this time I thought—"

"You thought I was pulling your leg. It takes an open mind to understand the ways of tribal people. You're only now beginning to appreciate your journey."

"Does that mean strange things are going to keep happening to me?"

Connie cocked her head. "What do you mean, *strange?*"

"That bird. The sounds I hear now. I don't know. I just feel different."

"How so?"

Delta struggled with the right words. "Connected, I guess. Yeah. That's it. When people talk about getting their act together, I feel like I have."

"What a wonderful feeling," Connie said.

"Wonderful and scary."

"Why scary?"

Delta inhaled the freshly washed air. "Because I don't think I can go on living the same life I left. Everything's changed now. I guess that's the scary part; I don't really know what that means."

Putting her arm around Delta's waist, Connie squeezed her. "You'll figure it out. Once we get home, you'll be surprised how clear you'll see things."

Delta sighed. "Thanks."

# 35 ——

It was nearly noon when the river finally met the Caribbean. With relief, the women realized that their arduous journey was almost at an end. "Look!" Sal shouted, pointing in the distance. "The ocean!  We've made it to the coast!"

Delta, Connie and Megan joined Sal at the forest's edge, and it was like stepping out of a dream. Standing high above the beaches, the four looked down and saw the sea pounding against the side of the cliff.

Delta drank in its wild beauty. "Now it's Panama or bust, you guys," she said. They grinned at each other in spite of their weariness.

Connie whistled at the sight below them. "Incredible."

"Yeah, but the cliff means slower going," Megan added. "We'll have to follow the forest line to Panama."

Delta stopped to listen to a distant noise filling the air. She couldn't name it, but the sound was out of place.

"We'll just follow the cliff to the border, just like Tamar said," Connie continued. "If all goes well, we should be there before nightfall." Stopping suddenly, Connie cocked her head and listened too. "You guys hear that?"

Sal listened intently. Eyes wide, she grabbed Delta and Connie and pushed them back toward the jungle. "It's a chopper! Run!"

All four women turned as one. Legs pumping, they sprinted the hundred or so yards from the cliff's edge in the direction of the rain forest. With fifty feet to go, they watched a large military helicopter lift over the rain-forest canopy and circle around for another pass.

"Did...did he see us?" Megan panted as they crouched behind dense forest foliage.

Delta looked through the leafy greenery. "Hard to tell. Jesus, don't these guys ever give up?"

Megan shook her head. "Zahn is a very proud man. If my escape embarrassed him, he'd stop at nothing to bring me back."

"We must be closer to Panama than we thought," Connie said.

"Maybe they're not even looking for us," Sal offered. "Maybe they're Costa Rican."

Megan looked at Sal and shook her head. "Costa Rica has no army."

Sal frowned. "That's absurd. Everybody has an army, right, Connie?"

Connie shook her head. "Not Costa Rica."

"Then I'd say that bird was definitely looking for us." Sal pulled her binoculars out and peered through them. "They're soldiers, all right. Fatigues and all." Sal reached for her weapon and checked her ammunition.

Delta and Connie studied each other for a moment.

"The coast is too dangerous and open," Connie said. "And it's too slow through the jungle."

"We've done pretty good so far," Sal said. "Well...sort of." Picking up the three other weapons they'd liberated from the poachers, Sal checked each one for ammo. "Couple hundred rounds. That's about it."

"I say we take our chances in the rain forest. I don't want to be in a position where we can be cornered." Delta listened to the hum of the rotors from the helicopter. It made her very uneasy.

"Fine," Connie said. "If we get separated, we'll meet at the American Embassy in Panama City. We wait twelve hours for the rest to show."

"And after that?"

"After that, we bring the Panamanians and everyone else we can to come after anyone who hasn't made it. Agreed?"

Everyone nodded.

"Stay on the coast or follow a river if we get separated," Sal added. "That way, we'll be able to narrow down our search possibilities."

Delta reached over and squeezed Megan's hand. "Everyone ready? Good. Then let's get the hell out of here."

# 36 —

Delta first sensed them when the hair on the back of her neck started tingling. It was subtle at first—she'd had this feeling often enough to know what it meant. It didn't matter whether she was in the city or here in the jungle, one thing Delta could feel for miles away was imminent danger.

It had been less than an hour since they'd heard the chopper, but something told Delta they had been seen. And where there was a military chopper, you were sure to find militia with binoculars, heat sensor scopes and a variety of other technologies aimed at finding people in the jungle.

"Hey, guys, I have a—" But before Delta could finish, a bullet split the air and lodged deeply in a tree nearby.

"Take cover!" Delta cried as another bullet thudded into a tree in front of her. Suddenly, leaves, branches and bushes were being pounded by lead. Sal suddenly catapulted forward, landing hard on the ground. Scrambling over to her, Delta looked up and saw Connie push Megan towards cover.

"Sal? Sal?" Delta barked, rolling the tiny woman over. When she was completely on her back, Sal forced a grin.

"Ouch."

"Where are you hit?" Delta asked.

"Let's just say he barely missed my cute butt." Wincing, Sal rolled to her side, revealing a bullet hole in the back of her leg.

Rolling Sal back over, Delta pulled off her own shirt and pressed it against Sal's leg; it was quickly covered with blood.

"Leave me," Sal said.

"Like hell. Hold on, damn it."

Chuckling under her breath, Sal inhaled. "Hold on? For what? An ambulance? Save yourselves, Storm. Leave me here."

"No way." Grabbing her stolen rifle, Delta squeezed off a few rounds in the direction of the gunfire.

"Bet that surprised them," Sal muttered. "Bastards."

Delta looked down at Sal's profile and realized the tiny woman might go into shock. Pulling Sal's pants down, Delta recoiled at the hole near Sal's left butt cheek. *Gotta stem the blood flow and keep her from going into shock, or she'll end up just like Tamar,* Delta thought.

"Come on, Storm, think!" Delta growled, looking around for something, anything...And then, she remembered. Manny had put some sort of leaf on his wound. It was one of the red-and-yellow leaves she'd seen strewn about the forest floor.

Seeing the tree with the red-and-yellow leaves, Delta quickly crawled on her stomach over to it and ripped a few leaves from a low branch. Immediately, there was a yellowish sap oozing from the base of the stem and, instinctively, Delta scooped up the sap in the leaf. As she crept back to where she'd left Sal, more gunfire exploded, ripping bark off the trees around her. Connie returned fire, laying enough fire cover for Delta to return to Sal.

"A favor," Sal whispered.

"Anything."

"Don't leave my bare ass hanging out next time."

She pulled down Sal's pants, gently placed the sappy leaf over the wound, then pulled her pants up again. "Who'll notice?" Delta teased.

"Three dykes," Sal said, chuckling. Suddenly, her chuckle faded, and she inhaled a ragged breath. "Delta?"

"What, Sal?"

"This is suicide for you guys."

"That's your unwanted opinion," Delta whispered back. "Now shut up and save your strength."

Turning her back over, Delta placed Sal's cap back on her head. With one arm around her neck, Delta slung Sal across her shoulders like a yoke.

"Shit," Sal grumbled. "Think you're taking this Amazon warrior crap a little too far?"

Delta ignored her as she scooted behind a few trees before reaching Connie. To her surprise, no shots rang out. This meant one thing—the shooters were moving closer. Delta knew from experience that it was too hard to move and shoot at the same time. It would merely waste ammunition.

"How is she?" Connie asked, as they squatted down behind a cypress tree.

Delta's eyes burned into Connie's face. "She needs help *now*. We have to do something, Connie. Sal is *not* going to die in this fucking jungle."

Megan touched Sal's clammy face. "We have to get her out of here."

Connie thought for a second and then a slow smile played on her lips. "If she needs a taxi, I suggest we hijack the only one in town."

Delta looked up at the canopy. "I like it so far."

A dozen more shots pierced the surrounding trees and Connie rose to return fire.

"You're going to hijack the helicopter?" Megan asked, incredulously.

Connie nodded. "Sal could go into shock and die if we don't get her to a hospital soon. It may be our only chance."

Delta nodded. "Con's right. If we don't try, she'll die here." Delta adjusted Sal on her shoulders, her right knee cracking under the strain. "I'll leave her at the cliff clearing. Lay some ground cover until I get back. If we can get the chopper to land, we can attack it."

"Be careful, Del," Connie said, firing a few more rounds. "If you get hit, we're done."

Chugging through the dense jungle, Delta huffed and heaved until she came to a clearing safe enough to leave Sal. Gently laying Sal on the ground, she touched her face. "I'll be back," Delta said, mimicking Arnold Schwarzenegger's Terminator.

"If they get to me first—"

"They won't," Delta promised.

"But if they do, I'm gonna do myself. The idea of...gross sexual torture doesn't...do much for me."

Delta pulled Sal's combat knife out and handed it to her. "If that happens, take one or two with you, Slugger."

Sal grinned. "Will do. Now get out of here."

Delta ran back through the jungle and rejoined Connie and Megan. "How many?"

"Could be six, could be sixteen. Hard to tell. How's Sal?"

"Hanging in there."

"For how long?"

Delta shrugged. "We need that chopper now. I say it's time we go on the offensive. Ten to one these clowns on the ground have a radio and have told the chopper where we are. I say we get that radio, we get that helicopter. Everyone else is expendable." Delta looked hard at Megan. "Can you do this?"

"Kill someone?" Megan laughed. "In a heartbeat, my love."

"Then I guess this is it. We spread out, take a sixty-degree angle and take out as many as we can until we get the radio. Everyone okay with that?"

Megan and Connie nodded.

Delta inhaled slowly. "We can't afford to blow this."

Connie laid her hand on Delta's shoulder. "Then let's finish this and go home."

As they spread out, Delta watched Megan regrip the smaller AR-18 rifle. It was such an odd picture, it had a surreal quality to it. Megan hefted it to her shoulder in the same fashion she did her purse.

As Delta crept through the forest, rifle poised, finger ready on the trigger, she knew this was really it. If they failed here, it was over. For good. They would never leave this place.

Suddenly, bullets peppered the surrounding foliage. Delta flattened on the ground and peered through the brush, locating her attacker.

"Gotcha," she said, seeing one of the Colombians in her cross hairs. Slowly squeezing the trigger, Delta sent a bullet that entered his neck and blew out the other side. As soon as he dropped, Delta crept over to him. No radio.

A second series of gun-bursts prompted Delta to seek cover. Peering from behind the tree, her breath caught in her throat. Thirty feet from her was the radio man. As she hoisted the rifle to her shoulder and took aim, she felt something jab her in the back. Delta froze. Slowly looking over her shoulder, she saw the sadistic smile of a soldier with rotted front teeth.

"*Hóla, señorita,*" he said, and motioned for her to drop the rifle.

Delta turned toward him, quickly weighing her limited options. "Do the words 'Fuck you and the burro you rode in on' mean anything to you?"

The soldier grinned maliciously. "*Puta!* Beetch."

Delta shrugged, her mind racing to find a way out of this. "Why can't men across the world find some original derogatory remark for women? You're all so damned uncreative."

The soldier cocked his head. "Te *voy a matar, señorita.*"

Delta shrugged again. "*No comprendo,* asshole,"she said.

As the soldier lifted his rifle to strike Delta, she heard *crack*...and his head exploded. Bone fragments and gray matter scattered all over her shoulders and face. She looked up from the headless corpse and saw Megan perched in the crook of a tree, her AR-18 arching quickly to the left as it fired once more.

Delta saw her chance. She moved around the tree quietly, then made her way a few yards over to the radio man,

LINDA KAY SILVA

who was fumbling with the handset when she approached him. He reached for his holstered pistol and pointed it at Delta. Forcefully, she jabbed the muzzle of her rifle into his chest. *"Silencio,"* she said, for lack of anything else to say. Delta watched the barrel of his pistol shake. She lifted the muzzle of her rifle to his face. For a long, tense minute, neither budged. Finally, the radio man dropped his pistol and held his hands in the air. "Okay, okay. *No problemo,*" he babbled.

Delta motioned with the rifle for the man to get on his knees. He did, and laced his fingers behind his head. He repeated, *"No problemo. Sí?"*

Delta frowned at him. "We'll have to see about that." Then she yelled, "Connie! I found him."

Connie quickly maneuvered through the brush. "Excellent."

Delta glanced over at the tree Megan had been in. *Gone.* "Where's Megan?" Delta asked.

"We'll round everyone up once we bring that chopper in." Connie told the soldier what to say. The soldier nodded and reached a quivering hand for the mike.

"I told him to tell the other men to cease fire. That there is friendly fire and they are all shooting at each other."

"Brilliant," Delta said, nodding.

Connie issued more orders to the radio man, who repeated her words into the mike. After giving a few more instructions in Spanish, to Delta's surprise, the radio man started taking his clothes off.

"What's he doing?" Delta asked.

"I told him to tell the pilot we have to bring the wounded to the chopper. If we're going to get close to that bird, we're going to need uniforms."

"Excellent."

Connie grinned. "I thought so, too. Keep your gun on him, will you?"

Aiming her rifle at the near-naked man, Delta watched Connie transform herself into a Colombian soldier; she looked the part with her hair tucked in under the hat.

"Amazing," Delta murmured.

Connie pulled her belt out of the pants on the ground, bound the soldier's hands behind his back and took the radio. "Actually, I got the idea from your little diversionary tactic."

"Great minds..."

"Let's get Sal to that chopper."

"What about Megan?"

Connie stopped and leveled her gaze at Delta. "We *have* to get this chopper, Delta. We won't leave without anybody unless we have to, but right now, Sal's life hangs in the balance."

Delta cupped her hands to her mouth and shouted, "Megan! Go to Sal!" With that, Delta, Connie and a grumbling radio man made their way to the clearing on the cliff.

"Sal?" Delta asked, kneeling over her. She looked so tiny and pale that, for a moment, Delta thought they'd lost her. "Sal?"

"Leg hurts," Sal groaned, shivering. "Think I'm in shock."

Connie grinned. "Can you stay awake long enough to take a few more out?"

Sal swallowed hard. "Point me to 'em."

Delta carried Sal back to the edge of the jungle and sat her on a soft cushion of moss. Leaving Sal, Connie and the radio man, Delta ran back to the headless corpse Megan had shot, pulled off his bloody clothes, and brought them back to Sal.

"Put these on," Delta said, handing the heap to Sal.

"But they're all bloody."

"So are yours."

Sal looked at herself. "Oh yeah."

When the roar of the chopper blades could be heard, Connie had helped Sal change into the Colombian uniform.

"Everybody ready?" Connie asked, hoisting both her own and Sal's rifle over her shoulders.

Delta stared back into the rain forest. "Damn it, where is Megan?"

"We'll get her, Del. That's who we came here for."

Taking Sal under her arms, Delta helped load her onto Connie's shoulders. "You sure you can still shoot?" Delta asked, positioning one of the rifles in Sal's hands. "You hit the instrument panel, and we're history."

"Duh," was Sal's only response.

Delta adjusted Sal's cap and stepped back to examine the finished product. "You'd fool their mamas."

As the helicopter neared, Connie smiled at Delta. "Sounds like our taxi is here." With Sal over one shoulder and a rifle over the other, Connie touched Delta's hand. "I don't do good-byes," Connie said quietly.

"Me either."

"Just know—'whither thou goest, so goest I.'"

Nodding, Delta looked over Connie's shoulder as the helicopter landed. "Well, goest and get that bird."

While Connie ran the distance to the helicopter with Sal yoked around her neck and shoulders, she bowed her head so the pilot and any others in the aircraft couldn't see her face. The wind from the rotors beat against her face, as her uniform flapped against her arms. This was definitely her gauntlet, and if she could pull this off, it would be the miracle of her life. As the door of the chopper slid open, Connie saw two men in the doorway waiting to help. There were probably others.

"There's three for sure, Sal, but that's all I can see for now." Connie adjusted Sal across her shoulders as she approached the helicopter.

"How heavily armed?" Sal asked.

"Can't tell." As they neared, Connie realized that she couldn't see the pilot's hands, but the two men she could see had their rifles hanging limply at their sides. "Watch the pilot, Sal."

"10-4."

With five feet to go, Connie regripped the rifle and swung it toward the soldiers at the door. She shouted something in Spanish, and the two men backed up away from the door with their hands in the air. Laying Sal inside the chopper, Connie pointed her rifle at the men.

"*Tieren sus armas,*" Connie yelled at the men.

"You, too," Sal said, motioning at the pilot with her rifle. As the pilot came out of his seat, he aimed his small-caliber pistol at Connie. A flash from Sal's gun, and the pilot slumped down onto the floor of the helicopter.

"Shit!" Connie cried, "Now who's gonna fly us outta here?"

"I will," Sal said.

Connie motioned the men outside, pointing to the ground near the chopper and ordering them to lie down. "You know how to fly a helicopter?" she asked Sal, keeping her weapon trained on the men.

Sal nodded as she rolled to her side. "Sure. Went with my dad all the time."

Connie gently handed Sal her rifle as she pulled a coil of rope from behind the pilot's seat. "I'm not surprised. If they move, shoot them." Connie jumped to the ground and tied the soldiers together. "Thank God your dad loved his little girl."

Rising to her hands and knees, Sal winced. "There's only one problem."

Connie looked up at Sal.

"I have to sit down to do it."

Connie looked at the wet blood on Sal's pants. "Oh. Shit."

Suddenly, bullets started peppering the side of the helicopter. Sal quickly dropped into the pilot's seat, and let out a howl that could be heard above the roar of the rotors. "Goddamnit!" Sal yelled, as perspiration rolled down the side of her face. Grimacing from the pain, she reached for the controls. "Hang on, Connie, we're gettin' outta here!"

Neither Sal nor Connie heard the distant gunfire over the roar of the whirling blades, but they did hear the pinging noise as the bullets sprayed the helicopter. "Can you see either of them?" Sal yelled, wiping the sweat from her brow.

"Not yet!"

Somewhere out there, more soldiers were bearing down on Delta and Megan. As the gunshots got louder, Delta looked up from her position behind a palm tree and saw they were from Megan's rifle; she was racing toward the clearing.

"Megan!" Delta yelled over the roar of the chopper and the rifle blasts. "Over here!"

For endless moments, Delta waited until she heard the heavy footsteps of someone plunging through the jungle. Sweat dripped down her chest, wetting the center of her bra; she wished she still had her shirt on. Lifting her rifle, she took aim. Through the cross hairs, she saw Megan's sweaty, bloody face. "Over here!" Delta yelled, keeping her rifle poised and ready.

As Megan stumbled forward, out of the jungle, Delta shot two soldiers in hot pursuit. Both men's backs blew out as two well-aimed bullets tore their bodies apart. Moments later, Delta helped Megan up and checked her rifle's ammunition.

When she finished examining the AR-18, Delta looked at Megan's bloody face. "You're bleeding. You okay?"

Megan nodded. "A bullet grazed my cheek. Think I was unconscious for a moment, but I'm back. Nothing to worry about, love."

Delta nodded. "Get to the chopper." Delta scanned the edge of the jungle, waiting for more soldiers to appear.

"What about you?"

"Right behind you, love." Quickly kissing Megan on the lips, Delta gave her a shove toward the chopper.

"Delta?"

"Yeah?"

"Don't leave me."

Delta grinned. "Never. Now move it!"

With that, Megan sprinted toward the chopper. When she was a step away from the helicopter, the rain forest suddenly exploded with a hail of gunfire, as a second squad of soldiers appeared at the edge of the clearing.

With both rifles against her hips, Delta backed out onto the cliff area, firing steady rounds at the oncoming soldiers. She couldn't see anything except the muzzle flashes. It was only a matter of time before one of their rounds hit its mark. There would be no cover as she made her way to the helicopter; she would be completely vulnerable, even with cover fire from Connie. With both barrels blazing, Delta backed quickly toward the chopper until her final round was spent. The she flung the rifles down, whirled around and ran for her life.

Legs churning, arms pumping, Delta watched as Megan and Connie fired into the forest. Round after round of bullets shattered the ground, kicking up dirt and sand. Zigging and zagging, Delta tried to keep her five-nine frame low. Sixty yards to go and the chopper started off the ground, wobbling from side to side. One leg touched back down briefly before lifting off again. It looked like the chopper was being flown by a drunken pilot as it rocked back and forth. Megan was now in the rear bay of the chopper with a rifle in one hand and the other outstretched toward Delta. She was yelling something Delta couldn't hear.

Forty yards to go. Delta's lungs were ready to burst.

"Run!" Megan yelled above the noise. But the helicopter lurched forward, and Delta knew why: bullets were pelting the side of the helicopter and Sal was trying not to be a sitting target.

*Is that Sal?*

Delta shook her head. It sure looked like Sal sitting in the pilot's seat.

Twenty yards to go. Suddenly, Delta went down hard, a burning sensation searing the back of her leg.

"Shit!" she cried, grabbing her thigh. One of the bullets finally found its way into her flesh. Painfully rising, Delta turned and saw a half dozen soldiers coming at her. Looking back at the helicopter, she saw it rise ten feet as if suddenly incapable of hovering. It bobbed up and down and went from ten to five to twenty feet in seconds, as it wobbled unsteadily in the air. As more gunfire rang out, Delta limped closer, but the chopper was too high.

"Lower!" Megan yelled to Sal.

Delta could hear the bullets as they pinged into the chopper. She had to get up on one of those legs before a stray bullet hit the gas tank.

Delta visualized herself leaping up to grab the leg as it dipped toward her. Bearing down on the chopper, Delta leapt and grabbed a leg of the helicopter as it wobbled and lurched uneasily, nearly throwing Megan out the cabin door.

"Go!" Delta yelled. "Go!"

The wind created by the rotors pummeled Delta. Rising, the chopper spun around, quickly gaining altitude and speed. Dangling from the helicopter, Delta tried to regrip her tenuous hold, but couldn't get a better grip. With increasing blood loss and a bad grip at best, Delta looked down at the blue water below. As the helicopter turned away from the cliff and out over the sea, Delta saw Megan reaching out to her.

"Take my hand!" Megan yelled over the wind, her long blonde hair blowing wildly about. The soldiers continued firing at Delta and the chopper.

Connie tossed her rifle to the floor of the chopper and knelt down. "Take her hand!" Connie yelled.

Delta looked up at Megan; her face was intense as her sweat mingled with the blood from the wound in her cheek. Trusting that Megan had the strength to hold her, Delta reached one hand up. Just as their fingertips touched, a bullet ripped through Delta's shoulder, causing her to release her grasp of the chopper's leg. She couldn't, wouldn't take Megan with her. Delta had no other choice; she let go.

In horror, Megan screamed a heart-piercing "D-e-l-t-a-a-ah," as she watched Delta plummet into the blue water below.

"Delta's down!" Connie frantically yelled to Sal, whose face was bathed in sweat. "She's in the water!"

"She's what?"

Megan pointed down. "She's in the water! I think she's been hit! Go down!"

Sal turned the chopper around as more bullets battered the side. "Can't do it!" Sal yelled. "They're already making Swiss cheese out of us. If we take one in the tank, we're all dead. We gotta get out of here!"

Connie's eyes grew wide as she looked at Megan.

"Con, please...," Megan pleaded.

Connie looked down at the water below.

"Connie, *please*. For God's sake! It's Delta!"

Connie looked over at Sal, who shook her head. Swallowing her bitter decision, like a jagged pill, Connie's eyes filled with tears. "Sal's right. We can't risk it."

Megan's face paled. "You can't mean that!"

"We'll try landing on the beach down the coast and see if we can go after her from there, but we can't let these guys keep shooting at us."

Megan looked down at the water. They were too high to see anything except the crest of the waves as they broke.

Reaching out for her, Connie held tightly to Megan's arm. "Don't even think about it."

"My lover is down there, goddamnit!"

Nodding to Sal to go, Connie turned back to Megan. "I'm sorry, Megan, but this is what Delta would want us to do."

"That's bullshit!"

Tears rolled down Connie's face. "I'm sorry, Meg. But if we go down there to get her, we'll all end up dead. We'd be a sitting duck."

Megan glared at Connie before turning away and staring down at the ocean beneath them. "If she dies, Consuela, I'll never forgive you."

Connie nodded sadly, as more tears rolled down her cheeks. "Don't worry, Meg. I'd never forgive myself."

# 37——

**The** chopper landing wasn't pretty, but they made it.

Just five minutes after they landed in Panama, Sal was whisked away in an ambulance.

"You going to be okay?" Connie asked, laying her hand on Sal's head, as the ambulance sped along.

Sal nodded. "I'll be fine...can't even feel it anymore. You going back for Del 'n' the others right away?" she asked.

"The Panamanians will probably have a lot of questions first, but when they hear our story, I'm sure they'll help."

"They better hurry. There's not much time."

Connie squeezed Sal's hand. "Going back with help ought to be a whole lot easier than the way we left."

Sal nodded. "Think Josh is at the embassy?"

"We'll check it out right away," Connie said. "He'll be frantic when I tell him you were shot."

Sal grimaced as the ambulance hit a huge pothole. "Make sure you tell him it's only a flesh wound, or he'll hurt everyone who slows him down on his way over."

Connie grinned. "Will do."

Connie kissed the top of Sal's head. "Thank you so much for all you've done."

"Hey, I didn't do anything except get shot. Now...go find Delta!"

❦ ❦ ❦

Several hours later a crisply-uniformed Panamanian army lieutenant pulled up in front of the hospital. He escorted Megan and Connie to army headquarters.

Almost as soon as they walked in, an officer began firing questions at them.

"What's he saying?" Megan asked.

"They want answers, Megan. Answers only we can provide, and they're not letting us go until they're satisfied."

After hours of interrogation, Connie and Megan finally convinced the captain who was grilling them of the truth of their story. At last, he agreed to send a search party...but not until the morning.

While the women waited for a taxi to take them to a hotel, Megan washed her face and looked at herself for the first time in weeks. She looked much older, and the white butterfly bandage on her cheek stuck out against her bronze skin. She had lost weight, and her face appeared sunken and hollow. But she'd made it. Well...she'd almost made it. It wasn't a success without Delta. Megan pushed the thought away. She would not allow herself to think about a life without her.

Delta was a survivor.

She was a powerful swimmer.

She was a champion.

Hell, Delta Stevens had just become a *warrior.*

She *couldn't* be dead!

# The End

## More Fiction to Stir the Imagination from Rising Tide Press

**RETURN TO ISIS**
Jean Stewart
It is the year 2093, and Whit, a bold woman warrior from an Amazon nation, rescues Amelia from a dismal world where females are either breeders or drones. During their arduous journey back to the shining all-women's world of Artemis, they are unexpectedly drawn to each other. This engaging first book in the trilogy has it all—romance, mystery, and adventure.
**A Lambda Literary Award Finalist**    $9.99

**ISIS RISING**
Jean Stewart
In this stirring romantic fantasy, the familiar cast of lovable characters begin to rebuild the colony of Isis, burned to the ground ten years earlier by the dread Regulators. But evil forces threaten to destroy their dream. A swashbuckling futuristic adventure and an endearing love story all rolled into one.    $11.99

**WARRIORS OF ISIS**
Jean Stewart
At last, the third lusty tale of high adventure and passionate romance among the Freeland Warriors. Arinna Sojourner, the evil product of genetic engineering, vows to destroy the fledgling colony of Isis with her incredible psychic powers. Whit, Kali, and other warriors battle to save their world, in this novel bursting with life, love, heroines and villains.
**A Lambda Literary Award Finalist**    $11.99

**EMERALD CITY BLUES**
Jean Stewart
When the comfortable yuppie world of Chris Olson and Jennifer Hart collides with the desperate lives of Reb and Flynn, two lesbian runaways struggling to survive on the streets of Seattle, the forecast is trouble. A gritty, enormously readable novel of contemporary lesbigay life which raises real questions about the meaning of family and community, and about the walls we construct. A celebration of the healing powers of love.    $11.99

**ROUGH JUSTICE**
Claire Youmans
When Glenn Lowry's sunken fishing boat turns up four years after his disappearance, foul play is suspected. Classy, ambitious Prosecutor Janet Schilling immediately launches a murder investigation which produces several surprising suspects—one of them her own former lover Catherine Adams, now living a reclusive life on an island. A real page-turner!    $10.99

**NO WITNESSES**
Nancy Sanra
This cliff-hanger of a mystery set in San Francisco, introduces Detective Tally McGinnis, whose ex-lover Pamela Tresdale is arrested for the grisly murder of a wealthy Texas heiress. Tally rushes to the rescue despite friends' warnings, and is drawn once again into Pamela's web of deception and betrayal as she attempts to clear her and find the real killer.    $9.99

### DANGER IN HIGH PLACES
**Sharon Gilligan**
Set against the backdrop of Washington, D.C., this riveting mystery introduces freelance photographer and amateur sleuth, Alix Nicholson. Alix stumbles on a deadly scheme, and with the help of a lesbian congressional aide, unravels the mystery. $9.99

### DANGER! CROSS CURRENTS
**Sharon Gilligan**
The exciting sequel to *Danger in High Places* brings freelance photographer Alix Nicholson face-to-face with an old love and a murder. When Alix's landlady turns up dead, and her much younger lover, Leah Claire, is the prime suspect, Alix launches a frantic campaign to find the real killer. $9.99

### HEARTSTONE AND SABER
**Jacqui Singleton**
You can almost hear the sabers clash in this rousing tale of good and evil, of passionate love between a bold warrior queen and a beautiful healer with magical powers. $10.99

### PLAYING FOR KEEPS
**Stevie Rios**
In this sparkling tale of love and adventure, Lindsay West, an oboist, travels to Caracas, where she meets three people who change her life forever: Rob Heron a gay man, who becomes her dearest friend; Her lover Mercedes Luego, a lovely cellist, who takes Lindsay on a life-altering adventure down the Amazon; And the mysterious jungle-dwelling woman Arminta, who touches their souls. $10.99

### LOVESPELL
**Karen Williams**
A deliciously erotic and humorous love story in which Kate Gallagher, a shy veterinarian, and Allegra, who has magic at her fingertips, fall in love. A masterful blend of fantasy and reality, this beautifully written story will delight your heart and imagination. $9.95

### NIGHTSHADE
**Karen Williams**
Alex Spherris finds herself the new owner of a magical bell, which some people would kill for. She is ushered into a strange & wonderful world and meets Orielle, who melts her frozen heart. A heartwarming romance spun in the best tradition of storytelling. $11.99

### DREAMCATCHER $9.99
**Lori Byrd**
This timeless story of love and friendship illuminates a year in the life of Sunny Calhoun, a college student, who falls in love with Eve Phillips, a literary agent. A richly woven novel capturing the wonder and pain of love between a younger and an older woman.

### DEADLY RENDEZVOUS $9.99
**Diane Davidson**
A string of brutal murders in the middle of the desert plunges Lt. Toni Underwood and her lover Megan into a high profile investigation which uncovers a world of drugs, corruption and murder, as well as the dark side of the human mind. Explosive, fast-paced, & action-packed.

## DEADLY GAMBLE
### Diane Davidson

Las Vegas—city of bright lights and dark secrets—is the perfect setting for this intriguing sequel to *Deadly Rendezvous*. Former police detective Toni Underwood and her partner Sally Murphy are catapulted back into the world of crime by a letter from Toni's favorite aunt. Now a prominent madam, Vera Valentine fears she is about to be murdered—a distinct possibility, given her underworld connections. Flamboyant characters and unsavory thugs make for a cast of likely suspects... and keep the reader guessing until the last page.　　　$11.99

## CORNERS OF THE HEART
### Leslie Grey

A captivating novel of love and suspense in which beautiful French-born Chris Benet and English professor Katya Michaels meet and fall in love. But their budding love is shadowed by a vicious killer, whom they must outwit. Your heart will pound as the story races to its heart-stopping conclusion.　　　$9.95

## SHADOWS AFTER DARK
### Ouida Crozier

Fans of vampire erotica will adore this! When wings of death spread over Kyril's home world, she is sent to Earth on a mission—find a cure for the deadly disease. Once here she meets and falls in love with Kathryn, who is enthralled yet horrified to learn that her mysterious, darkly exotic lover is...a vampire. The ultimate lesbian vampire love story!　　　$9.95

## EDGE OF PASSION
### Shelley Smith

This sizzling novel about an all-consuming love affair between a younger and an older woman is set in colorful Provincetown. A gripping love story, which is both fierce and tender, it will keep you breathless until the last page.　　　$9.95

## YOU LIGHT THE FIRE
### Kristen Garrett

Here's a grown-up **Rubyfruit Jungle**—sexy, spicy, and sidesplittingly funny. Take a gorgeous, sexy, high school math teacher and put her together with a raunchy, commitment-shy, ex-rock singer, and you've got a hilarious, unforgettable love story.　　　$9.95

## FEATHERING YOUR NEST: An Interactive Workbook & Guide to a Loving Lesbian Relationship
### Gwen Leonhard, M.ED./Jennie Mast, MSW

This fresh, insightful guide and workbook for lesbian couples provides effective ways to build and nourish your relationships. Includes fun exercises & creative ways to spark romance, solve conflict, fight fair, conquer boredom, spice up your sex lives.　　　$14.99

## TROPICAL STORM
### Linda Kay Silva

Another winning, action-packed adventure/romance featuring smart and sassy heroines, an exotic jungle setting, and a plot with more twists and turns than a coiled cobra. Megan has disappeared into the Costa Rican rain forest and it's up to Delta and Connie to find her. Can they reach Megan before it's too late? Will Storm risk everything to save the woman she loves? Fast-paced, full of wonderful characters and surprises. Not to be missed.　　　$11.99

## HOW TO ORDER

**TITLE**     **AUTHOR**     **PRICE**

- ❑ Corners of the Heart-Leslie Grey 9.95
- ❑ Danger! Cross Currents-Sharon Gilligan 9.99
- ❑ Danger in High Places-Sharon Gilligan 9.95
- ❑ Deadly Gamble-Diane Davidson 11.99
- ❑ Deadly Rendezvous-Diane Davidson 9.99
- ❑ Dreamcatcher-Lori Byrd 9.99
- ❑ Edge of Passion-Shelley Smith 9.95
- ❑ Emerald City Blues-Jean Stewart 11.99
- ❑ Feathering Your Nest-Gwen Leonhard/ Jennie Mast 14.99
- ❑ Heartstone and Saber-Jacqui Singleton 10.99
- ❑ Isis Rising-Jean Stewart 11.99
- ❑ Love Spell-Karen Williams 9.99
- ❑ Nightshade-Karen Williams 11.99
- ❑ No Witnesses-Nancy Sanra 9.99
- ❑ Playing for Keeps-Stevie Rios 10.99
- ❑ Return to Isis-Jean Stewart 9.99
- ❑ Rough Justice-Claire Youmans 10.99
- ❑ Shadows After Dark-Ouida Crozier 9.99
- ❑ Sweet Bitter Love-Rita Schiano 10.99
- ❑ Tropical Storm-Linda Kay Silva 11.99
- ❑ Warriors of Isis-Jean Stewart 11.99
- ❑ You Light the Fire-Kristen Garrett 9.95

Please send me the books I have checked. I enclose a check or money order (not cash), plus $3 for the first book and $1 for each additional book to cover shipping and handling. Or bill my ❑Visa/Mastercard ❑Amer. Express. **Or call our Toll Free Number 1-800-648-5333 if using a credit card.**

CARD # _____ EXP.DATE_____

SIGNATURE_____

NAME (PLEASE PRINT) _____

ADDRESS _____

CITY_____ STATE_____ ZIP_____
- ❑ New York State residents add 8.5% tax to total.

RISING TIDE PRESS 5 KIVY ST., HUNTINGTON STATION, NY 11746